But He's My Fake Fiancé

ANNAH CONWELL

This one is for all the readers who fell for Grayson the first time they saw his name in One Last Play.
And to Gray's Girls, Rachel and Sarah, who love him probably too much. Thank you for your endless encouragement, inspiration, and most of all, friendship.

All's well that ends well to end up with you, swear to be overdramatic
and true to my lover.
-Lover, Taylor Swift

Contents

Content Warnings

This is a closed door romance with some steamier make outs.

There is discussions of grief and anxiety, as well as panic/anxiety attacks depicted. There is also a minor altercation that occurs on page.

CHAPTER ONE

Sloane Covington

It's much harder to bust out a car window than one would think. The movies and songs about tearing up someone's car for revenge make it seem easy. But in reality, it takes a few solid hits before you get a good crack in the glass if you don't have the right tools or enough strength.

I grunt as my crowbar connects with the driver's side window. The glass shatters everywhere, making me glad I wore gloves and a long-sleeved shirt. Now that I have a good technique, I skip around the car, twirling the crowbar with a smile before smashing another window. It's quite a cathartic experience. Now I understand the appeal of those rage rooms I keep getting ads for. After all four door windows are busted, I lean the crowbar against the front right tire and pull my voice recorder from my back pocket.

"Character would need to exert significant physical force in order to do damage to a car. Crowbar worked better in comparison to the heavy rock used previously. Also, there is a notable dopamine rush whenever one accomplishes an act such as this."

I slide the recorder back into my pocket, then take the crowbar and start to hack at the tires as well, noting how many times it takes me to puncture them. Much like a Hollywood method actor, I prefer to get in my characters' heads as much as possible. I'm a romance author, so usually, that means touring a beautiful vineyard or learning how to paint. But, my next novel is a romantic *suspense*. Which means I have to learn villainous tendencies as well.

So far, it's been rather interesting. I've listened to *way* too many true crime podcasts, gotten into the stalker mindset by following my best friend Myla–with her consent–and as of now, I've demolished a car. My high school English teacher who made us *act out* our vocabulary words would be proud of my creative approach to research, even if my ex-boyfriend Christopher hated it. But that's why he's an *ex* now. Another reason was he wanted me to give up my career as a romance author to be a trophy wife, who drinks mimosas at the club with my stepmom all day, and pretends to run charities that are really just excuses to buy a new designer gown. As much as I love the billionaire trope, I'm not giving up my dream to be a part of a world I hate.

My denial of his proposal–and by proxy my father's wishes–was the first time in the course of my shy, soft existence that I stood up for myself. Today, when I meet my father and stepmother for lunch, will be the second. I'm glad I chose today to destroy a car. The boost of adrenaline and release of pent-up emotions is going to help my mood significantly.

My phone alarm goes off, letting me know it's time to head to lunch, so I take a selfie with the gnarled vehicle to tease the book to my readers on Instagram. They've been pumped about me branching out into romantic suspense from my usual sweet romance, so I've been trying to let them see behind the scenes as much as possible to fan the flames of their excitement.

"Thanks again, George!" I yell to the man supervising the junkyard as I head out. He waves from his post nearby, his reflective vest glinting in the afternoon sun.

I found George through a Facebook community group. Neighborhood groups are the best. It makes for good entertainment–by way of all the drama–and great connections like this one. He was advertising his car-crushing services, so I reached out to see if I could pay him to demolish one of his cars. The kind old man decided to let me come for free, saying it didn't hurt anything for me to go in the yard and beat up the old cars before he smashed them.

My phone buzzes in my pocket as I near my car. I tuck my gloves under my left arm, then pull my phone out.

Dad: Where are you? It's 1 PM.

I let out a heavy sigh. My dad is also a fan of intense punctuality. When I told him I'd get to the club *around* one, he heard I'd be there at *exactly* one.

Sloane: I just finished up some research I was doing. I should be there soon.

Dad: Okay.

A man of many words, my father.

I get in my silver BMW convertible and throw my required hard hat into the passenger seat. It knocks against my laptop bag and rolls onto the floor. With a shrug, I pull down my visor mirror to inspect my hair.

Yikes. This Georgia humidity is not doing me any favors. I redo my ponytail, grabbing a hair wax stick from my purse to smooth my flyaways down. Thankfully, my mascara is waterproof and the rest of my makeup is on the subtle side today, so I look glowy and fresh-faced after a few strategic dabs of a napkin from my console.

My dad won't care if I arrive looking less than runway-ready, but my dearest stepmother will likely tell me I look like a sweaty troll. Okay, she might not say those *exact* words but she will say something like *"Are you feeling okay, dear? You look a little warm."* Which is code for sweaty troll status in Monica Covington speak.

I strip off the long-sleeved shirt I'm wearing, exposing the soft pink tank top underneath that I've paired with black yoga pants and white sneakers. It's not a glamorous look, but since it's from Lululemon maybe Monica won't nitpick it too much. Who am I kidding? She'll spend the first thirty minutes of lunch trying to convince me to go shopping with her and her daughter, Brooke.

When my dad married Monica, I tried to befriend her by going on one of her many shopping trips. She and Brooke spent the entire time judging every person who passed us, ordering around the sales staff, and making weird faces at the clothes I chose. They didn't even let me go into the *bookstore*. From that point on, I avoided going out with them.

Once I look less sweaty, I pull out of the parking lot and drive through the Atlanta suburbs with my music blasting. I create a custom playlist for each novel I write, and I spend the entire time I'm writing said book listening to that playlist on repeat.

This one is filled with powerful and sultry hits with deep bass. Something that makes you want to wear leather and red lipstick, face off against the killer in one scene and make out with your love interest in the next. By the time I pull up to the valet station I feel good, or maybe *bad* is a better word for it. I'm ready to take on the world, including my judgmental stepmother.

I hand my keys to the valet, then walk inside the doors to Willowbrook Country Club, the place where both my father and stepmother spend much of their time. My father stays on the course or in the card room, while my stepmother can be found on the patio or in the spa. When seen together, they're often dining in the esteemed Willowbrook Hall, where I'm headed today for lunch.

My sneakers squeak on the tile floors, earning me a look from the receptionist. I avert my gaze and squeak faster down the hall to the dining room. This whole place reeks of judgment. I never liked it here growing up. My mom rarely came, but sometimes we'd have to make an appearance as a family and I'd have to wear an itchy dress and sit up tall while my parents pretended to like each other.

They used to *love* each other, but once my dad got a taste of wealth, my mom says he turned into someone she didn't know. They lived like roommates for most of my life, finally divorcing after I graduated high school. My dad married Monica not long after–a little *too* soon if you ask me, but they won't admit there was any overlap–and then a few years later my mom married Vince, who I like. He wears graphic t-shirts with puns on them and makes my mom happy, which she deserves after all those years of loneliness. I much prefer their company to my dad and Monica's.

The hall opens up into a dining room with crystal chandeliers and a wall of windows. The room overlooks the golf course, and it truly is a magnificent view. I'd love to sit by the window and write, if it weren't for the feeling of being constantly watched. Almost every table is full, with it being toward the end of the lunch rush, but no matter what time of day it is, there's always a few gossips in here ready to spread a tale.

I spot Monica and my dad sitting in the center of the room, likely so everyone can see them. I hate the idea of being the center of attention. So I can't imagine wanting all eyes on me, but I suppose not everyone is like that.

Monica raises a thin brow as I sit down across from her, checking the silver watch on her wrist.

"We didn't agree upon a specific time." I go on the defense immediately, hoping to get ahead before she starts trying to tear me down.

She sniffs, looking to my father as if he should reprimand me for not arriving when she preferred for me to.

"Next time, please be punctual," my father says in a monotone voice. The same voice he uses during conference calls. If he looked down his nose at me just a tad more, it would be the same way he addresses all of the staff who've 'served' him over the years. I always said we should have treated them like family. I guess he took that statement to heart.

"I'm sorry, I will do better." I tell myself that I'm just choosing my battles, but it feels as though I'm already giving up. Might as well slap the word *welcome* on my forehead because I'm a certified doormat.

My father nods as if this pleases him, while Monica purses her lips. The waiter comes before any of us can speak again. Judging by his wavering expression, my table has already given him plenty of trouble.

"Could I please have a water and the lemon chicken salad?" I order in the kindest tone possible.

"No substitutions?" he asks and I resist the urge to sigh. I'm sure he had a list of requirements from Monica. My dad will likely send his steak back twice before deeming it appropriate to eat.

"No, how it comes is perfect." In all reality, it's not perfect. It's a bowl of arugula with barely seasoned grilled chicken and a squeeze of lemon juice. I'd much rather have their Wagyu burger with truffle parmesan fries and extra garlic aioli on the side. But if I ordered that, I'd have to listen to Monica go on a speech about how *health is wealth* and *a minute on the lips is a lifetime on the hips.*

After hearing that speech the first time, I went to my mom's house and hugged her, thanking her for never telling me that eating a burger was detrimental to my health. I couldn't imagine going through years of dance without feeding myself properly.

The waiter fills my water glass before he leaves, and I immediately regret not ordering what I wanted. At least I would have gotten a good meal out of this terrible meeting. *Why can't I ever make my own decisions?*

"Now that you're here, your father and I have something we'd like to discuss with you," Monica says. I clasp my hands together beneath the table, bracing myself.

"Yes." My father sits up in his chair, clearing his throat. "We've been speaking with the Williamsons and we think it's time you quit this little charade of yours and return to Christopher."

I stare at him in shock.

"You want me to get back together with *Topher*?" I lace Christopher's ridiculous nickname with acid. My father flinches at the name, because even he knows it's ridiculous. Christopher Williamson the third wasn't bad enough, his mother had to nickname him Topher. When I first met him, I thought the nickname was endearing, if a bit childish. Now that he's my ex though, I'm free to dislike it all I want.

"You've given us quite a headache," Monica chimes in. "The Williamsons are offended by your refusal to marry Christopher. Vicky was positively distraught at brunch last weekend, afraid that you truly meant what you said to him."

"I did." They stare blankly at me, so I continue. "I told Topher that I wouldn't give up my career as an author to be his trophy wife. I meant it when I said it two weeks ago, and I still do now."

"We're your *parents*, Sloane." It takes all my willpower not to cringe. "You don't need to pretend with us. If you want a bigger diamond, just say so. I had your dad get me a bigger one, too. Vicky said that she'd have the stone on her grandmother's ring replaced for you."

I blink at her. Were those real words? Did I just hallucinate? I look to my dad, who is downing the rest of his whiskey like the fountain of youth is at the bottom of it. *Swell*.

"I don't care about the ring, Monica. I care about the fact that Topher doesn't have the same vision for a future as me." There are many, many other reasons I don't want to be with Christopher Williamson the third, but if I say any more they'll think I'm attacking him.

"No married couple has it all figured out right away. Isn't that right, Charles?"

"Right," he says in a distracted voice, as he signals down a waiter for more whiskey.

"Your father and I are happier than ever, but we didn't know what we wanted when we met." She places a hand on my dad's arm, her large diamond ring glinting in the light. "Don't you want to be like us?"

Bile rises in my throat at the thought. That is the *last* thing I want. I shoot to my feet, knowing that the longer I stay here, the more likely I am to give in to what they're saying. Their manipulation and heavy handed suggestions are the reason I stayed with Topher for so long in the first place.

"I'm not feeling well, I need to go home."

I turn on my heel and rush out the door, panic setting in with every step I take. Monica calls after me once, but stops, likely to keep from causing a scene.

The valet gives me a strange look when I ask for my keys and tell him I'll get my car myself. But I can't risk waiting around for them when my dad and Monica might try to stop me from leaving. Hopefully the guy won't get in trouble for letting me get my own car.

I jog toward my convertible, starting it as soon as I slide inside. Usually I'm the kind of girl who takes ten minutes before she leaves to set the mood with a playlist and adjust the air vents to the perfect angle, but not today. Today I peel out of the parking lot in a way that would concern my mother.

Once I'm out of the lot and on the road, I release a breath.

"You did it," I say to myself, then cringe. "Sort of." I had hoped to be a bit bolder today, maybe tell Monica off, or tell my dad how hurtful it is that he doesn't acknowledge the fact that I'm an author or support my career choice. I did none of those things, but I also didn't make a life-altering decision that I'd regret today either. So that's a win.

My pent up emotions start to weigh on me. The adrenaline from destroying the car earlier quickly wore off. Now I'm left with an ache in my chest and a heaviness on my shoulders. I consider heading home, maybe talking things out with my roommates Myla and Simone will help. But I find myself turning toward The Secret Door, a local bookstore that stole my heart the first time I stepped inside.

It's a dangerous thing to go into a bookstore while in an emotional state, but I know it'll help soothe my nerves and cheer me up. So while it's probably financially irresponsible of me, I pull up to the quaint little shop, a smile already growing on my face.

CHAPTER TWO

Grayson Carter

"Come on, old man, don't be like that," I say, staring at the silver mustachioed man across from me.

"Like what?" he grumbles, crossing his arms and glaring at the chess board.

"Cantankerous, ill-tempered and–dare I say–*crotchety*."

His bushy eyebrows rise as he points a knobby finger at me. "Now you listen here, sport. I've been playing chess longer than you've been alive. There's no way you've beat me."

"Again," I fill in for him. "I think you meant to say there's no way I beat you *again*, and whether you believe it or not, it's true." I smile and sit back in my chair, crossing my arms.

"This is preposterous! You cheated." He taps the table with a scowl.

"Prove it," I challenge. He sputters for a moment before his brows lower, practically covering his eyelids.

"Fine, you didn't cheat. But you shouldn't have won either." And here comes his usual spiel to get me to play him again. I know he's lonely, so I come in as often as I can to 'challenge' him, but I didn't plan on staying for long today. I guess Juliette and Dahlia can go on without me whenever they're done shopping. Though, there's a good chance that I'll play another game and they'll still be browsing. My future sisters-in-law do love to shop for books.

I open my mouth to tell him I'll play another round, when a familiar face turns the corner. Sloane Rose, my favorite author *and* the woman who sadly turned me down a month ago at the gym we both frequent.

A smile grows on my face at the sight of her, even though it shouldn't. *She has a boyfriend*, I remind myself. But it's still difficult to hold back from admiring her. Since the first time I saw her, I've been enamored with her. There's something about the way she moves. It's like she's floating rather than walking, as if she's an ethereal being gracing us mere mortals with her presence. And yet, even with that graceful air about her, she never seems like she thinks too highly of herself.

"Hey, Rose, it's been a while," I call. Sloane looks in my direction, her brown ponytail swinging with the movement. Her soft pink lips pull up into a smile, but it's not a full one. It's not even the adorably shy one she gave me when I approached her at the gym. There's a tiredness lining both it and her eyes.

"Hey, Gray," she replies in a soft voice. I'm drawn back to when we spoke for the first time. She signed a few books for Dahlia and Isa, while my copies burned a hole in my gym bag. I told myself I'd ask her to sign them, but then our conversation evolved into something much different.

"Is your name really Sloane Rose?" I ask as she signs another copy with a flourish. She was shy when I approached her, and still is, which surprises me. I would have thought the woman who wrote some of the most beautiful prose I've ever read wouldn't be so timid.

"Sloane is, but I added Rose as a sort of pen name."

"That's surprising, considering how well Rose suits you." It more than suits her, actually. Her beauty and demeanor surpasses that of a simple rose, but the similarities are still unmistakable. She's delicate and beautiful, yet resilient. I don't know what she's been through, but I know her words. I know that if her pen reveals her heart then she's known pain and stood tall as she walked through it.

"Your name suits you as well," she says, meeting my eyes from across the table. "I assume it's your real name?"

I lean in conspiratorially, "Yes, but don't tell anyone, because I usually don't blow my cover like this."

She leans in as well, mimicking my posture. "Don't worry, your secret is safe with me."

"I knew I could trust you, Rose." She smiles and it's the kind of smile you could see every day and it would never get old.

"So I'm Rose now?"

"Naturally, we need code names."

"Naturally," she repeats, her hazel eyes bright and warm, like sunlight filtering through amber glass. "I'll call you Gray, then."

"So when I call you tonight, I'll say Gray is calling, to assuage any suspicions."

The light in her eyes dims, as if someone pulled the curtains shut over them.

"I–" She looks down at the stack of books, then forces out, "I have a boyfriend."

I blink back to the present.

"I'll have to play you again another day, old man," I say to my chess rival as I stand, and he nods. There's a mischievous light in his eyes when he regards Sloane, the same look he had when I sat across from him the first time.

The old man–still yet to give me his name–hobbles off with a tip of his newsboy cap. Sloane gives him a polite smile, curiosity shining in her eyes.

"We play chess together whenever I have time to spare," I explain to her. "He's the only real competition I've come across."

Her eyebrows raise. "That's rather cocky of you."

I cross my arms and lean against a nearby shelf. "I know my abilities."

"Is that so?" Her hazel eyes rove over me, perusing in a way that doesn't seem like someone in a relationship would. *Interesting.*

"I've been called a prodigy once or twice."

Her lips quirk up at the edges like she's holding in a smile.

"Funny, I've been called the same quite a few times after matches." Her tone borders on flirty, and a thrill rushes through me. I shouldn't feel this way, not without confirming my suspicion that she's no longer in a relationship. But she's beautiful, intelligent, and plays my favorite game.

"You play?"

"Only when there's someone worthy of playing."

I gesture to the board. "Care to put both of our words to the test, Miss Rose?"

She looks at the board, then back at me. "Maybe you misheard me ... I only play *worthy* opponents."

I place a hand on my chest. "*Ouch*. I would have worn a bullet-proof vest if I'd known I'd be shot in the heart today."

She giggles and the whole store brightens. The sound embodies pure joy and I'm convinced it could chase away rainclouds on the darkest, stormiest day. I smile at her, catching her warm gaze. Maybe I'm giving myself too much credit, but I swear she looks happier than she did when she came in.

"We can play a game, if you have time," she says, mirth filling her voice. She takes a seat, flipping her long ponytail over her shoulder.

I pause before sitting down, hating that I haven't already asked her. I'm not the kind of guy who flirts with another man's girlfriend.

"Before I sit down, I have to ask: Are you still with your boyfriend?" She looks up at me, surprise evident in the widening of her eyes. "I only ask because there's no way I can sit across from you for the next twenty minutes and not flirt with a woman as beautiful as you."

Her face flushes and she looks down at the board, toying with a pawn. "We broke up two weeks ago."

"Good," I say, then cringe. "Well–not good, just–" I rake a hand through my hair, wondering when I became such an idiot. I'm never like this around women.

"It's okay," she says with a laugh. "It is good. He was a jerk."

"Oh." I sit down across from her and we start to set up the board. "I'm sorry about that. Do you want to talk about it?"

She shakes her head. "I don't want to think about it anymore."

"I can be a great distraction," I say and she smiles.

"Is that meant to be a line?"

"Do you want it to be?" Her gaze drops. She spins a knight 180 degrees, then does the same to a pawn.

"No," she answers. A hot poker of disappointment prods at my heart, but I don't let it show on my face. "I'm not ready to start anything new right now." Her quiet words are a balm to the burn of rejection. Maybe this means I still have a chance, just in the future. I'm not known for patience, but for Sloane, I can challenge myself.

"Then let's be friends." The look she gives me is not encouraging. "What? You don't think we can be friends?"

"I've seen you flirt with every woman you cross paths with at the gym, so forgive me if I'm a little doubting of your capability of being *just friends*," she drolls. I chuckle at her attitude.

"Have you been watching me, Rose?"

Her cheeks deepen a shade, but then she points at me. "*That* was flirting. See? You can't help it!"

"I wasn't flirting. I was asking a question."

"In a flirty tone," she accuses.

"What makes a tone flirty?"

"Don't pretend like you don't know what I mean." She rolls her eyes. I can't help but smile at this newfound spark within her. I much prefer this over her shying away from me. "Do you even have any female friends?"

"I have many, thank you very much." Sure, all of those women might be in serious relationships, two of them being engaged to my brothers, but that's neither here nor there.

"Don't lie to me, Grayson Carter." Hearing my full name on her lips gets my blood pumping. I can't decide if I love that or the nickname she gave me more.

"I'm not," I say with a laugh. With impeccable timing, my two sisters-in-law round the corner, tote bags filled with books slung over their shoulders. "Here's two of them now, actually."

CHAPTER THREE

Sloane Covington

I look over my shoulder, half expecting Grayson to laugh and say he was joking. Two stunning women carrying bulging tote bags walk toward me. One is a petite blonde who looks like she spends her days studying in the library of a mystical academy. The other looks like an explosion of color with a dash of 1970s flare. They're both much more fashionable than I am in my sweaty workout clothes.

"Oh. My. Gosh," the woman who embodies everything bright and colorful stops in her tracks. "You're Sloane Rose."

My stomach tightens like a fist inside of me. I tuck a stray hair behind my ear and muster a smile. "That's me."

"Rose, these are my *friends* Dahlia and Juliette," Grayson says as he stands. I follow suit, shifting from one foot to the other as the colorful girl twirls a silver ring and bounces on her toes in excitement.

"I signed books for one of you, right?" I ask in an attempt to make coherent conversation. The girl who recognized me nods, her short waves bouncing with the movement.

"You signed my books. I'm Dahlia, and you're my favorite author. I have wanted to meet you for years now but you never do signings–which is totally fine, I'm not saying you should–so I can't believe that you're here right now–"

Grayson cuts her off by placing a hand on her shoulder. "Breathe, Dahlia, you're scaring her," he says with a laugh, then looks at me. "Sorry about her, you'd think a therapist would know when she was overwhelming someone."

I force a laugh, tugging on the hem of my tank top. I love talking to readers online, but in person? Not so much. I've turned down countless book signing events and conferences because I get too nervous meeting people.

"I'm so sorry," Dahlia says with wide eyes. "I got a little overexcited."

"You're fine." I wave her off. "I'm flattered that you think so highly of my books." There, that was a full sentence, and I didn't stutter!

"I've convinced everyone I know to read your books, including Juliette and Grayson." She gestures to each of them.

My eyebrows shoot up. "You've read my books?" I ask Grayson.

All eyes are on him now, but he doesn't look the least bit ruffled. He shrugs, a casual grin spreading across his expression.

"I had to see what the hype was about," he says. I want to press him for more information, but since we have an audience, I don't.

"I usually only read classics, but Dahlia convinced me to read yours and I fell in love," Juliette chimes in. Her voice is gentle and sweet, matching the softness of her style. "You put words to feelings I wasn't able to articulate. I'm so glad I get the chance to thank you in person."

"Oh," I say, my voice coming out in a higher pitch than I'd like. I cringe and clear my throat. "I don't know what to say," I admit, my face flushing in embarrassment.

Why can't I have a normal social interaction? Maybe I should have gone through those etiquette classes my dad tried to force me into when I was younger. Though I doubt they covered dealing with social anxiety.

My gaze is drawn back to Grayson. He's looking at me with curiosity shining in his blue eyes. Why was it so easy to talk to him, of all people? I should have been fumbling for words around him, what with how unbelievably gorgeous he is. But he puts me at ease. I wish that ease transferred over to this situation with his friends.

"You don't have to say anything," Juliette replies with a sweet smile. "I'd love to get a photo with you though, if you don't mind."

"Me too!" Dahlia says. She holds her phone out to Grayson. "Will you take the photos?"

"I'd be happy to." He meets my eyes. "As long as Sloane is okay with having her picture taken."

It feels as though champagne is bubbling through me, sweet and sparkling. I can't remember the last time someone besides my two roommates checked on how I felt about something. Sure, a photo request is nothing big, but he still wanted me to be comfortable. I tilt my head to the side, a smile tugging at the corners of my mouth as I try to decipher who the man standing across from me is.

He's clearly a flirt and the kind of extrovert I couldn't even dream of being. But he's also read my books–if only to support his enthusiastic friend—and is thoughtful enough to pause and check in. It has me intrigued, which isn't good. I can't afford to end up enamored with a man who has no problem flirting with one woman one day, and a different one the next. If he's gone through as many girls as I suspect, he either thinks commitment is synonymous with the plague or has standards so high I'd never make the cut.

"Oh!" Dahlia cringes. "I got overexcited again. If you don't want to take photos, that's perfectly fine. You signing my books was enough to make my whole year."

"No, it's okay, thank you for asking though," I direct my gratitude toward Grayson.

Juliette and Dahlia choose a romance bookshelf nearby as our backdrop, and I try not to look nervous as I smile for the pictures.

"Thank you so much," Dahlia half-speaks, half-squeals into my ear as she wraps me up in a hug. I stiffen for a moment but hug her back so she doesn't think I'm rude.

"Thank you for reading my books," I reply, then accept Juliette's hug.

Grayson opens his arms with a smirk. "What about me?"

"This feels like a trap," I say and the girls laugh.

"Friends hug," he defends his actions with his arms still open wide.

"Are you going to hold your arms out until I hug you?"

He shrugs, his smirk morphing into a playful grin.

"You're going to be holding them up for a long time because I'm not falling for this game."

"There's no game," he says in a tone that makes it seem like there very much is a game afoot. "And I can hold this pose for a while; you've seen me at the gym."

Translation: *You've been watching me, Rose.* My face flushes because, well, I have been watching him. Only because it's hard not to admire a tall, dark-haired, sculpted masterpiece. Especially when said masterpiece also has a smile as bright as the sun and makes everyone he comes in contact with laugh.

"I hug Dahlia and Juliette all the time," he adds. His words make me realize the two women are still here too. Grayson seems to have an uncanny ability to make me forget other people are around.

"Are both of you really *just* friends with him?" I ask.

Dahlia laughs. "We're about to be family. I'm marrying his older brother."

"And I'm marrying his twin," Juliette says.

I raise my eyebrows, shooting Grayson a look. "They do not count as female friends if they're your *family*."

"Why not?" He lets his arms drop. "We're friends too, right?" He gives them a look that screams *back me up.*

"Of course!" Dahlia immediately says, but Juliette just smiles, amusement flickering in her eyes.

"Could the both of you please tell her I'm capable of having female friends without dating them?"

Dahlia spins her ring, while Juliette tugs at the sleeves of her sweater.

"I'm not hearing any confirmation," I say in a teasing tone.

"Really, you two? I'm not defending either of your excessive book purchases to my brothers anymore," Grayson says with a huff. They both just laugh, and I join them.

"I'm sorry, Grayson, you're an amazing friend," Juliette tells him and pats his arm. "But you have a tendency to flirt with every woman you come across."

"That's what I told him," I say.

Grayson sighs. "I'm *friendly* with everyone; that doesn't mean I'm trying to date them."

"Wait," Dahlia says, her eyebrows pushing together. "Why are you trying to convince Sloane that you can have female friends?"

I cross my arms over my chest, suddenly feeling self-conscious. What will they think of me now that I've turned their future brother-in-law down?

"We were having a little debate before you two showed up," Grayson answers, his tone nonchalant.

Dahlia and Juliette look between us, their eyes lighting with some sort of mutual understanding. I can guess what conclusion they ended up at, and it's not good.

"I should get going," I blurt out. I could stay here until closing time if I wanted to, but none of them have to know that. "It was nice meeting you both," I say to the girls. They respond in a similar fashion.

I avoid looking at Grayson and turn to leave, walking fast in the opposite direction. I think I hear him say my name, but I ignore it and rush out the door into the sticky spring air. As I drive home, I'm torn between wishing I would have stayed to see what could have happened, and being grateful I made it out of there before I embarrassed myself any further.

"I'm home and I've decided I'm never going out in public again," I announce as I kick off my sneakers by the front door of our apartment.

"I'm guessing that means your lunch with your dad didn't go well?" One of my roommates, Simone, asks as I walk into the living room. She's propped up on our blush pink couch, her laptop balancing precariously on a flower-shaped throw pillow as she twists her auburn hair up into a claw clip. She must be in the middle of writing. Simone is of the belief that like Violet Baudelaire from Lemony Snicket's *A Series of Unfortunate Events*, she thinks better with her hair up. Last time I checked, she was nearing the end of the latest installment in her fantasy romance series, so it makes sense that she's doing all that she can to focus.

"It went terribly, but I don't know if that's even the worst thing that happened today." Her eyebrows shoot up at my words. I sit down in my favorite circle chair and our cat Roman—short for Roman C. Kitten—jumps up next to me. I hold him to my chest and sigh.

"Well, spill," Simone says, setting her laptop on the curved acrylic coffee table next to a half-empty iced coffee and a bag of goldfish.

"Have you eaten more than goldfish today?" I ask her, both to avoid talking about my embarrassment and because there's a chance that she hasn't eaten enough today. All of us—me, Simone and our other roommate Myla—have a tendency to get locked into our writing and forget the world around us exists. So each of us has to help the other remember important things like food, going outside, and drinking enough water.

She waves me off. "I had lunch earlier. Now tell me what happened that has you even more antisocial than usual."

I frown. "I'm not antisocial, I'm just socially inept."

"Quit stalling, S," she says in her usual no nonsense way. Simone is a blunt realist. However, even though she's a realist, she writes incredible romantic fantasy novels. So while she keeps her feet firmly planted on the ground about this world, she spends her days writing about a fantasy land where nothing is as it seems.

"*Fine*, but where's Myla? Because there's no way I'm telling this story twice."

"I'm right here." Myla walks out of the kitchen, a bag of gummy worms in hand. "I heard everything while I was searching for a snack. Let the show begin!" She flops down onto the couch, her tulle skirt fanning out around her. Myla treats every day like it's dress-up day. She's the only one I know who can pull off a tiered tulle skirt as everyday fashion.

"It's fitting to compare this disaster to something that would happen on a stage. Though I'm not sure people would buy tickets if they knew they'd be cringing from secondhand embarrassment the whole time," I say.

"It's probably not as bad as you think," Myla says, ever the optimist. Of the three of us, she's the most sensitive and tenderhearted. She writes sweet and light romantic comedies and believes the best of everyone. Simone and I call her Princess Myla sometimes whenever she starts waxing poetic about romanticizing her life.

I cuddle Roman closer and embark on the tragic tale that is my current social life. After relaying the lunch with my dad and Monica, I jump right into the bookstore story. Myla and Simone know enough about my family to not be surprised by them insisting I marry Topher.

"So then Grayson's sisters-in-law come up, and they've both read my books–"

"Wait a minute, I think we need to pause right there," Myla says, while Simone smirks.

"Why?" I ask, even though I know.

"Because Grayson was flirting with you! And you were totally flirting back." She smiles like this is the best news she's heard all day.

"I was not," I say. Simone and Myla share a look, then turn back to me.

"You were," Simone confirms.

"You're both wrong, and that's not the point of the story."

"Haven't we heard of Grayson before, too?" Myla asks, tilting her head like she's thinking. Nerves bubble up within me. I was hoping they wouldn't remember. Myla snaps her fingers. "Oh! He's the one who brought you his friends' books to sign. The one who you said made you realize that Topher was the worst."

"Those were not my words." I give her a flat look. "I told you that a stranger being so flirty and forthcoming with me made me realize that Topher had never truly acted that way. Which was only a *part* of why we broke up."

"Yes, well, that part sounds cute and like he still wants to date you," Myla shoots back with a grin.

"It doesn't matter, because I'm not interested in dating anyone. And I'd never date a guy like Grayson."

Simone and Myla frown in unison.

"Didn't you just say he showed you something you were missing in your relationship with Topher?"

I look down at Roman, running my fingers over his soft orange fur as I contemplate how to convey what I'm thinking.

"Grayson is..." *Magnetic, charming, kind, funny?* "Too flirta-tious. I've seen him around the gym. He's not flirting with me because he wants a genuine connection. I'm just another girl to chat up."

"How can you be so sure?" Myla asks.

"I've seen him flirt with countless women at the gym. He has a line for everything and his own sisters-in-law both admitted he isn't capable of female friendships. The underlying message: he's a player. Well meaning or not, that's what he is." I try to infuse certainty in my words, even if they don't seem entirely right.

"I suppose you know more about him than we do," Myla con-cedes.

"We just want you to be happy, and not settle for another To-pher," Simone adds.

"I know, and I won't," I promise them. "But Grayson isn't hus-band material, and that's what I'm going for after wasting so much time with Topher."

They nod in understanding, thankfully content to drop the sub-ject for now. As I tell the rest of my story, I can't help but recall the time when Grayson stopped everything to make sure I was com-fortable. There's a part of me that wants to push aside my doubts and give him a chance, but I shake off that feeling. Grayson treats everyone that way, and I don't want to be one of many.

CHAPTER FOUR

Grayson Carter

"Looking good, ladies!" I call out as I walk past the elderly Zumba class. They all titter and wave.

"We've missed you!" Doris, one of the most talkative class members, shouts out.

I pause at the door, leaning against the frame. They're all stretching to prepare for the next hour of dancing. "I'll have to sign up for the next class. I've been busy with work and only had time for my regular workouts," I say, earning an admonishing look from most of them.

My excuse is true, though. Running my private security company alongside my brother Adrian makes for a busy schedule at times.

"Our classes aren't the same without you," Cheryl–another one of my gym favorites–says.

"Stephanie doesn't let us film our TikToks when you're not here," Doris grumbles. I shoot an apologetic look to the instructor

Stephanie, who's watching patiently at the front of the room. They wouldn't even attempt to film themselves if it wasn't for me.

She likely doesn't let them try to film because none of them know how to do anything other than FaceTime their grandkids on their phones, and they barely know how to do that.

"Y'all be nice to Stephanie, she works hard to keep you ladies looking as good as you do," I say. Stephanie smiles, while the ladies in the class fluff their hair and giggle.

"Has anyone told you that you're a bit of a casanova?" Cheryl asks.

"Once or twice." I wink. "I've got to go now though, you young ladies have fun for me."

Their giggles follow me down the hall. I pass by the next classroom and look through the window to see what class is going on. A line of women hold a ballet barre with one hand as they bend their knees into a plié—a term I know thanks to the show *Dance Moms* and my niece Maddie's love of dance.

I plan to keep going to the end of the hall, where my mobility trainer is waiting on me, but a familiar face catches my eye, making me pause. Sloane is at the front of the line, facing the mirror. She's wearing a long-sleeved top, a sheer skirt, tights, and leg warmers, all in various pastel shades. The softness of her attire contrasts with the strength of her movements. Every lift of her arm and bend of her knees showcases her elegance. The instructor—an older woman dressed in all black—walks around correcting everyone but Sloane.

The pliés stop and the instructor gestures toward me, though I'm sure she's really gesturing toward the cubbies holding the water bottles. But since I'm standing here, all of their eyes land on me. I recognize a few faces other than Sloane, but hers is the only reaction I'm looking for.

Her eyes widen when she sees me. I shoot her a grin. The women in the room go over to their water bottles and bags, but Sloane walks out the door to me.

"What are you doing here?" she asks, placing her hands on her hips. I let my eyes rove over her for a moment, taking in her beauty up close.

"This is my gym too, you know."

She rolls her eyes. "I meant here as in outside of the window of my class."

"I was passing by and saw you," I tell her. "Your beauty distracted me." Honesty is usually the best policy, but considering I'm supposed to be convincing her we can be *just friends*, it's probably not wise to voice my thoughts.

She flushes under my gaze, her cheeks turning a pretty pink that matches her ballet shoes. But her full lips are downturned.

"You're flirting again."

"You don't compliment your friends?" I counter and she gives me an unamused look.

"*Gray.*"

I chuckle, trying to ignore the way my chest warms at that nickname. "I'll stop." *For now.* "You did look like a professional in there, though. Everyone was following your lead."

She tugs at the sleeves of her top, not meeting my gaze. "I'm sure they weren't all following me."

"I was watching. They were."

She shrugs off my compliment. "You're just saying that."

I shake my head. How can a woman so breathtaking and utterly brilliant be unsure of herself? Seeing her fidgeting in front of me makes me want to find whatever is causing this insecurity and rip it apart.

She glances over her shoulder and I follow her gaze. The other class members are moving the barre to the back of the room.

"We're about to start again," she says, then looks back to me. "Go do whatever you came here for and quit spying on me." Her lips are turned up at the edges, even though her words are shooing me away.

"What if I came here to watch you?"

She pushes my shoulder, fighting a smile. "*Go.*"

"All right, all right. I'll go. See you around, Rose." I back away, holding her gaze with a grin. She turns to go into the classroom with a smile on her lips. The sight makes me feel like there are Pop Rocks in my chest, a sweet fizzy feeling that I don't want to lose.

I don't know if I've ever felt this way about a woman before. I've barely spoken with her, but I'm anxiously awaiting our next meeting. Her laugh is on repeat in my head, and I can already tell it's going to be one of those songs you can play over and over and it never gets old. And if I think about her books on top of all of that, I'm a goner.

Every word of hers is crafted with masterful intention. Nothing is ever merely filler. I've reread her books, thinking that the allure would wear off, but it never does. Time and time again, she draws me into her stories and makes me feel every emotion alongside the characters. Her words have stuck with me, and now that I've met her in person, I want nothing more than to get to know the woman behind those words. If only she'll give me the chance.

"I don't know why I bother," I say with a sigh as my brother Levi sinks the eight ball into the pocket of my pool table.

"Me either." He chuckles. "But it keeps my wallet full, so keep it up."

"Why did you bet money on a game you were likely to lose?" my twin brother, Adrian asks.

"Because I thought putting money on the line would make me play better." It did not. Or at least not better than Levi. He's way too good at this game, but that doesn't stop all of us from trying to beat him. My whole family is competitive, so the opportunity to dethrone Levi never loses its appeal.

"Hey guys, sorry I'm late, had to close the bakery myself today," another one of my brothers–Maverick–says as he walks down the stairs of my basement.

Most of the time, if all of us brothers are getting together, we end up down here in my basement. I bought a two-story home in a quaint, family-friendly neighborhood because I felt like buying a 'bachelor pad' was foolish when I knew I wanted a family one day. But I also am a bachelor, and like having my brothers over, so I turned my basement into a man cave of sorts.

There's a giant TV on the wall, every gaming console available, a pool table, a huge sectional, and a closet full of board games that have caused many fights between all of us. I've even got a Georgia Thrashers helmet that's been signed by all of the players of the last championship-winning team on display in a glass case, perks of my sister marrying their coach.

"It's no big deal. I thought you stopped doing that though?" I ask as I put my cue on the mounted wall rack.

Maverick runs his own bakery, and as it's grown in popularity he's hired a few employees to help him. He still likes to go in early in the mornings to do a lot of the baking himself, but he rarely works the counter anymore.

"I did, but both my employees who usually work today called in sick, so I figured I could work or close up shop, and since I already had most of the baking done, I worked the whole day."

"You should probably be home asleep," I say and he shrugs, heading over to slump onto my sectional.

"It's been a while since we all got together," he says.

"Yeah, that's because Adrian and Levi are lovestruck." I grin as I sit on the couch. Levi and Adrian follow suit. "They don't have time for us anymore."

"We see you plenty," Levi says with an eye roll. "I saw you last weekend at MJ's house." Our sister, who's the youngest, has the biggest house out of all of us, having married a millionaire football coach. She lives in a secluded mansion with her husband Sebastian and their adopted daughter Maddie. Most of our family gatherings are at her house or our dad's. They'd probably all be at her house if our dad wasn't such a hermit.

"And I see you too much," Adrian grumbles, but I just smile. Working with my twin wasn't in the plan years ago, but after being away from family for a while traveling as an Air Marshal, I wanted to settle down. Luckily, Adrian felt the same way about his position in the CIA. So, we both retired and opened a private security company together.

"What would you do without my bubbly presence around the office?" I ask him with a grin.

"Get more work done," he answers in his usual gruff tone. Maverick and Levi both chuckle at us.

"I thought getting engaged to Juliette would make you nicer to everyone, but I guess you're just nice to *her*." I shake my head like I'm disappointed. The corner of his mouth twitches, but he doesn't let himself smile.

"Speaking of Juliette," Levi jumps into the conversation. "How's wedding planning going?"

Adrian shrugs. "Fine."

Levi stares, waiting for him to elaborate.

"Did you think he was going to gush over floral design with you?" I laugh.

"I thought he'd give me more than a one word answer!" Levi leans back, kicking his feet up on the ottoman.

"Because he's known for lengthy monologues," I deadpan. Adrian watches us in silent amusement.

"Fine, I'll ask Dahlia. I'm sure she and Juliette have shared every detail with each other."

"How's *your* wedding planning going?" I ask Levi. He and Dahlia got together in the fall, after being apart for five years. Now they're planning a late summer wedding with a few friends and family.

"It's going great. We just booked the condo for our honeymoon in Rosemary."

"That's not wedding planning," I say and his lips stretch into a crooked grin.

"No, it's not."

I shake my head, laughing at his thinly veiled enthusiasm for what comes after their wedding.

"In all seriousness, it is going great. Dahlia got The Secret Door to agree to let us book a private event there so we can get married amongst the shelves."

"That's great, I know she'll love that."

Levi continues talking about the planning process, telling a story about how he found out he was allergic to hydrangeas when they visited the florist's shop. I listen and laugh when appropriate, but there's an uncomfortable sensation in my chest, like a pin pricking at my heart. Unfortunately, I've come to know this feeling well as of late. Jealousy, with a tinge of loneliness.

Seeing my baby sister happily married, and two out of three of my brothers engaged, has created this concern that I'll be the odd man out. If Maverick finally moves on from the pain of his ex, he's bound to find someone too. Images of me sitting alone at each of my siblings' weddings and being the 'fun uncle' at every family party, come to mind. They only add to the discomfort.

I try to keep a smile on my face as I take a few deep breaths. The last thing I want is to follow these thoughts into a spiral that leads to an anxiety attack. My mind races as I search for something positive to ground me.

Interestingly enough, the image that finally slows down my thoughts is Sloane's smile.

CHAPTER FIVE

Sloane Covington

I don't know why I'm still here. I sigh and swirl my straw around in my mostly melted strawberry banana smoothie. My ballet class ended a half hour ago, but I can't bring myself to go home. I know when I get there, I'll go into my room and see my laptop on my desk taunting me. I haven't been able to write all week. Every time I sit down, I get the urge to throw my laptop into a trashcan, pour gasoline on it, and light a match.

My eyes wander around the gym, finding their way to where Grayson is working out in the free weights section. *Again.* Because even though my silly brain knows that he is trouble, I can't help but be drawn to him. He picks up two large dumbbells and starts lifting them, doing lateral raises. I'm not close enough to pick up on the details of his appearance, but even from here, I can see his muscles working and the sheen of sweat on his skin.

His head lifts and I whip back toward my smoothie, taking a drink to hide my flaming face. There's no way he saw me watching from this far away, but somehow I think he would know. He probably already does.

My face twists up at my room-temperature smoothie. What a waste of eight dollars. Simone makes better ones, and would probably make me one if I asked. But again, home is where my laptop is, so it must be avoided at all costs. Even if the cost is an overpriced smoothie.

I look up once more, determined to look everywhere but the free weights section. I take in the lines of treadmills and stairclimbers, the stationary bikes with TVs mounted on them, and the kickboxing area with multiple punching bags suspended from the ceiling. When my gaze lands on the front desk area, I stiffen.

Topher is here. *And* my stepsister Brooke. They take their passes from the front desk clerk, then look around as if they're searching for someone. They must be here for me. My delusional, overbearing father and stepmother must have sent them to find me and convince me to marry Topher.

Anger surges to life within me, drowning out my anxiety. I push to my feet, grab my smoothie cup, and throw it into the trashcan before walking over to them. I can feel the adrenaline in each step I take. Brooke's eyes land on me first, her perfect face twisted into a smirk as per usual.

"I cannot believe you two are here," I say as soon as I'm close enough to them. Topher's eyes blow wide, likely not expecting the venom in my voice. I've always been soft-spoken, and he tended to talk over me even when I wasn't.

"Mom told us–"

I cut Brooke off, my disbelief at my stepmother's audacity fueling my boldness. "I don't care what she told you. I'm not marrying Topher. So you can turn around and leave. Nothing you can say would convince me to marry him."

Brooke's eyes light up, her lips pressing together like she's trying to contain laughter. My stomach drops. She should be frowning, or angry, but she's not.

"That's not why we're here."

"What?" My brain buffers, unable to comprehend any other reason why these two are standing in front of me. "The club has a gym, so I know you aren't here to work out. Don't lie to me, Brooke, I know you're just here to help Topher win me back."

"Why would I be helping my fiancé get back with his ex?"

My mouth falls opens, then shuts. What did she just say?

"Y-your fiancé?" I look to Topher, then back at Brooke. She smiles, shoving her hand out in the space between us. Weighing her slender finger down is the same ring Topher proposed to me with, except with a larger diamond nestled into the decades-old setting.

"Topher realized after his parents tried to force him to marry you, that he's been in love with *me* all along," Brooke says, leveling me with a superior look. "He proposed yesterday, and Mom thought it was best we break the news in person."

I try to swallow, but my throat is too dry.

"You're going to marry my *stepsister*?" I ask Topher.

"We want the same things," he says. If he looked down his nose at me any more he'd be cross-eyed.

My anger starts to dissolve like paper in water. I never loved Topher, but it still hurts to think that he could move on so easily, and with a member of my family no less.

"We'll be getting married next month," Brooke squeals, then calms herself and flips her platinum hair over one shoulder. "Oh, and Mom also wanted me to invite you to the engagement party this Saturday. I'm assuming you won't have a plus one?" Brooke asks, still wearing her shiny, smug grin.

Her question stings. She's won and she knows it. They came here with the intent to catch me off guard, to hurt me, and then leave me feeling alone and unworthy. I glance away, trying to gather my thoughts, and my eyes land on Grayson. He's walking toward a machine nearby. Before I can talk myself out of it, I call out to him.

"Gray!" I say and his head snaps in my direction. A grin spreads over his face, bringing a rush of warmth over my skin. If only he didn't look at everyone like that, like they're the best thing he's seen since he opened his eyes this morning.

I wave him over and he saunters up to us. His confidence is infectious, and I find myself standing a little straighter. My boldness from before returns, and a very, *very* stupid idea comes into my mind. But when I glance back at Brooke to find her nuzzling Topher's arm like a cat, I throw caution to the wind.

"Brooke, Topher," I say, then take a deep breath of courage. "I'd like to introduce you to my fiancé, Grayson Carter."

Brooke's mouth drops open, and Topher looks as though someone took a crowbar to his Porsche. Their shocked faces boost my mood, but there's one more reaction I need to check. I look up at Grayson, and he smiles down at me like I didn't just blatantly lie about our relationship. Then he throws an arm around my shoulders, pulling me into his side.

"You're engaged?" Brooke squeaks out and I smile big, hoping it hides the way my entire nervous system is malfunctioning.

"Yep! He proposed just last week, and we haven't told anyone yet. We wanted to keep the news to ourselves for a little while, enjoy our moment in private." The last part is a dig, and by the way her expression tightens, she knows it.

For once in my life I'm not thinking before I speak. I'm sure I'll regret that immediately after this conversation, but right now I feel powerful–like I have the upper hand.

"Then where's the ring?" Brooke asks. I look down at my bare left hand, my mind just as blank as my ring finger.

"She doesn't like to wear it to the gym," Grayson says, squeezing my shoulders. "She hates the idea of potentially damaging it."

"That's right," I say, my smile returning. "I couldn't bear it if something happened to it."

"I didn't get a chance to ask." Grayson's fingers trace circles on my shoulder as he speaks, making a pleasant shiver go down my spine. "Who are you to Sloane?"

"I'd think she would have told you about her sister," Brooke says, sounding like she's caught me.

"*Step*sister," I clarify, leaning into Grayson. "And you didn't come up. Neither did my ex-boyfriend, Topher." I gesture to Topher, who's still glaring at the both of us. "They came by to tell me that they're getting married next month. Isn't that wonderful news?"

I tilt my head back, meeting Grayson's eyes. They're gleaming like sapphires, not a trace of annoyance in them. In fact, he looks amused, maybe even *excited*. Like this is some game that we're in together, instead of an unplanned ruse I sprung on him.

"I guess love is in the air." His eyes don't leave mine and I can't help the fluttery feeling in my stomach.

"I guess it is," Brooke says through gritted teeth, drawing my attention–reluctantly–back to her. "I'm *so* happy for you two." Her smile looks frozen on her face. Topher doesn't look much better. He's trying to seem intimidating by puffing his chest and standing tall, but it doesn't work next to Grayson. It's a sight that would make me laugh if it wasn't for the fact that I'm a breath away from spiraling.

"Thank you, I'm happy for you too." The words burn like acid coming up my throat, but I make it through the sentence.

"So we'll be seeing you two at the engagement party, then?"

Oh no. I'd forgotten about the whole reason I made up this engagement in the first place. What am I going to do now?

"Of course," Grayson answers for me, cool as a tropical breeze.

"Great, that's just great." Brooke's fingernails are digging into Topher's bicep. That's got to hurt. "I'll send you the details."

"Sounds good," I say, feeling numb.

Brooke drags a brooding Topher away. As soon as they're out the door, I step away from Grayson, my hands shaking.

"So," he begins while I'm trying to wrap my head around what I've just done. "Have we set a date yet?"

CHAPTER SIX

Grayson Carter

"Personally, I think next spring would be great. Both my brothers are getting married this year, so we probably shouldn't overshadow them," I joke after Sloane doesn't say anything.

She stares blankly at the door that her ex and stepsister just walked out of. I can't blame her for being in shock. I'd be shocked too if I was her. This level of toxicity is new to me since I come from a good family. It makes me want to go home and hug all of my siblings. It makes me want to hug *her*, but I'm not sure she's ready for that level of physical affection after everything that just happened, so I settle for something more subdued.

"Rose," I say in a low voice, taking her hand and running my thumb over her knuckles. "Take a breath." Her pink lips part as she drags in a shuddery breath. "It's okay."

She looks up at me with wide hazel eyes. They're a touch more green today, the color brought out by the emerald workout set she's donning.

"It's not okay," she says, panic lacing her words. "I just lied about being engaged!" Her voice goes up an octave, and I look around to make sure no one is looking over at us.

"Come on, let's go outside." I guide her out, still holding her hand and enjoying it far too much.

Once we're outdoors, I walk us to my car and open the passenger door for her.

"Where are we going?" she asks but gets in the car.

"Nowhere, I just thought we needed some privacy," I reply before shutting the door and going to get in on the driver's side. I quickly turn on the air conditioning before the Atlanta humidity can suffocate us.

"How are you so calm right now?" She turns in the seat, positioning her body toward me. "I just grabbed you and forced you into a fake engagement. And that's another thing–why did you go along with it?" Her words come out rapidly, tumbling one after another.

"It's not a big deal. Friends help friends." I smile at her, but she doesn't return it.

"This is too much. I shouldn't have brought you into this." She puts her face in her hands. "I'm going to have to tell everyone I lied."

"Why?" My one word question hangs in the air between us.

She lifts her head, her eyes glassy. "Because I can't ask you to be my fake fiancé, Grayson. It was sweet of you to play along, but meeting my family?" She shakes her head.

"I think it sounds fun," I tell her and she lets out a disbelieving laugh. "I'm serious. That ex of yours seemed like a jerk, and your step sister would definitely fit into the cast of Cinderella. It would be awesome to help you stick it to them."

Her lips turn up in an uncertain smile. "We can't stay fake engaged forever though. Eventually, the show has to end."

I shrug. "So, you say we broke up. You're a brilliant author, I'm sure you can come up with something. Tell them I got obsessive and you had to get a restraining order. Or that we had a falling out because we both like to eat just the marshmallows out of Lucky Charms instead of being the perfect balance of one liking the cereal and the other liking the marshmallows."

She lets out a real laugh this time, and all I want to do is ensure that she does it again and again. Her laughter fades, and her expression turns thoughtful. "Let's say we keep this up. It would help me face my family, but what do you get out of it?"

More time with you, I want to say.

"A chance to practice my acting skills," I joke instead and she laughs.

"I'm serious, Gray. My family..." she trails off. "They aren't pleasant to be around. This isn't going to be a fun time."

"That, my dear future wife, is where you're wrong. I can make anything fun. That will be my reward, proving you wrong."

"So, it'll be like a game for you," she says.

"Yeah, a game. I'll prove that I can make even the most awful parties fun, and you don't have to face your family alone."

She bites her lip. I sit through a minute of agonizing silence before she sighs, then shrugs. "Why not? It's better than telling them I lied."

Excitement rushes through my veins like I just drank an energy drink and a coffee back-to-back—neither of which I'm allowed to have anymore, according to my family.

"This is going to be a fantastic summer." I grin. Sloane's smile is wary, but there's a light in her eyes that assures me she's a little excited too.

"I don't think you know what you've signed up for, but I'm glad I don't have to do this alone." She reaches across the console and touches my forearm, sending warm sparks all through me. "Thank you, Gray."

"You're welcome, Rose," I tell her with a smile.

I should really be thanking her, though. She's given me a chance to spend time with her and this will be the perfect distraction from my family shifting and changing.

"So, I guess I need to prepare you for this weekend," Sloane's voice pulls me from my thoughts. "You are free on Saturday, right?"

I nod. " Luckily, I am. But I do have some work to do today, so how about I pick you up tonight for dinner and you can tell me everything I need to know?"

She tucks a stray hair behind her ear. "Sure, that sounds good. I can give you my number, then text you my address."

I hand her my phone and she opens up the contacts. Pauses. Then looks at me.

"There are other girls' numbers in here," she says in a stilted voice.

"There are," I reply, confused at her tone.

"If we're going to do this, you can't—I mean—" She cringes. "Are you okay not dating anyone while we're together? I'm sorry—I'm not trying to be controlling of your personal life—but if someone saw you..."

I ignore the sting of her implications. She doesn't know me, but I wish she didn't think I'd be the type of guy to date around while I'm dating her–fake or not.

"Rose." I meet her eyes. "I won't date or flirt with anyone while we're doing this. I'm not that kind of guy. I'm yours for the summer."

"Thank you," she breathes out. Then she types in her number and hands my phone back to me.

"I guess I'll see you tonight, then." She grabs the door handle, and I can see her confidence beginning to wane.

"Do you like the marshmallows or the cereal better?" I ask her as she opens the door. She smiles at my question, and I know my method of drawing her out of her thought spiral has worked, if only for a moment.

"Marshmallows, definitely. You?"

"The cereal," I lie with a grin.

"Really?" She gives me a questioning look. "You seem like a guy who would have a sweet tooth."

I do, big time. But if she likes the marshmallows, I'll eat the mushy cardboard-tasting bits.

I shrug. "When it comes to cereal, I don't."

"We have a lot to learn about each other before this weekend if we're going to convince everyone." She starts to slide out of the seat.

"Yes, we do. Prepare to share all your secrets, wifey," I say, and she shakes her head, giggling.

"Please don't tell me that's my new nickname."

"I think it has to be now."

"I prefer Rose." She gets out of the car, then bends down to look at me with a playful scowl.

"One thing about me that you should know, *wifey*, is that I love nicknames. There will be no shortage of terms of endearment this summer."

"You like nasty cereal and terms of endearment, got it."

I place a hand over my heart. "It feels like you've known me for years."

She laughs. "I'll see you tonight, Gray."

"See you, honey bunches of oats." I can still hear her laughing even after she closes my car door and steps back onto the sidewalk.

I watch her walk back inside the gym, then I Google search jewelry stores nearby.

"Time to make it official."

Rose: I don't have an engagement ring.

I smile down at my phone. I just texted Sloane so that she had my number after getting back to my desk post-engagement ring shopping.

Rose: Oh, hi. I should have started with that.

Before I can type a reply, my phone buzzes again.

Rose: Also, I'm attaching my address to this message before I forget.

Rose: Oh no, you're at work, aren't you? I shouldn't be texting you so much! I'm sorry.

I chuckle, leaning back in my chair, watching the three little dots appear once more to let me know she's not done.

Rose: Where do you work? I should probably know that.

Rose: I DID IT AGAIN. Please stop me. I'm so sorry.

Grayson: Hi, Rose.

Rose: Hi. I'm sorry. Again.

I can't stop smiling. I don't think I've stopped since I left the gym this morning.

Grayson: Don't be. Now I know you like to send multiple texts instead of one long one. That's a key detail for me to know as your fiancé.

Rose: And now I know that you can spin anything to make it positive. That will come in handy while you're engaged to me.

Grayson: See? We make a great couple. I got you an engagement ring, by the way. I'll show it to you tonight at dinner.

Rose: Should I be concerned that you bought something without me? You didn't need to do that. I hope you didn't spend a lot of money.

I spent more than I thought I would when I walked in there, but that will be another harmless little detail I'll keep to myself. Go big or go home, as they say.

Grayson: Don't worry, I got something reasonable. But I just realized I never asked, what ring size are you?

Rose: I have no idea. I haven't worn a ring since I was a kid.

I guessed in the store because I didn't want her to offer to buy her own. And then once I was in there, I found myself drawn to a ring that seemed so very *her*. Said ring was also a real diamond when I planned on buying a fake one, but what's the point of having all this money if I don't spend it on an elaborate ruse every once in a while?

Grayson: Then I suppose we'll see if I guessed correctly tonight. If it doesn't fit, we can get it resized. Can I pick you up at 7?

Rose: Yes, that works. Where are we going?

Grayson: Do you like surprises?

Rose: I'd usually say no.

Grayson: But?

Rose: But I kind of want to see what you'd do if I say yes.

Grayson: Surprise it is then, wifey.

Rose: I hope I don't regret this.

CHAPTER SEVEN

Sloane Covington

There's no way I can sneak out without my best friends seeing me. Especially since Myla invited me to have a movie night after dinner. I stammered out a yes because I hadn't worked up the courage to tell her or Simone what happened today. I'm not even sure if I should tell them. Then they'll have to lie for me if they end up seeing any of my family in the coming months.

Once again, I'm second guessing my decision to go on this date. When Grayson asked to pick me up tonight I was in the middle of writing. Or rather *trying* to write. Even after all my research, it's been difficult to wrap my head around this new genre. I had all these ideas, but the execution has been ... questionable to say the least. So, I almost said no to him in order to stay home and bang my head on my desk the rest of the night. But I figured I got myself into this fake engagement, so I should commit. Plus, I'd be lying if I said I wasn't looking forward to seeing Grayson again.

I sigh and open my bedroom door, walking down the hall into the living room. *Might as well get this over with.* Simone is curled up on the couch, writing in her Sudoku book. I don't get the appeal, but she says it keeps her mind sharp and is different enough from writing that it feels like a break. She looks up when I enter the room, her brows furrowing.

"Where are you going?"

I knew she'd call me out immediately. Around the house I'm usually in pajamas, and anywhere else I go I wear athleisure. So coming out in a yellow sundress is akin to hanging a flashing neon sign over my head that reads *look at me, look at me*!

"I'm meeting a friend for dinner," I say, trying to keep my voice level.

Simone narrows her eyes. "Who?"

"You sound like an owl." I let out a nervous laugh.

Myla comes out of the kitchen, a frilly red apron with white polka dots pulled on over her pastel blue dress. She's wearing matching red lipstick that makes her teeth look extra white when she smiles at me.

"Are you dressed up for girls' night too? How fun! Simone, you should go change. We can take photos before the sun goes down all the way."

"Sloane is going out with a friend," Simone says and Myla frowns.

"We're her only friends."

"Hey, I have other friends," I defend myself, though I can't think of any.

"Again I ask: Who?" Simone's voice conveys her suspicion.

A knock sounds at the door and my stomach flips. The dainty gold watch on my wrist reveals that Grayson is eight minutes early.

Another detail about him to file away. Despite his lackadaisical attitude, he is punctual.

"If I tell you, you can't ask any questions or talk to the person on the other side of that door."

"Or I can go answer the door right now," Myla says and takes a step in that direction.

"No!" I hold my hands out. "I just need time to explain. Time I don't have because Grayson Carter is waiting outside that door."

Simone blinks. Myla's mouth drops open.

"You're going on a date," Myla squeals and claps her hands. "Why didn't you just say that?"

"It's ... complicated."

"It must be, considering you told us you had no plans of dating him." Simone eyes me, and I fidget under her gaze.

Grayson knocks again, saving me.

"I'll explain soon enough, I promise." I walk toward the door, grabbing my brown crossbody bag and sliding on my gold sandals.

"You better!" Simone calls out as I open the door.

Grayson grins down at me. I place a hand on his chest, pushing him backward so that I can walk out into the hall, and shut the door behind me.

"Hello to you too, wifey," he says with a laugh. I grab his hand and start to drag him down the hallway.

"Come on, we need to go."

"What are you in such a rush for?" He lets me tug him to the elevator, smiling the whole way. "If you're anxious to get to the post-date kiss, I'm happy to oblige you now."

I hit his arm, then press the elevator call button three times in a row.

"We are not kissing." I pull him into the elevator as soon as it opens. "We are making sure my roommates don't talk to you."

"I can't believe my betrothed is embarrassed of me."

Once the elevator doors close, I sigh and look at him. He's wearing navy blue shorts and a white linen shirt with a few buttons undone, exposing a triangle of smooth, tan skin. The sleeves are rolled up too, which I'm convinced is every woman's kryptonite.

I realize I'm still holding his hand, and I drop it. It's suddenly much too warm in here.

"I'm not embarrassed of you. I simply don't know how to tell my two best friends that I'm *engaged*."

"Do you want to tell them it's fake? I assume you can trust them, since you live with them."

"I don't know if I want to drag them into this, but I also hate the idea of lying to them."

"I think you should tell them. You shouldn't have to keep up the story in your own home." His reasoning is sound. I don't want them to lie for me, but it's rare that they'd run into anyone they'd have to lie to on my behalf, now that I think about it.

"That's a good point. I'll tell them, then."

"Good." He pauses, and I fiddle with my watch. "You look lovely, by the way."

"Oh, thank you." I blush. "You don't have to compliment me, though. I know it's all a game."

"Complimenting you will never be a game, Rose."

I look up at him, meeting his sparkling blue eyes. His sincerity hits me like a tidal wave, stealing my breath. The elevator dings, saving me from having to formulate a coherent reply. I step off and Grayson follows. We walk through the ice-cold lobby, goosebumps breaking out over my arms and legs.

Thankfully, we're not in the cold long. The warm evening air washes over my skin and I can't help but shiver at the sudden temperature change.

"My car is this way." He gestures to the left and we walk in silence under the setting sun. The scent of azaleas floats on the breeze, the bright pink blooms dotting the bushes that line the building. My fingers continually twist my watch around my wrist, my stomach feeling like a popcorn machine of nerves.

"I'm worried," I say, and he glances over at me, concern lining his face. "You're too quiet. I haven't known you long, but that can't be good." My words come out less joking than I want. It sounds like I'm worried he's going to kill me, not that he's simply up to something mischievous.

"Your beauty stole my words." He gives me a crooked grin, and I roll my eyes. "I was really just thinking about our date. I'm hoping you'll enjoy yourself. Though you are gorgeous enough to render a man speechless."

My cheeks heat and I duck my head, focusing on my feet walking down the sidewalk. My stomach backflips, but the blossoming giddiness within me withers when I realize that he's not serious. He's like this too often for his words to have meaning.

"What do you have planned?" I ask him, working to not sound as breathless as I feel.

"It's a *surprise*, remember?" he teases as he walks to his silver car to open the passenger door for me.

"I think I changed my mind. I'd rather know." I slide into his car.

"Too late." He shuts the door with a wide smile. I buckle my seatbelt while he walks around the front of the car.

"Can you give me a hint?" I ask him when he gets in. A fresh out of the shower scent fills the car. It's citrusy and bright, but mellowed out by a musky sweetness that makes me want to breathe a little deeper to savor it. *Of course* he would smell fantastic on top of looking like a model and having the confidence of one.

"If I did, I'd give it away. Don't worry, it's nothing elaborate."

"Am I dressed for the occasion?"

"I would have told you if you weren't. Though, admittedly you didn't give me much time."

He pulls out of the parking spot, then out of the lot and onto the road.

"I'm sorry for manhandling you," I say. A wicked grin spreads over his face.

"You can handle me any way you like, wifey."

I groan. "Is this how it's going to be all summer?" I feign exasperation, but beneath my skin is a sweet hum. The kind of buzz I could easily chase for the next month.

"You walked into that one."

"I have a feeling that you could come up with a line in response to anything I say."

"I'd be up to the challenge, if you want to test me."

I bite back a smile and look out the window, trying to decipher where we're headed. Every time I think he's going to pull over, he doesn't. We pass several restaurants, an arcade, and a movie theater. We're nowhere near the aquarium, so that's out too.

He finally pulls off in front of a small pizza place. From the looks of it, it's not even big enough to have tables.

"Be right back," he says and hops out. I watch him jog inside, make the clerk laugh, then come back out and put two large boxes in the backseat.

"What if I don't like pizza?" I ask once he's back in the car.

"Then I guess we'll need to make another stop," he answers like he knows I'm teasing. "Do I?"

"No," I mumble, making him laugh.

"We'll be there soon, then your curiosity will be satisfied."

True to his word, we pull into a suburban neighborhood not long after grabbing our pizza, and then he pulls up in front of a gorgeous craftsman home.

"Is this your house?" I ask him. He unbuckles his seatbelt, and I follow suit.

"Yes. I hope that's okay. I thought it was better to have some privacy since we're going to be divulging our life stories."

I didn't plan on giving him my whole life story, but I suppose he's right about needing privacy. I don't want to run into anyone I know before we get our story straight. Atlanta is a big city, but with my luck, I'd end up running into my dad.

We get out of the car and I smooth down my dress.

"Why do you have such a large house? Do you have a secret family I should know about?"

He chuckles while grabbing the pizza from the backseat.

"No, but I do want a family one day, so I thought it made the most sense to buy a home for one."

I wait for a joke, or the explanation of a missed punchline, but it doesn't come. He can't be telling the truth, can he? I study him as he walks to the door, balancing the pizza in one hand while fishing his keys out of his pocket with the other.

I don't think he'd lie to me, but this new information doesn't fit with the playing-the-field-bachelor image I have of him. I thought I had him figured out, but now he's changing things. It's like getting halfway through writing a book only to remember a key point I forgot. It changes the rest of the story, and forces me to go back and rewrite what I thought I knew.

"Everything okay?"

I blink, realizing I've been standing a few feet away staring.

"Yes, I was just admiring the house."

"It's okay if you think it's a weird purchase, most people do."

I walk in behind him. He throws his keys in a bowl on a table by the door.

"It's unusual, but sweet, too."

"I'll take it." He laughs, but it doesn't sound the same as his usual one. There's a touch of tension in it, like he's as nervous as I am that I'm here. "I can give you a tour another day if you'd like, but we're out back for tonight."

We walk through his living room. It's spacious and cozy, with no TV in sight. Instead, there's a large painting of a field of sunflowers, surrounded by photos of what looks to be friends and family and a few smaller art pieces. If Grayson wasn't heading for his sliding back door, I'd stop and look closer at the wall. Instead, I follow him outside back into the warm summer air.

I suck in a breath when I step onto the porch. The entire backyard has string lights hanging over it, and there's a picnic blanket in the center of the yard.

"Gray," I whisper, but he's too far away to hear me. He sets the pizza boxes on the blanket then turns to look at me. "What is this?" I speak louder this time.

"It's a picnic," he says like it's nothing. "I know it's not much, but I thought if I went elaborate you'd be overwhelmed." He sits down and gestures for me to come to him.

Considering I am overwhelmed, that was a good call on his part. I walk over, trying and failing not to get lost in the magic of the deep blue sky and the warm lights. The picnic blanket has a cooler on it, and some extra blankets in a folded stack.

"This is beautiful," I say as I sit down beside him. I grab one of the extra blankets and pull it over my legs, in case my dress rides up. "Did you hang these lights just for me?"

He opens a pizza box, setting it in between us. The fragrance of warm, melty cheese and sweet basil fills the air.

"I've been meaning to, but you coming gave me the extra push."

He tears a slice of pizza, oblivious to my emotional undoing. This is nothing to him, but this is the sweetest thing a guy has ever done for me. Topher always took me to the most expensive restaurants, like that's what would make me happy, but Grayson's picnic beats out every five star restaurant I've been to. It's romantic and private, and free of all the pressure to perform that those restaurants usually induce.

He glances up, catching me staring. "You don't have to stare, I'm happy to pose for a photo."

And there it is, another flirty line that has me wondering how many girls he's said that too. I'm certain he's been stared at before.

I roll my eyes and steal his slice of pizza from him.

"I wasn't staring at *you*, I was staring at the pizza." I take a bite and he laughs.

"Whatever you say, Rose." He pulls off another slice, setting it on a paper plate. "Are you ready to talk about this weekend, or do you want to avoid it a little while longer?"

I sigh, my stomach tightening with anxiety. I'd much rather eat pizza under twinkle lights while Grayson makes me blush and laugh for hours, but it's probably best that we talk about this weekend instead. I don't need to get caught up in all of this and forget that it's fake. *A game*, he'd said earlier today. It's just a game for him to pass the time this summer.

"Let's do this."

CHAPTER EIGHT

Grayson Carter

I'm not a man known for my self-control. I'm responsible, sure, but I've also bought a jet ski because I saw a TikTok of a guy doing a handstand on one and thought to myself *hey, I could do that*. I did, by the way, but that's not the point. The point is I deserve a medal, a trophy, or at least a gold star for my restraint around Sloane right now.

I don't know what I was thinking, stringing twinkle lights above us. They only serve to make her tan skin glow and her hazel eyes glitter. There's a softness about her that begs to be held. If this was a real date, and not some prep course for this weekend, I'd lay her down on this picnic blanket and kiss her soft and slow until we were both breathless and dazed.

But it's not real, so I pull at a string of the picnic blanket, watching the checkered seam unravel.

"What's your favorite color?" Sloane asks, making me look up from the blanket. "I figured we could start with the easy stuff." She pauses. "And I really don't want to talk about my family yet."

I smile at her while I think. I've never bothered to choose a favorite color. My soon to be sister-in-law Dahlia says that she loves all colors, but I can't say that's true for me. My eyes trail over her golden dress, and I make my decision in that moment.

"Yellow. What about you?"

"It depends on the season. But right now I love lavender and blush."

"And in the fall?"

"Burgundy and chocolate brown," she says with an air of certainty that makes me feel as though she's thought this through. I bet her wardrobe reflects her choice too. Imagining her in autumn, browsing books and smiling over a coffee cup makes my chest tight with longing. Will we be together when the leaves change? Or will all I have be memories of sundresses and summer breezes?

"What's your favorite dessert?" I ask her in an attempt to derail my unpleasant train of thought.

"Tiramisu," she says and I grin.

"That's mine too. You have good taste, wifey."

We trade facts back and forth for a while. I learn that she loves 90s and early 2000s rom coms, screaming to breakup songs in the car, and if she built her dream home it would have a two-story library and a wrap-around porch. I confess my love of *Dance Moms*, which makes her throw her head back and laugh. In return she tells me that she grew up loving ballet, but she gave it up in college to please her dad by focusing on school. She started taking adult classes at the gym last year and wishes she would have never given it up.

"Speaking of your family," I say as she wraps a blanket around her shoulders. The night air is cooling down enough to need it, but not enough to head inside. "Why don't you tell me about them?"

She sighs, begins. "My stepmother is an older version of Brooke, except she possesses a touch more tact. Not much, but some."

"And your dad?"

"He's proud, and thinks he knows best about everything. He hates my job, so try not to bring it up around him." I frown at this, but she continues. "Brooke sent me the details earlier, and the party is at the club where they're all members, so I'm sure all of their elite friends will be there. They'll suffocate you with their pretentiousness, but if you keep things surface level we can make it through the night relatively unscathed."

I'm used to dealing with pretentious rich people at the events I go to for work. There's a strong chance I've met some of the people we'll see this weekend. As the owner of a private security company, I spend a lot of my time networking.

"Surface level, got it." I nod. "Are they going to ask us any questions?"

"They'll likely ask how we met, and how you proposed, if only to catch us in a lie. So, I guess it would be good to get our stories straight."

"Okay, Miss Bestseller, what's our story then?" I glance over at her. There's a sweet smile playing on her lips.

"As fun as an elaborate plot would be, I think keeping it simple is best. We met at the gym after I broke up with Topher and fell in love from there." She stumbles over the word *love*, like it's an unexpected crack in the sidewalk.

"And our proposal?" I ask her. She tilts her head side to side.

"Hm, I'm not sure about that one. Nothing public. Anyone who knows me knows I don't do lots of people."

"Then, how about we say I asked you right here?" I reach for the ring box that I set behind the cooler. "Under twinkle lights, on a picnic blanket. You looking breathtaking in a yellow sundress, me debonair in my button down." She rolls her eyes when I compliment myself, but her smile is wide and genuine.

I open the ring box, holding it out between us. She gasps, immediately reaching for it. Her fingertips brush mine ever so softly, like flipping the page of a worn book.

"It looks so real," she murmurs.

"It does," I say, keeping my voice level. *Because it is*, I should say, but I don't. If I did, I'd have to explain why I bought a three carat pear-shaped diamond ring for my fake fiancée. And since my main answer is *I don't know*, it's probably not the best time to reveal that detail.

"It's beautiful, Gray. You chose well." She goes to remove the ring, but I take the box back from her.

"Not so fast, wifey. We're going to do this right."

I help her stand up, then get on one knee in front of her, and hold up the ring box. A breeze toys with the hem of her yellow dress. The lights above create a golden aura around her. I take a steadying breath of evening air, the scent of basil mixing with the fragrance of my lemon tree. I trail my gaze over her, memorizing the way her dress cinches in at her waist and how her bare feet nervously shift on the blanket. I'm not sure why I want to remember this, but something deep inside tells me I'm going to look back on this one day.

"Sloane–" I cut myself off with a little laugh. "Wait, what's your middle name?"

"Elizabeth," she answers in a breathy voice. The air around us is heavy with an emotion I can't quite place.

"Sloane Elizabeth Covington," I begin, then smile up at her. "Rose," I start once more and the smile she gives me in return could light all of downtown Atlanta. "Will you do me the incredible honor of becoming my wife?"

"Yes," she whispers, her voice soft as a feather, but her answer heavy with meaning. Though what the meaning could be, I'm not sure. I slip the ring on her finger. Perfect fit.

I stand up, suddenly not knowing what to do. Sloane shifts on her feet like she feels the same way. If this was real, I'd pull her into my arms and kiss her. There would be a photographer hiding nearby, capturing the moment for years to come. And our closest friends and family—the ones Sloane would be happy to see—would be somewhere close by, ready to celebrate with us.

"I'm not sure how people celebrate fake engagements," she says with a nerve-tinged laugh.

"Me either." I scratch the back of my neck. "Maybe with ice cream?"

She checks her watch, then looks back up at me.

"Actually, I should probably get back home. I'm sure Myla and Simone are going to be waiting for me to explain all of this."

Her story makes sense, but I'm still not convinced it's true. I think she felt what I did and she's scared of it. While I'm not scared, I'm not exactly standing on solid ground either. I love a good game, but I also genuinely want to get to know Sloane, to date her. And I'm not sure this is the best way to do that. It'll either be the perfect push to get her to give me a chance, or it'll be too much too soon.

"Okay, we'll have to celebrate another day then."

She looks relieved as I guide her back through my house and to the car. I'm glad we don't spend much time inside. I'm worried if I see her here long enough, my imagination will get the better of me. I tend to get carried away, and the last thing I need is to be picturing Sloane in my kitchen sipping coffee, or snuggled up on my couch. Or worse, in my bed with a sleepy smile and messy hair. I need to remember this isn't real.

It's not real, I tell myself as I open the door for her. *Not real*, when I catch her admiring her ring under the light of a streetlamp. *Definitely not real*, when I drop her off by her door, clenching my fists so that I'm not tempted to touch her. *Please, let this become something real*, when she smiles over her shoulder as she disappears back into her apartment.

MJ: Maddie says she misses her uncles. She wants to have everyone over this Saturday. Who's free?

Levi: Dahlia, Jasmine, and I can make it if you do it in the evening.

Maverick: I'll be there. Do I need to bring anything?

My desk chair squeaks as I lean back in it with a sigh. I stare at my family group chat, debating what to do. I haven't told any of my siblings about Sloane. I've been trying to figure out exactly *what* I'm going to tell them. But either way, I can't make it this weekend, so I guess I can start there.

Grayson: Tell Mad Dog I'm sorry, that I'm busy on a quest to fight Blaze on Mount Inferno. I'll come by and see her soon though.

'Mad Dog' is the stage name turned nickname I gave my niece Maddie during the first dance competition of hers I attended. I had t-shirts made that said *Mad Dog's crew* for my whole family, and everyone who joins the family or attends a dance event even as a friend, wears one now.

Sebastian adopted Maddie after her mom–his sister–died during childbirth. They'd been making it on their own, when Sebastian met and fell in love with my sister MJ. Now they're a happy family, with a big extended family too. I'd do anything for my whole family, but Maddie is definitely at the top of my list. Which is why it pains me to say no to her.

MJ: I'll let her know you've been keeping up with your buddy read. Adrian? Can you and Juliette make it?

I smile at MJ getting my reference to the middle grade fantasy series I've been reading with Maddie for the past month. It's centered around dragons, hence all of the fire-related names.

Levi: Wait, just the other day you were giving us a hard time and now you're the one missing out on family time?

I sigh, having expected this.

Grayson: I have plans I can't break, or else I'd be there.

Levi: Do you have a work event or something?

Adrian: Jules and I will be there. There's no work events this weekend, so Grayson must have personal plans.

I scowl at my phone, tempted to go over to my twin's office down the hall and throw something at him. I've no shortage of choices, between the rubber band ball I keep on my desk, the mini basketball and matching hoop on my door, plus the darts that go with my electronic dart board on the wall. I think best when I'm moving or playing a game, so I like to have a variety of choices in my office.

MJ: Do you have a date?

Levi: He'd never bail on family for a date. He must be up to something.

Grayson: I'm accompanying a friend to an event for moral support.

There, that's vague enough. Maybe they'll leave me alone now.

Levi: Adrian, go to his office and make him tell you why he's being so secretive.

Or not.

Adrian: Some of us actually work during the day.

For once, I'm glad for my brother's obsessive work ethic. My whole family is very dedicated to their respective professions, but Adrian takes it to another level. If he wouldn't have met Juliette, he'd still be working late every single night, plus working on the weekends.

I put my phone on do not disturb, then turn back to my emails. After sending a few replies, I'm tossing my rubber band ball back and forth between my hands when I feel someone watching me. I glance up, only slightly surprised to see Adrian standing in my open doorway. Our siblings must have pestered him until he gave in.

"Where are you going on Saturday?"

"Good afternoon, brother dearest. How's your day been?"

"Fine. Where are you going?"

I lean back in my chair, throwing the ball up toward the ceiling, then catching it. Adrian has always been straightforward, bordering on blunt if not fully crossing over into it.

"To an engagement party," I answer.

"With who?"

"A friend."

"It's not like you to be vague." He eyes me.

"That's not true. I can be mysterious."

"You tell me about every date you've ever been on. In the morning, you come into my office and relay your morning commute, down to how many red lights you had to stop at. Last week you texted the group chat that you got a new deodorant. There has never been anything mysterious about you."

Okay, he's got a point. Though I keep more secrets than they think.

"I've decided to become a brooding enigma like you. Can you teach me how to scowl?"

He gives me a flat look. "Whatever you're hiding, you won't be able to keep it a secret forever."

"I thought you gave up the whole intimidation bit when you left the CIA."

He sighs. "You're insufferable."

"That's a good word choice. Tell Juliette that reading all those classics together is really paying off."

He shakes his head, then turns on his heels and walks out. *Success.* I can't avoid my family forever, but that should buy me enough time to see what Sloane wants me to tell them. We spent so much time talking about her family, we never touched on mine. And I have a feeling that if we tried to fake it, my family would not be easily fooled.

Chapter Nine

Sloane Covington

They're your best friends, just talk to them. I stand with my hand hovering over my bedroom door knob. As soon as I walk out into the living room, I know I'm going to be bombarded with questions. When I came in last night, I told them I needed time to myself, then ran to my room and locked the door before they could corner me.

I've holed up in my room most of the morning, but the half-eaten granola bar and lukewarm water on my desk only held my hunger at bay for so long. The scent of maple syrup and butter has been taunting me for the last hour. I'd think Myla made pancakes on purpose to lure me out, if it wasn't Friday. Fridays are for pancakes.

Myla's mom had always made pancakes every Friday as a way to celebrate getting to the weekend when she was growing up. Myla kept up the tradition now that she lives on her own, and Simone and I are very grateful she did.

With a deep breath of sugary air, I open the door and barrel into the living room with as much confidence as I can muster.

"Finally," Myla shouts, making me jump. "We've been waiting for hours."

"You haven't been up for hours," I say to her. She hops up from the couch and grabs me, pulling me to the circle chair I usually occupy. After shoving me into it, she lays a blanket over my legs and spins on her heels.

"I will bring you a plate of pancakes, and then you will tell us everything." She strides toward the kitchen, a blur of pink silk and feathers. Myla's fashion sense doesn't take a break when she sleeps. This morning she's dawning shiny pink button-down pajamas, with white feather trim.

I look over at Simone, who sets down the large fantasy novel she was reading and eyes me expectantly.

"I'm going to talk, don't worry," I tell her.

"I know you are. And you're going to start with the engagement ring you're wearing."

I look down at the ring in question. It sparkles in the morning light, casting tiny rainbows when I tilt my hand side to side. A smile stretches my lips as I recall Grayson kneeling under the twinkle lights. But my smile falls when I remind myself that it's not real.

Myla comes back in the room with my plate, setting it in my lap.

"Okay, I'm going to tell you everything, but you have to promise not to freak out."

"We're not going to promise anything," Simone answers on behalf of Myla. "Because last night you left with who we know to be an acquaintance at best, only to come back engaged!"

"How did you see my ring? I practically sprinted to my room."

"It's big enough to notice," Myla says, her pupils practically turning into hearts as she takes my hand and looks at it.

"It's not a real diamond, or a real engagement."

Myla frowns at my words. Simone's brows pull together in confusion.

"Explain," Myla says as she sits on the couch.

So, I do. I explain the Brooke and Topher situation first.

"I'd like to introduce both of them to my fantasy collection," Simone growls. I laugh at her protectiveness. A while back, I noted that Simone's larger tomes would make great weapons, so it became a running joke for us to all threaten to use them against people we don't like. She doesn't sound like she's joking, though.

"That won't be necessary, because I came up with a plan," I say. Both of my best friends raise their eyebrows at me. "I sort of, kind of ... got Grayson Carter to agree to be my fake fiancé for the summer."

Simone's mouth drops open, while Myla gasps and claps her hands together in glee.

"I love the fake dating trope!" Myla's smile is infectious, drawing one out of me.

"So let me get this straight," Simone says. "You're going to pretend to be engaged until after Brooke and Topher are married?" I nod. "What happens after that?"

"I formulate a breakup story, and we go our separate ways. Or I guess, we can be friends."

"*Or* you fall in love and get married." Myla lets out a dreamy sigh. "You'd make a beautiful springtime bride."

It's not lost on me that Grayson joked about getting married in the spring. My stomach flips at the thought. I scold my inner romantic, then Myla.

"I'm not getting married. I know better than to catch feelings for someone like Grayson. This is just going to be a way to get through these family events without feeling like dirt on the bottom of Brooke's Louboutins."

"If you say so," Myla singsongs. Simone looks skeptical herself.

"I do."

The twin smirks that spread across my best friends' faces make me groan. My word choice was not ideal, but the sentiment was sound. I will not–*cannot*–fall for Grayson Carter.

I stare at the blinking cursor on my screen, begging the words to come. I haven't been able to write since after my conversation with Myla and Simone. All I can think about is last night, and wonder what Grayson is doing. I assume he's working, but I don't even know what he does. He never answered me when I asked him over text. I should probably know that before the party tomorrow night.

My phone buzzes next to my laptop, Grayson's contact flashing on the screen as if I summoned him with my thoughts. I answer it, wondering what he could be calling me about.

"Good afternoon, dearest betrothed." Grayson's voice is warm and smooth, drawing a smile from me right away.

"Good afternoon, Gray," I reply. "I was just thinking about you."

"Is that so? Was I shirtless in this daydream of yours or fully clothed?"

I let out a surprised laugh. "Excuse me? I didn't say I was day-dreaming of you!"

"Mmmm, denial makes me think I was shirtless."

"I don't even know what you look like without a shirt, so there's no way I could imagine it." Except now I am, and my mind is filling in the blanks *just fine*. My face is so warm it feels sunburnt. I'm glad this conversation is over the phone so that he can't see me.

"We can remedy that," he says in a low voice.

"You are positively rakish, Grayson Carter."

"I love it when you talk bookish to me."

I have to bite my lip to hold in a giggle. "What did you call me for, Gray?"

"You've thoroughly distracted me. I'm imagining you imagining me now. How can I move on?"

"*Gray*," I say through laughter.

"Okay, okay." He chuckles, and the sound warms me to my core. "I called to ask what I should wear tomorrow night."

"Dress pants and a button down are fine. I'm wearing a lilac-colored dress."

"Okay, that's easy enough. Do you need me to pick up anything? A gift for the evil stepsister, perhaps?"

I smile at his moniker for Brooke. "No, you don't need to get anything. Thank you. I was wondering though, what do you do for work? I feel like I should know that before tomorrow. Someone is bound to ask."

"I co-own a private security company with my twin brother, Adrian."

My eyebrows go up. "That is not what I expected you to say."

"What did you expect?" I can hear the amusement in his voice.

Model, personal trainer, author of a series of books that teach men how to flirt. Any of those would have surprised me less than a security company executive.

"I'm not telling you, because it'll go to your head."

"Me? I'd *never* let a compliment go to my head."

"Your track record says otherwise, *hubby.*"

"Daydreaming of me *and* calling me hubby? I need to buy a lottery ticket, because today must be my lucky day."

"I've officially had my fill of your antics," I say, but I'm laughing as I say it. "I'm hanging up now."

"Wait!"

I pause, about to press the red end button.

"What is it?"

"Can you call me hubby again? I want to record it and make it my ringtone–"

I hang up on him. My phone immediately dings with a text.

Gray: See you tomorrow night, wifey ;)

I shake my head, trying to contain my smile and the accompanying butterflies. *He's a flirt*, I remind myself. *This is what he does.*

But no matter how many times I repeat it, I can't help but feel giddy when I think of seeing him tomorrow night.

CHAPTER TEN

Sloane Covington

I almost fall trying to get to the door before Myla and Simone. The wedges I'm wearing tonight aren't exactly conducive to running.

"We don't have time for an interrogation," I tell them before I open the door. Myla tries for an innocent smile, but it comes off mischievous, while Simone gives me a look that says she'll do what she wants, like always. "I'm *serious*. If I'm late, I'll never hear the end of it."

I give them one last warning look over my shoulder, then swing open the door. Grayson lifts his head as I do, his blue eyes bright with excitement. He's wearing cream pants, with a matching blazer and a white button-down underneath. His hands are tucked into his pockets and his hair is perfectly tousled. *This* is why it was hard to believe he was an executive and not a model.

He looks like he belongs in a cologne ad, standing in front of the ocean while a beautiful supermodel hangs on his arm. Every woman who saw him would buy a bottle in hopes that their boyfriend or husband would resemble him in some way, if only by scent.

Myla hip checks me, then steps in front of me. "Hey!" I complain from behind her.

"Good evening," Grayson says with all the pomp and air of a prince. "You must be one of Rose's roommates."

"Rose?" Myla questions, hands on her hips.

"Every good fake fiancé gives his betrothed a nickname. I call her Rose and wifey, mostly. Though I plan on expanding my repertoire over the course of the summer. She calls me Gray, and if I'm really lucky, *hubby*." He looks at me over Myla's shoulder and winks. I shake my head at him, trying not to smile.

Myla's hands fall off her hips. "That's so cute!"

"I try." Grayson smirks.

"I'm Myla, and this is Simone," Myla introduces with a flourish. Simone merely nods at him. I think she's going for some kind of silent intimidation tactic. It's unlikely to work on Grayson, but it is serving to make *me* uneasy.

"It's nice to meet you both," he says, his smirk morphing into a genuine smile.

"Okay, we're all acquainted now. Time to go." I grab my purse off the hook by the door, then push past Simone and Myla.

"Have a great night!" Myla says in her sweet, cheerful voice as I close the door.

I let out a breath. "Ready?" I ask Grayson.

"You said you weren't embarrassed of me, but this is the second time you've kept me from talking to your friends." His expression reads more amused than hurt.

"You met them, that's more than what happened last time," I say before grabbing his hand to pull him down the hall. "We don't have time for their inevitable interrogation of you. If we're late to the party, my stepmother will spend most of the party dropping passive aggressive insults about our lack of punctuality. I'd like to minimize the amount of things she can criticize."

"We're not going to be late," he assures me as we step on the elevator, still hand in hand.

"There could be traffic."

"There won't be. And if there was, we're still leaving plenty early."

"We could get a flat tire."

"I've got pit crew level tire changing skills. It won't take long to fix."

"We could–"

Grayson cuts me off by pulling me to his chest. I squeak, my palms flattening against his lapels.

"Rose, everything is going to be fine," he tells me, staring into my eyes.

"How do you know that? You can't know that. Which is why I hate when people say that phrase." I'm babbling, as per usual. Why am I like this?

He runs a hand up and down my arm, the action both soothing me and sending flames across my skin.

"That's a fair point, but we've got each other. That counts for something, right?" he asks in a low voice.

"It does." I sigh and look down. "I'm sorry for spiraling. I mostly avoid this side of my family, so it's hard for me to not freak out about seeing them."

He tilts my chin up, making my heart skip.

"Don't apologize. I understand what it's like to be on a carousel of emotions. To feel like you can't get off no matter how badly you want to." His expression is soft and sincere. It makes me wonder what he's been through to know that kind of feeling.

The elevator dings and I take a quick step back, putting distance between us. A kind-looking elderly woman is waiting for the elevator. She smiles at us as we step off. Grayson holds the door for her so she can slowly make her way over the threshold.

"Such a gentleman. You hold onto this one, dearie," she says to me.

"Yes, ma'am," I reply, forcing brightness into my tone. Hopefully she doesn't see through me. It's not her fault she doesn't know that I can't hold onto a man that isn't mine.

Once she's safely on the elevator, we walk out toward Grayson's car. Surprisingly, he doesn't make any teasing comments about being called a gentleman, or about holding on to him. He simply opens the passenger door for me with a small smile. I get in, unable to smile back at him.

Is he upset that I didn't respond to his moment of vulnerability? I twist my engagement ring. He gets in the car, same carefree smile on his face as he starts it and begins to back out.

"Thank you for what you said on the elevator," I blurt out.

"You're welcome, Rose," he says in a smooth voice.

There's nothing in his tone or demeanor that gives away any negative emotions on his part. Except for his fingers tapping out a made up beat on the steering wheel. Is he nervous? It's hard to believe that *Grayson Carter* could be nervous. No, it must be something else. I, on the other hand, am quite anxious. But since it's not his job to manage my emotions, I don't share how I'm feeling.

Instead, I look down, watching my ring glimmer in the afternoon sun as I twist it round and round. I try to count each turn as a way to calm my nerves, but since the ring is a symbol of what I'm nervous about, it doesn't help all that much.

In my peripheral vision, Grayson's hand appears. His palm is facing up, his large hand placed on the console between us. I hesitate for a second. No one is here to see us, and our relationship isn't real, but ... I could use the comfort. He keeps his eyes on the road, but when I slip my hand in his, the corner of his mouth tips up. He adjusts my ring with his thumb, then rubs circles on the back of my hand as he drives.

I count each circle now, and take in deep, slow breaths. My anxiety starts to fade, becoming white noise in the back of my mind rather than a song blaring at full volume. Eventually, my eyes fall shut. I focus on the warmth of his hand and the soft purr of his car engine. I'm close to drifting off to sleep when the car comes to a halt.

"We're here," he says quietly. I bite the inside of my cheek as anxiety swiftly flares back up.

The valet opens my door for me, not giving me the option of sitting in here and panicking until I chicken out and ask Grayson to take me home. I step out of the car, murmuring a quiet thanks to the man. Grayson hands him the keys and waits for the tag he'll get in return so that we can come retrieve his car later. I'm back to twisting my ring, staring at the entrance, when Grayson steps up beside me.

"Are you tired?" he asks and I frown.

"What?"

"Because you've been running through my mind all day."

A laugh bursts out of me. That was the last thing I expected him to say right now. "That was terrible, surely you can do better than that."

"If you were words on a page, you'd be what they call *fine* print."

I groan. "No, that one is worse."

He places a hand on my lower back and leads me up the stairs toward the door.

"If being sexy was a crime, you'd be guilty as charged." Even he can't make it through that one all the way before laughing. I'm in a fit of giggles by the time he's opening the club's door for me.

He looks down at me with sparkling eyes as I walk through the door.

"Why all the cheesy lines?" I ask him. He takes my hand in his like we've been together for years instead of faking it for a few days.

"I wanted to see your smile," he answers, making warmth spread over my face and neck.

"More like you're trying to distract me from our impending doom."

"Maybe it won't be as terrible as you think."

We walk through the halls to the dining room that was rented out for the occasion. The doors to the dining area are open when we get to them, conversation and laughter spilling out. There are a lot of people here already, all of them milling about in their designer dresses and suits. The whole room is glittering and covered in expensive floral arrangements. Each table has a large centerpiece that will making seeing the person across from you impossible. I'm sure that was intentional, though. Every time someone has to crane their neck to see, they'll be reminded of just how much money my dad and Monica spent.

I scan the crowd of people, my stomach churning with anxiety. Brooke stands with Topher, my dad, and Monica in the middle of the room. Her smile is so wide it hurts my face by proxy. I recognize the people they're talking to, some club members that I've known since I was a little girl.

Brooke glances about the room, her smile shifting into something brittle when her gaze lands on us.

"It will be." I sigh. "It always is."

Brooke says something to my dad and Monica, then their eyes are on us too.

"Are you ready to swim with the sharks?" I ask Grayson.

Before he can answer, my family is upon us. I feel trapped, not unlike a cage diver in the middle of the ocean. Grayson squeezes my hand, reminding me that for once I'm not alone.

"Hello, Sloane," Monica says, her eyes narrow.

"Monica." I nod to her. "Dad," I say next, looking up at his impassive face. I don't greet Brooke or Topher, instead choosing to wait on them to speak first. The less I say, the better.

"Brooke tells us you're engaged. You'll have to forgive us for not offering to host you a party, considering we've never heard of or met your fiancé."

My dad's jaw ticks at this, making me swallow. He's not happy, which I knew would happen. Even a good dad wouldn't be happy their daughter got engaged to a man he's never met.

"It happened so suddenly, I'm sorry for not introducing you sooner." I gesture to Grayson, who's wearing a smile that makes it look like he doesn't have a care in the world. "This is my fiancé, Grayson Carter. Gray, this is my dad, Charles, and my stepmom,

Monica." I again choose to ignore the smirking Brooke and brooding Topher.

"It's a pleasure to meet you both." He shakes both of their hands. "I know my just now meeting you isn't ideal, but when I fell in love with Sloane, I had to ask her to marry me right away. I hope you'll forgive me for not coming to you first."

Monica sniffs at this, while my dad looks mildly placated by Grayson's manners.

"Yes, well, we weren't thrilled by the way we found out. And it is rather *interesting* that you're engaged so close to Brooke and Topher," Monica says. I work to keep my expression blank.

"Almost as interesting as their engagement happening right after we had lunch in this very room," I reply in a cool tone. Monica's haughty expression falters.

Brooke's brows pull together. It's clear she doesn't know about the lunch where her mother begged me to reconsider marrying her new *fiancé*.

Monica clears her throat. "We need to make a few more rounds." She tips her chin up, avoiding my eyes.

"I hope we get to talk more later," Grayson says with a bright smile.

"Yes, we can't wait to get to know you," Monica drolls. She walks away, my father, Brooke, and Topher following after her like ducks in a row.

"They were pleasant," Grayson says once they're out of earshot. I huff out a laugh.

"As pleasant as a bee stinging your eye."

"Very nice–and disturbing–metaphor. I can see why they pay you the big bucks."

I can't help but smile. "Thanks, hubby."

"My favorite nickname twice in one week? I'm so happy I might float away." He lets out a contented sigh and I hit his arm, laughing.

"These reactions make me want to never say it again."

"You wouldn't deprive your betrothed of such monumental happiness, would you?"

I try and fail to stop myself from smiling. I'm incapable of holding it in, though that seems to be the trend around Grayson. "I would if my *betrothed* was being incorrigible."

"You insult me, and yet you're smiling. I wonder what that means."

One of Monica's friends starts walking our way, waving. My smile falls. If I had to guess, she's coming to interrogate us on Monica's behalf.

"Our fun is over once more," I say on a sigh.

Grayson squeezes my hand. "Not on my watch."

CHAPTER ELEVEN

Grayson Carter

Sloane pushes her chicken around her plate. We've gone through endless questions about our relationship, my job, and–unfortunately–her job. Mostly whether she was going to give up on her career once we got married. I did my best to talk her up, and explain that I'd never want her to quit, but no one seemed to listen. Sloane took every hit with her chin held high and a placating smile on her lips. None of these people deserve her kindness.

I've not come through on my promise to make these events fun. There's no dance floor to pull her onto, which is something I was counting on. We've not even had dessert yet, that comes *after* the slideshow of Brooke and Topher's individual accomplishments. I keep thinking it will be over, but it hasn't stopped. Endless photos of each of them accepting awards and showing off expensive purchases are being displayed on a large projector. The same annoying instrumental song being played over and over.

I've tried to joke with Sloane, but the people at our table–work friends of her father's–give me a dirty look every time I lean over. I wouldn't care if it didn't make Sloane shrink in her chair each time they did it.

An idea comes to mind as my eyes catch on the champagne tower nearby. I lean down to whisper in Sloane's ear.

"Come with me."

She blinks in surprise.

"Where are you going?" she whispers back, then cringes when another nasty look gets shot her way.

"Somewhere not here," I answer. She pauses for a second, as if she's thinking, then shrugs and throws her napkin on her plate.

We both slip out of our chairs as quietly as possible, and I take her hand before leading her around the back of all of the tables. The lights are off for the slideshow, and we were seated far away from Brooke and Topher. I think it was to slight Sloane, but it's working in our favor.

Light spills out of the kitchen, and I head toward it. We push through the swinging door. A few workers are bustling about, but they don't pay us any mind as they clean.

"What are we doing in here?" Sloane asks in a low voice.

"I needed a few things."

I snag a champagne bottle out of an ice bucket nearby, then my eyes land on a tower of cupcakes. *Perfect.*

"Grab a few of those, will you?" I ask her, nodding my head toward the display before searching for something to sit on. I doubt they have blankets anywhere in here, but–ah! Tablecloths. I grab one, then turn to find Sloane staring at me.

"We can't steal cupcakes," she whispers. A worker wiping down one of the stainless steel counters looks over at us. I give him a good natured smile. He nods at me, then returns to his work.

"It's not stealing, we're just taking the ones we were going to eat." She doesn't respond, just looks at the cupcakes and bites her lip. I wait, holding my breath to see what she's going to do. I could convince her, or grab the cupcakes myself, but I want to see what she'll decide on her own.

"I can't believe I'm doing this," she mumbles, then snatches two cupcakes off the tower. She turns toward me with wide eyes. "What now?"

"Now, we get out of here before someone comes in and catches us." I spot an exit sign nearby and head toward that.

"Catches us?" she hisses. "I thought you said we weren't stealing."

I don't reply, instead choosing to push through the exit door and hope it leads us somewhere good. I blink as my eyes adjust to the sudden change in lighting. It led to stairs. Hopefully the stairs lead us somewhere better. Our steps echo in the stairwell, but we don't meet anyone on our way down. At the bottom is another door with a glowing exit sign.

Warm summer air blankets us as we step outside. There's a dumpster to our left, but an opening to the right that should lead us ... well, we're about to find out where that leads us.

"Gray, seriously, what are we doing?" Sloane asks, worry seeping into her tone as she follows me toward the opening.

"Right now we're trying to find the golf course. Which shouldn't be this hard." I walk toward the opening with Sloane at my heels.

She throws a hand out in front of us. "This *is* the golf course. And if we stay in this vicinity, anyone who looks through the restaurant windows will *see us.*"

I look up to find that she is correct, the room we were just in overlooks exactly where we're standing. A vast expanse of rolling green hills is in front of us, blanketed in golds and rich red as the sun sets. It's exactly what I was hoping for, minus the *on display for everyone to see* part.

My lips stretch into a grin when I see an unattended golf cart. Based on the courses I've been to over the years for networking purposes, I know that it's highly likely that cart has keys in it. I head in that direction.

"Grayson, I'm really trying to be spontaneous and adventurous, but I am neither of those things, and I'm also in heels," Sloane says, and I can't help but chuckle.

"You're plenty adventurous, you stole cupcakes. What's more adventurous than a heist?" I ask and then hop up into the golf cart. "As for your heels, we now have transportation, so no more walking in them."

I grin at her. She stares at me.

"There's no way they just left the keys in there."

I pull the keys out and lift them to show her. "Golf is a gentleman's sport. They expect everyone to act accordingly. But I'm no gentleman." I wink and get what I was hoping for, a laugh.

"Now come on, before your stepmom looks down and sees us."

She gets into the cart, cupcakes in hand. I tuck the bottle of champagne in between us, and Sloane gasps when the cold hits her leg. I set the tablecloth in my lap, then look over at my partner in crime.

"Are you ready, Agent Rose?"

She giggles. "I suppose I have to be, Agent Gray."

"Then hold on, beautiful."

"I can't hold on because of the c-" Her words turn into a squeal as I hit the gas.

The scent of fresh cut grass and evening air fills my lungs as we race down the fairway. Sloane's laughter is stolen away by the wind, and each time she slides into me my grin widens. After we've driven for a while, I find a spot near a pond and slow to a stop.

"That was amazing," Sloane breathes out, sounding like she can't believe it. I look over at her, intent on saying some cheesy line, but it dies as soon as I see her.

Her hazel eyes are a kaleidoscope of green, gold and brown, shining bright with excitement. The wind has tousled her hair into something wild that begs for my fingers to be tangled in it. And her smile–*wow* her smile. It's the kind of thing poets spend their whole lives trying to capture into words. But their efforts are in vain. No words could ever do this–do *her*–justice.

"You stayed true to your word about making this fun," she continues talking when I don't say anything. I snap out of my daze and step off the cart with the tablecloth in hand.

"Did you doubt me?" I ask as I spread the cloth out like a picnic blanket.

"I'll admit I did a little. I was sure we'd be stuck at that terrible table all night."

"My own wife has no faith in me," I lament, looking up toward the sky.

"I'm not your wife, I'm your *fiancée*," she corrects. "Now hurry up, the icing is melting all over my fingers."

"So demanding," I tsk, then grab the bottle of champagne off the cart. It's only then that I realize I didn't grab anything to drink out of.

"You forgot glasses, didn't you?" Sloane asks, humor lacing her words.

"Maybe."

"It's okay," she says with a soft smile. "I don't mind sharing if you don't."

It might kill me to know our lips have touched the same bottle, but I suppose death is worth it when she's looking at me the way she is right now. Like I'm some superhero who rescued her out of a burning building, instead of a reckless guy with a half-thought out plan.

I pop the bottle of champagne, watching as bubbles cascade down the side since it was shaken up during the drive. After it's open, I set it beside the tablecloth and walk over to where Sloane is still on the golf cart. She holds out a cupcake for me, but I get on a knee in front of her instead of taking it.

"I think you'll be more comfortable with these off." I gesture to her wedges. "May I?"

She nods, eyes transfixed on me.

I unhook one of the belt-like clasps, my fingertips brushing her ankle. Her skin is smooth and warm. If this were real, I'd give into the temptation to kiss where I've touched. The shoe slides off, and I set it aside while trying to get ahold of myself. I've been on countless dates, but never have I felt so undone in the presence of a woman before. And all I'm doing is *taking off her shoes*.

I make quick work of the other one, then set her shoes on the cart and stand up. The more distance between us, the less likely I am to take things too far.

"Thank you," she whispers.

"What are fake fiancés for?" I ask with a wry smile before taking a cupcake from her.

We sit on the tablecloth across from each other. Sloane tucks her legs to the side, smoothing her dress with one hand. She peels the paper down on her cupcake before taking a bite. Frosting gets on her thumb and she licks it off. My brain short circuits in response. Her eyes flick up, and I turn to grab the bottle next to me so I don't stare.

"Champagne?" I offer, sounding like a waiter at a restaurant.

"Why not?" She takes the bottle from me and tips it up to her lips for a long drink. In her party dress, half-eaten cupcake in hand, and wild hair, she looks like a real rebel. A chuckle escapes me at the thought.

"What?" she asks, eying me.

I take the bottle from her and drink. The sparkling liquid warms my chest, and I know I won't have more than this since I'm driving.

"You look like a wild child," I tell her and she laughs. She takes the bottle back from me.

"I'm nothing close to *wild*."

I slip my phone out of my pocket and snap a photo as she tilts the bottle back again. A memory to look back on at the end of the summer. Hopefully, it's one we look at together, and not something I stare at late at night, wishing things would have gone differently.

"Are you sure about that, wifey? We stole champagne, a table cloth, cupcakes, *and* a golf cart. That's pretty wild."

"You did most of that," she points out before drinking some more.

"You'd still be charged as my accomplice," I retort.

"I'll claim coercion," she shoots back, a smirk on her pink lips.

"The jury won't buy it."

She laughs, but it fades as she looks off in the distance. "I wouldn't have done any of this without you, you know. I'd be up there, walking on eggshells and praying that no one spoke to me." Her face twists up. "Sometimes I feel so pathetic." Another long drink from the bottle and I have a feeling the bubbly has already gone to her head.

"You're not pathetic, Sloane."

Her glassy eyes lock on me. "Then what am I?"

"Human," I answer. "Learning, just like everyone else."

"I don't like being human."

"If it helps, you look like an angel," I say in an attempt to cheer her up.

She gives me a small smile. "You're too smooth, hubby." Her words blend together, and it's clear that among stealing cupcakes and hijacking golf carts, drinking is another thing Sloane doesn't usually do.

"All right, Bubbles, I think you've had enough to drink." I reach for the bottle and she pulls it back, giggling.

"I'm *fine*." She draws out 'fine' until its eight syllables instead of one, her sentence punctuated by an adorable hiccup. "Isn't that what you said earlier? I'm *fine print*." Her smile is wide and relaxed. I reach again, snagging the bottle from her. It's much lighter than before, practically drained.

"I did say that, but now I'm saying you're *cut off*."

She lets out a dramatic sigh and lays down on the tablecloth, flopping onto her back. I chuckle and set the bottle to the side before laying next to her. Stars are beginning to blink awake in the indigo sky above. I turn my head to find Sloane already looking at me.

"Gray," she whispers and tingles race down my spine.

"Yes, Rose?"

"I-"

Cold water. *Freezing* cold water sprays all around us. I suck in a breath and Sloane squeals. The sprinklers have been turned on, and we're right in the middle of them. I scramble to my feet, and pull Sloane with me. She careens into my chest, looking up at me with wet lashes. Water rains down on us, and I know we're going to be soaked to the bone if we stand here any longer. But I can't bring myself to move.

I wrap my arms around Sloane's waist. Her hands slide up until her arms are draped over my shoulders. My eyes fall to her lips, the tiny droplets of water present making me want to kiss her more. *She's had too much to drink*, I tell myself. I won't kiss her like this. No matter if every part of me is begging to.

"I've always wanted to be kissed in the rain," she says. My fingers clench the fabric of her dress. She pushes up onto her tiptoes, a breath away from me.

In my peripheral vision I see movement, making me turn my head. Her lips brush my cheek and if there wasn't a golf cart heading in our direction, my self control would be shriveled up.

"We need to go," I say, turning back to her. She looks in the direction I was before, her dazed eyes widening. She freezes in place. I take her hand and pull her toward the cart. "Come on, Bubbles, we've made it this far. Can't get caught now."

We slide into the bench seat, our wet clothes squeaking on the plastic. She fists a hand in my jacket sleeve to brace herself as I floor it. We're flying toward the country club, water spraying us from all angles, and bouncing so much I worry we might flip at one point. Sloane is giggling the entire time, and I can't help but laugh with her.

The cart screeches to a halt right by the valet stand. The worker's eyes widen when he lands on us. I have no doubt we're a sight to see with drenched clothes and big smiles.

"Can you bring my car around?" I ask, my chest heaving. I fish the tag I got at the beginning of the night from my pocket and he takes it from me slowly. "The faster the better," I tell him, looking behind me to see if that other cart has found its way to us. I don't see anything yet, but I'm betting it's only a matter of time. Hopefully, they stopped to investigate our crime scene. I feel bad about not cleaning our mess. I might have to return and tip whoever was unfortunate enough to be stuck with the task.

The guy rushes off. We wait, bouncing on our toes to keep warm. Sloane is shivering, holding her shoes in one hand and rubbing her arm with the other. Right as my car pulls up I hear voices. I shove a hundred dollar bill into the valet's hands before helping Sloane into the car and jogging around.

"There! That must be them!" a voice shouts.

I jump in and hit the gas, buckling as I drive.

"That was one for the books," I say as I pull out of the parking lot and onto the road.

"This might be the best night of my life," Sloane murmurs, her head back against the seatrest, eyes closed. I put on the heat and her seat warmer so she doesn't freeze in her wet clothes.

"This is the first of many, wifey."

"I hope so."

Her words burrow into my chest, snuggling up next to the image of her smile, and the memory of the first time I read her books. If I'm not careful, my whole heart is going to be made up of her by the end of the summer.

CHAPTER TWELVE

Sloane Covington

My nose scrunches up as light pierces my eyelids.

"Ugh," I groan, then stick out my tongue in disgust at how my mouth feels. I definitely did not brush my teeth last night. Mascara crumbles against my fingertips when I rub my eyes, a reminder that I forgot to remove my makeup, too.

As the fog slowly clears around my brain, I begin to see why I abandoned my night routine. I did a lot of out of character things last night. Another groan escapes my lips, this time due to embarrassment. I feel around for my phone, wanting to see what time it is so that I can determine if it's too early to send an apology message to Grayson for getting tipsy and trying to kiss him.

What kind of woman acts that way after a little champagne? I'm sure he thinks I'm an awful mess and doesn't want to be seen with me ever again. I vaguely recall him being kind as he brought me to my apartment last night, but Grayson is nice to everyone. I'm not special.

I unlock my phone to see a few different messages on my screen. One from my dad–*definitely not checking that first*–and three from Grayson. I click on Grayson's messages. The first thing I see is a photo of me, champagne bottle to my lips, the sunset like a fire behind me. My hair is a mess, my dress wrinkled, and there's cupcake frosting all over my hands. But I still smile at my screen. Because I look … *free*. The second photo is me laughing in the front seat of his car, soaking wet with mascara running down my face. In this one I look more like a raccoon, but I'm a happy little trash panda, so that counts for something.

Gray: Good morning, Bubbles. Had fun celebrating our engagement last night. If you're already overthinking everything like I suspect, don't. I had more fun with you than I've ever had on a date.

My face heats and I press my lips together to keep from squealing in delight. I try to tell myself that he's just saying that. He can't mean it. But a part of me really wants to believe it.

Sloane: More fun than you've EVER had on a date? That's a bold claim considering how many you've been on.

Gray: I mean it. Also, are you judging me? Because it feels like I'm being judged for being likable and attractive.

I roll my eyes.

Sloane: Pride is not an amiable trait, Mr. Carter.

Sloane: Ps. Thank you for taking the photos. I love them.

I snuggle further under my lavender comforter, smiling as I wait for his reply. I should go get a long shower and brush my teeth.

Maybe find some food, too. But all I want to do is stay in my happy little bubble.

Gray: It's not being prideful if it's the truth, future Mrs. Carter.

Gray: Ps. You're welcome. I love them too. You look happy.

I lock my phone and set it on my chest, staring at my ceiling fan spinning round. He's too much. Too *perfect*. I'm scared I'm going to get caught up in this. Our relationship isn't real, but the fluttery feelings in my stomach definitely are. Biting my lip, I pick my phone back up.

Sloane: I was happy. I am happy. Thank you, Gray.

Gray: Anything to see you smile, Rose.

Why does he have to say things like that? I need to exit out of these messages before I do something dumb like ask him to be my *real* fiancé. As I'm swiping out of our text thread, I accidentally open up the one with my dad. My eyes catch on the first sentence, and I keep reading against my better judgement.

Dad: Your sister was highly disappointed that you left before the toast. I am as well. You should have stayed the entire time so that everyone would see us as a family unit. You know how important that is in my position. Since you missed the toast, you also missed the announcement that the wedding will take place in Hawaii two weeks from now. You are expected to attend. The wedding planner has emailed you all the details you need.

I'm glad I chose to open Grayson's message first, because my phone might have been shattered from throwing it if I started my day with this. I drag myself out of bed with a frustrated sigh.

"Coffee," I murmur to myself. "I need coffee before I deal with this."

I walk out into the living room where my two best friends are typing away on their laptops on opposite sides of the couch. There's a timer ticking down on the TV screen, so they must be doing writing sprints together. They both pause when I enter though.

"Good morning," Myla says with a too-wide smile. "There's coffee ready in the kitchen and a pot of oatmeal on the stove."

"You are a sweet, beautiful angel of a woman," I tell her, choosing to ignore the mischief in her eyes. I walk toward the kitchen.

"Wait!" Simone says, laughter in her voice. I turn around to face them. "I'm describing a goblin in the scene I'm writing and I need a muse."

Myla snorts and I scowl at both of them.

"You're terrible, both of you!" I turn back around with a huff and continue walking to the kitchen.

"I thought I was a sweet angel?" Myla calls out.

"Now you're a fallen one!" I yell back and hear more laughter in response.

After making my coffee and spooning oatmeal into a bowl, I head back into the living room. It's hard to maintain my scowl though when both of them are laughing so hard.

"Do I really look that bad?" I set my mug and bowl on the side table before snuggling up in my favorite chair under a blanket.

"You could use some makeup remover and a hair brush, but it's not too bad," Myla says, not bothering to disguise her amusement.

I grab my coffee and take a sip, closing my eyes as the sweet warmth hits my dry throat. When I open my eyes again, both of my best friends are looking at me with expectant expressions.

"Go ahead and begin the interview," I say with an eye roll.

"Grayson told us everything," Simone says. "But we would like to hear your side of the story."

"He told you *everything*?" I squeak and they both nod.

"He's an excellent storyteller," Myla says. "I told him he should take up writing, but he said he couldn't sit still long enough to write a book."

"I can't believe you stole a golf cart." Simone sounds impressed. "And that you got tipsy on champagne." She laughs.

"Gray stole the golf cart, I just tagged along." I take a fortifying sip of coffee. "I'm guessing he didn't tell you that I threw myself at him?"

"He did not," Simone answers with raised brows. "I thought you didn't want to date him."

"I don't," I say with a sigh. I set my coffee cup down and rub my eyes, not caring if it smears my eye makeup even more. "The romance of the moment swept me away. Not to mention the champagne." I cringe. "He texted me this morning telling me it was the best date of his life, but I'm sure he's just being nice."

"I don't know, he seemed really happy when he was telling the story last night," Myla says, then takes a sip of her coffee. "After you stumbled to your room mumbling something about needing to get out of your dress, he sat down right where you are now and told us everything like you both went on some adventure quest."

"That's just his personality. It doesn't mean anything."

"Sloane, he *likes* you. He flirted with you before this whole fake engagement thing, and he wouldn't have agreed to all of this if he didn't want something more than friendship," Myla says.

I shake my head. "He's a flirt, Myla. That's what he does. Even last night, he was charming everyone in the room. He may find me *attractive*, but that doesn't hold any value."

"You can't seriously think that he would go along with this plan for *any* woman?" Myla asks. Simone stays silent, but I can tell she's gathering her thoughts as she listens.

"He would have. He called it a game and made a joke about working on his acting skills. I think if any girl in the gym did what I did, he'd go along with it just to have something to do this summer."

Myla looks down at her floral mug. I trade my coffee for my oatmeal and take a bite, thinking that maybe I've proved my point enough for the conversation to be over.

"And what if that changed last night?" Simone asks, surprising me.

"What do you mean?"

"What if last night was the best date of his life and now he wants more, what do you say to that?"

"There's no way it was the best date of his—"Simone cuts me off. "Not what I asked."

I narrow my eyes at her, but she just stares me down.

"Even if he wanted more, I can't date Grayson," I say, looking down at my bowl of oatmeal. "He's someone to everyone. Everything he says is flirty, which is fun, sure, but also makes me wonder if any of his words mean anything. How could I ever feel special and treasured while knowing he could replace me within minutes if he got bored?"

And he would get bored. Because my life isn't stealing golf carts and racing through the sprinklers. Most of my days are spent on the couch with a book or my laptop. All of my exciting moments are fictional. Grayson is the kind of man who needs adventure. He'd tire of my homebody ways and leave me heartbroken.

"I think you're scared," Simone says, and Myla nods in agreement. "But that's understandable after all that time with Topher."

"I'm scared because I know I'm right," I say in a tight voice. "Now, I don't want to talk about this anymore. Please."

Simone and Myla share a look, but then nod.

"Thank you," I say before digging into my barely warm oatmeal. My phone buzzes in my lap and a notification from Brooke pops up.

Brooke: We need your RSVP within the day, or else there won't be a room for you. Topher told me you're scared of flying, though, so I understand if you can't work up the courage to join us.

I grit my teeth then click out of that thread and open up the messages between me and Grayson. The photos and messages on the screen embolden me. The girl in those pictures isn't afraid of anything.

I could turn down going to Hawaii, but then I wouldn't have the satisfaction of standing up to everyone who has stepped on me for years now. I can make it through one little flight to stick it to them. Sure, the mere idea of flying has me feeling itchy, like I might break out in hives any second, but I can get through it.

I type out a text to Grayson first.

Sloane: How do you feel about going to Hawaii in two weeks? For Brooke and Topher's wedding. No worries if you can't make it because of work.

Gray: If you're there, I'm there. How long is the trip?

I grin and forward him the details. Even if Grayson isn't boyfriend material, he's the *perfect* fake fiancé. I've never met someone so willing to go along with anything, before he even knows the details.

Gray: I'm good to go. Guess this means your daydreams of me being shirtless will come true after all.

I laugh at his text, then I RSVP for us both and open up my messages with Brooke.

Sloane: Grayson and I will be there.

She doesn't respond, even though it says the message was read. *Perfect.* I've already shaken her up. Now, I just have to get through the flight and then I'll have a week of fun with Grayson, with just a few wedding festivities to endure.

It occurs to me *after* I've sent the message that it's not the brightest idea to go on a tropical vacation with a man who I want to avoid falling for. I'll simply have to be careful, and make sure that I don't get swept up in Grayson, no matter how strong the pull.

CHAPTER THIRTEEN

Grayson Carter

I don't have to look up to know that my twin has entered my office. I fully expected him to storm in here demanding to know why I've taken off a whole week of work without talking to him about it first.

"Good afternoon, Adrian, how can I help you?" I ask in a calm tone while typing out an email to a client of ours who requested additional security for his home.

"Why didn't you tell anyone you're going on vacation?"

"I did. I told HR."

"Don't play games, Grayson."

I look over at him brooding in my doorway. "You're no fun, you know that?" He simply glowers. "I got asked to go by a friend *yesterday*, that's why I haven't told anyone." I turn my attention back to my screen.

"What kind of person invites someone on a vacation with only two weeks' notice?"

"The fun kind?" I spin in my chair so that I'm facing him. "Is there something wrong with me taking a vacation?"

"No." He sighs, crossing his arms and leaning against the doorframe. "I guess I shouldn't be surprised. You are the wandering type. I thought you were giving up those ways though."

"What made you think that?" I grab my rubberband ball off my desk, tossing it from my right hand to my left then back again.

"I don't know, maybe the fact that you pitched this whole company as a way for us to *put down roots*?"

I study him. He doesn't seem that upset, but he is tense. His jaw is clenched and his posture is far from relaxed despite his faux-casual way of leaning. It's likely that he's annoyed by how vague I've been as of late. Maybe it's time I reveal what's going on to my family. When everyone finds out about Hawaii there are bound to be questions. I need to figure out exactly how to broach the subject first. It's not exactly something you blurt out. They're unlikely to take me seriously if I do that.

"You can have roots *and* vacation, Adrian. If Juliette told you she wanted to go on vacation, you'd drop everything for her."

"That's different. We're engaged."

A slow grin stretches my lips. Now this is a way to reveal what's going on, but also have a little fun. I know Adrian won't believe that I'm actually engaged, but it will be entertaining to see how far I can take this.

"It's funny that you mention that, brother, because so am I."

Adrian stares at me. When I don't drop my smile or tell him I'm joking, he shakes his head in disbelief.

"You're lying." He frowns and pushes off the doorframe. "What I can't figure out, though, is *why* you're lying. What have you done that's worse than getting engaged without telling anyone?"

"I proposed to Sloane Rose–Dahlia's favorite romance author–and she said yes," I say instead of answering him.

The statement is more or less true. And I can tell by the way his eyes narrow that he determined exactly that. Adrian has always been able to tell when someone is lying, in part because of our family's observant nature but also as a result of his CIA training. He's not entirely perfect in his observations, but he's pretty close.

"Tell me the truth," he demands, making me laugh.

"The truth is that I bought a ring, got down on one knee, and asked Sloane to marry me in my backyard. I met her family Saturday night, and now I've been invited to go to Hawaii for her sister's wedding."

He places his hands on my desk, narrowing his eyes. "You're leaving something out."

"I've left a lot of things out, for the sake of brevity." I lean back in my chair, putting my hands behind my head. "And privacy," I add with a wink.

"I know you're not actually engaged, Grayson. You're impulsive, but you wouldn't keep something like that from the whole family. So tell me what's really going on." He takes on a more serious tone, letting me know that my charade is up. I could keep going with my little act, but it would only serve to make him more ornery.

"Fine, I'll tell you the whole truth." I take a deep breath in, drop my arms, then tell him–*almost*–everything. The gym situation, my backyard proposal, and our agreement to end things at the close of summer. I keep to myself how much I like her, and the moment we had on the golf course. By the end of my story, Adrian is sitting in the chair across from me looking unconvinced.

"I'm serious, Grayson, quit lying," Adrian says with an eye roll.

"I'm not lying." I look straight at him. "If you'd like to see the receipt for the ring, I can show it to you." I'd rather not, because when he sees the price tag he'll think I've lost it. Hopefully he takes me at my word.

He runs a hand through his hair, and that's when I know he's flustered. It's not like him to be visibly distressed.

"So you're telling me you're fake engaged to a practical stranger for *fun*?"

I shrug. "Yeah, pretty much."

"And this is just for the summer?"

"Yes. We'll part ways at the end of it, and she'll make up a story about our breakup to tell her family."

"You're fine with that? Parting ways like nothing happened?"

"Of course. It'll be a fun way to pass the time, then we'll go back to our normal lives." The lie tastes bitter on my tongue. Adrian's brows lift.

"You like her."

I force a laugh and shake my head. "Enough to do this for her, but that's all."

"Hm." He sits back in his chair. "A woman you're willing to lie for, that's new."

"I'm not—"

"I want to meet her," he cuts me off. "I know everyone else will too once they find out, so you might as well plan to bring her to MJ's house next weekend."

"Since when do you want to meet new people?" I shift in my chair. "And what if she's busy?"

"Why are you so afraid of her meeting us?"

I'm worried she'll fit in so well it'll be hard for me to imagine my own family without her in it.

"I'm not afraid," I lie again. "I just think it's a waste of time to bring a fake fiancée home to meet the family."

"It'll make everyone feel better to know who you're traveling so far away with."

"Dahlia and Juliette have already met her," I say, trying whatever I can to get out of this.

"The more you protest, the more I'm inclined to think you have feelings for her."

Sometimes I despise how straightforward my twin can be.

"*Fine*, I'll invite her, but I'm not going to push her if she doesn't want to come."

"Fair enough." He nods, wearing a hint of a smirk. "I look forward to meeting the woman who's got you so on edge."

The way I feel around Sloane is the opposite of *on edge*. I'm comfortable with her, free to be myself. But the idea of bringing her home to my hyper observant family? Yeah, that has me feeling like I'm one step away from tumbling down Mount Everest.

CHAPTER FOURTEEN

Sloane Covington

"Your sister is married to *Sebastian Holt*?" My voice rises several octaves. "Why didn't you tell me before now?"

I clench my hands into fists to keep from nervously toying with the frays of my distressed shorts. If I would have known his sister was MJ Holt, wife of the beloved Coach Bash, I'd have dressed up a little more. The sage green t-shirt hanging off my shoulder is not celebrity worthy.

"I didn't think it was an important detail," Grayson says, his eyes on the Atlanta traffic in front of us.

"They live in a mansion, don't they?" I ask and watch as he tries for a reassuring smile.

"They're normal people..." he trails off, his explanation falling flat. I turn toward my window with a sigh.

I'm going to a mansion in shorts and a t-shirt. I know mansions, I lived in one for most of my childhood. You don't show up to a multimillion dollar home in clothes you bought at T.J. Maxx.

I used to have a closet full of designer clothes when I lived with my dad, but not anymore. The most I spend on clothes is for ballet class, and even then I shop sales. It's never seemed worth it to spend money on clothes when most of my days are spent inside at my desk. Topher used to make not-so-subtle comments about how he'd buy me clothes if I wanted him to. Refusing was my way of rebelling before I gathered the courage to leave him. Now I'm wishing I would have let him buy me a few things.

"What's on your mind right now?" Grayson asks.

I roll my head over to look at him. "I'm wondering how badly it would hurt if I jumped out of your car to escape going to this." He comes to a stop at a red light. "Oh, look, perfect timing."

"You're very dramatic today," he notes with a wry smile.

"That's not a very nice thing to say to your betrothed."

"Then it's a good thing we're not actually engaged."

I gasp, placing a hand to my chest. "That *hurts*, Gray."

He smiles and shakes his head. "I think I'm rubbing off on you and I don't know how to feel about it."

This past week I've seen Grayson every day. Not because of any event or date but because of our gym schedules. I'm not sure if I saw him this much before we got fake engaged, but I'm happy I do now. He never fails to make me smile before I go into ballet class, and on the days when I do strength training, he makes sure to hang around whatever section I'm in.

It's become normal to have my abs hurting every day, and not because of core exercises but because he makes me laugh so much.

Yesterday I looked in the mirror during ballet and I was *beaming*, all because Grayson had mercilessly flirted with me before I walked in. If I think about how fun it is for too long though, panic starts to rise. And I only have enough room for the anxiety I have surrounding meeting his family.

"I wish your confidence would transfer over to me," I say as he turns down a winding road under a canopy of oak trees.

"Dahlia and Juliette already love you, so you don't have to worry about them. And if they love you, Levi and Adrian are forced to. So that's two out of four siblings covered already."

"How comforting. Half of your siblings are *forced* to like me." I shift in my seat to look at him better, my seatbelt twisting around me. "You're usually better at talking me down."

We haven't known each other long enough for there to be a *usual*, but considering most of our interactions involve him boosting my confidence or convincing me to let go of my fears, it seems like enough of a pattern to warrant the use of the word.

"I'm sorry to disappoint." His fingers tap the steering wheel.

I narrow my eyes at him. "Why aren't you being your usual flirty outrageous self?"

"I told you how beautiful you look when I picked you up." He glances to the right, a smirk on his lips as he makes a show of looking me over. "I can expound on that, if you'd like."

My skin flushes and I hit his arm. "That's *not* what I meant. Also, keep your eyes on the road," I scold him.

"Yes, ma'am," he says in an exaggerated drawl that shouldn't send a shiver down my spine, but does.

"You're avoiding my question." I frown, then it dawns on me. "Are you nervous?"

His eyes flick to me then back to the road, but he says nothing. I groan, letting my head fall back against the headrest.

"If *you're* nervous there's no hope for this going well. We might as well turn around and tell them I got sick on the way. I'll fake an illness to my family too. Brooke won't be able to get a condescending word in if I repeatedly fake cough into the phone."

His hand, palm up, crosses the middle of the car. It reminds me of the car ride to the engagement party, and I can't help but smile. I slip my hand into his. Another gesture I shouldn't get used to. These little moments will come back to haunt me at the end of the summer.

"I'm only a little nervous. This is ... new for me."

"What? Bringing a fake fiancée home?" I joke.

"Bringing *any* woman home," he says and my heart stutters. I'm the first woman Grayson Carter is bringing to meet his family. I could more easily imagine making the *New York Times* Bestseller List than this.

"Oh," I say, sounding as dumbfounded as I feel. "You should have told them no. I shouldn't be the first."

I'm sure Grayson's family knows of his bachelor reputation. They're going to expect a supermodel to walk in with him. The kind of woman who could get a man like Grayson to settle down. Not a romance author who can't string together a coherent sentence unless it's in a Microsoft Word document.

"They would have tracked you down if I didn't let them meet you."

"That's not weird at all."

He laughs, but I can't join in. My nerves are getting the better of me. I'm sure Grayson is going to need a towel from how much my palms are sweating.

The car slows, then Grayson turns the wheel with one hand until we arrive at a large gate with a security guard posted beside it. The guard tips his hat to Grayson, then the gate opens for us. At the end of a lane lined with magnolia trees is a large glass mansion that resembles a greenhouse more than a home, judging on the amount of plants I can see through the windows.

He parks in between a large truck and a peach Jeep with a dash covered in rubber ducks, then looks over at me.

"It's going to be okay," he says and squeezes my hand. "We're here together, which means we're going to be fine."

"I don't know how you think having me by your side is going to help with your nerves. I'm a wreck."

"You being by my side helps me more than you know." The sincerity in his deep blue eyes steals my breath. Could he really mean that?

Movement in my peripheral vision has me glancing toward the mansion. A girl with curly blonde hair is peering at us from inside. She jumps behind a large fiddle leaf fig.

"That's my—rather nosey—niece, Maddie," Grayson explains with a chuckle. "I'm not sure what everyone has told her in regard to our relationship. I can't see MJ telling her we're faking our engagement, but she also wouldn't lie to her. Either way, I'm sure she's bursting at the seams with excitement to meet you."

Grayson says all this with a casual air, but I can sense something brimming beneath the surface. I look closely at him, ignoring my own insecurities and anxious thoughts in favor of searching to see if he has any of his own. It's hard for me to imagine, but I also can't imagine him lying about being nervous.

His hair is messy, which isn't abnormal for him, but it looks a little more mussed than usual. There's a tightness around his eyes that doesn't fit in with the easy expression he's wearing. And he hasn't let go of my hand, but instead is hanging on tight like I'm a life raft in the middle of the ocean.

"Are you okay?" he asks me, concern rippling over his features, removing any traces of his own emotions. I wonder how often that happens.

"Are you?" I return his question. An emotion flickers in the depths of his eyes, but soon enough he's wearing the carefree grin I'm familiar with.

"I'm perfect." He lets go of my hand to grab his door handle. "Let's go beat everyone at Cornhole, wifey."

"I didn't know this was a game night," I say as I get out of the car.

"It wasn't supposed to be, but it is now."

CHAPTER FIFTEEN

Grayson Carter

The door flies open as soon as Sloane and I step onto the porch.

"Uncle Grayson!" Maddie yells and jumps into my arms. I laugh and swing her around, narrowly avoiding hitting Sloane.

"Hey, Mad Dog," I say as I set her down. "How's it going?" I ruffle her hair and she scrunches her nose, looking just like MJ even though there's no blood shared between them.

"Good," she says with a too-innocent smile. "Everyone is waiting on you. Mom said you were bringing a *friend*." Maddie turns to look at Sloane.

"Maddie, this is my friend Sloane."

"It's nice to meet you," Sloane says with a smile. "I love your outfit."

Maddie's grin widens, her eyes lighting at the compliment. She's wearing cobalt blue bellbottoms and a shirt with daisies printed all over it. Her blonde curls are pinned back with butterfly clips. It looks like she stole the whole ensemble out of Dahlia's closet. My sister-in-law is not one to shy away from color.

"Thank you! My aunt Dahlia helped me pick it out," Maddie says, confirming my thoughts. "She has the best style, but you know that because you met her already. She told me you're her favorite author. I haven't read your books because I like fantasy. Uncle Grayson and I are reading–"

"Maddie, sweetie, take a breath," MJ says with a laugh, walking up behind Maddie and putting an arm around her. "You can talk more later. Everyone else wants a chance to meet her."

MJ's eyes are calculating as she takes us in. I'm sure she's storing away information and formulating questions to ask me later when we're alone. My heart starts to pick up speed. What will she think of Sloane? I glance over at her. She's smiling, but shifting back and forth on her feet while twisting her engagement ring.

Her ring. My eyes widen and I start to usher my sister and niece inside.

"We'll be inside in just a minute," I tell MJ before she can say anything else. She frowns at me pushing them, but thankfully doesn't protest more than that.

Once they're inside and the door is shut, I turn to Sloane and grab her left hand.

"What are you doing?" she asks.

I slide off the engagement ring and hold it up. "I don't want Maddie seeing this and asking questions," I tell her.

I also don't want any of my siblings looking too closely at the ring. None of them are jewelry experts, but I don't want to take any chances.

"Oh, that's a good idea."

I pocket the ring, then grab ahold of her hand once more, this time for emotional support. Though I'm not sure who needs it more at this point. My nerves have me feeling like I just stepped off a rollercoaster. I'm not used to this kind of anxiety. Most of the time I'm anxious about the future, or for a reason that I can't seem to place. I've never been nervous about what my family thinks of me, or rather the person I'm with.

But you're not actually with Sloane. The reminder doesn't lessen the tightness in my chest. If anything it makes it worse. I'm bringing home a woman who has every intention of parting ways at the end of the summer. I open the door for her and try to breathe deeply. Hopefully once we're playing a game, I'll be able to calm down. That usually helps. If I stay busy, I can keep these feelings under control.

Sloane doesn't let go of my hand, even as we walk into the living room where my family is congregated. I know it will confuse them more to see us holding hands, but I can't bring myself to let go. I think that's how I'm going to be at the end of this summer, too. Unable to let go, and praying she won't want to.

"Why couldn't you have a smaller family?" Sloane murmurs and I chuckle.

With all of my siblings, their spouses, Maddie, and Dahlia's sister Jasmine here, it's a full house.

"That would make it too easy on you." I run my thumb along her knuckles. "But don't worry Rose, I've got you."

I take in a slow breath, then paste on a grin. "Everyone, this is Sloane, member of the winning Cornhole team. Who wants to lose first?"

Sloane's beanbag lands just short of the board, *again*. Levi ducks his head, trying to hide his laughter. He wouldn't bother hiding it if Sloane wasn't a guest. Somehow, Sloane is the worst Cornhole player to ever walk the earth. Dahlia is barely paying attention–her focus is on interviewing Sloane about her books–and is still managing to do significantly better. I'm the only reason we're not totally hopeless, but I can only keep us above water for so long.

"Wait," I call out and walk over to her. "Let me help you, please." I take the beanbag from her.

"I'm not doing great," she says, looking up at me with a sheepish smile. "It must be killing you."

"What makes you say that?"

"You cringe each time I throw, and your brother is going to pass out if he keeps holding in his laughter." She toys with the frayed edge of her shorts. "I'm sorry I'm not good at this."

I frown at how serious she seems. "It's just a game," I tell her. She gives me a skeptical look. "All of my family is overly competitive, and you know I'm a little cocky."

"A little?" Her lips turn up at the edges.

"Yeah, a little. And that little bit can get me in trouble sometimes. Mainly when I don't check to see if my partner of choice has ever played the game before."

"Hey, I've played before!" she defends.

"Don't say that too loud, you'll embarrass yourself."

She rolls her eyes and shoves my shoulder. "Shut up," she says, but she's smiling.

"Hey, are you two going to finish your turn or have you decided to admit defeat?" Levi calls out, and Dahlia giggles.

"Don't worry, Sloane, we won't blame you for having a poor teacher," Sebastian taunts from where he's sitting in a lounge chair nearby. Him, MJ, Adrian, and Jules are watching us play, while Maverick is tending the grill. Jasmine is teaching Maddie how to do various gymnastics tricks in a patch of grass farther away, but even they laugh at all of the taunting.

"It's okay, Sloane, I used to be terrible too! They made fun of me relentlessly the first few family nights," Dahlia says.

"Try the first ten," I reply with a laugh, then look at Sloane. "All right, wifey, are you ready for our comeback season?"

Sloane shakes her head. "I will never understand how you're so confident."

I place the beanbag in her hand. "Just follow what I say, and you'll learn."

"How to be confident, or how to play Cornhole?" she questions as I move behind her.

I slide my hand down her arm. She sucks in a breath. "Both." I guide her arm back. "We're just going to practice, so don't let go of the beanbag, okay?"

"Okay," she whispers.

I swing her arm forward once, then pull it back and do it again.

"Now, whenever you get to this point," I say, pausing on my third swing. "Let go. Not too early, but not too late. Got it?" I say in her ear.

She nods, and I step back, fighting the urge to stay pressed against her.

"Show them what you've got, Rose."

Her arm pulls back, just like I showed her, and then she throws the beanbag. I hold my breath as it soars through the air. It falls right into the hole. My hands shoot up above my head. Sloane whips around, surprise in her eyes and a smile on her lips. I dip down and throw her over my shoulder, making her squeal.

"That's my girl!" I cheer, spinning her around a few times. She hits my back, her laughter filling the air.

When I finally set her down, she clings to my shirt, gasping for breath in the midst of her laughter. Her eyes meet mine, flecks of gold shining bright within the swirling brown and green. I hold her waist, drinking in this moment. Her hair tousled from being upside down. Her cheeks rosy and lifted by her perfect pink smile.

"I can't believe I scored," she whispers.

"I can." I tuck a stray hair behind her ear. The need to kiss her blooms within me. *If only this were real.* I search her eyes. *Could this be real?*

"Hellooo love birds, you're blocking the board," Levi yells out.

Sloane quickly steps back, her expression shuttered. I rake a hand through my hair and take a step back as well. The gap between us feels larger than it actually is. Our moment is lost, and my surroundings come rushing back. When I look over at my family, they all wear smug, knowing looks. Maddie and Jasmine are giggling and whispering to each other across the yard.

Sloane steps behind the board and we watch as Levi takes his turn, unfortunately securing the win for his and Dahlia's team. He dips Dahlia back for a celebratory kiss. I avert my eyes, instead looking to Sloane. She's watching them with something like longing on her face. When she turns and catches me staring, she gives me a small smile.

"We'll get them next time," I say and she nods.

It's only after she turns to walk over to a chair that I realize there may not be a next time.

Chapter Sixteen

Sloane Covington

I really like the Carter family. I'm beginning to feel rather attached to them, which is not good. They tease and poke at each other, but it's clear they love and care for one another deeply. And no one has said a single condescending word to me. It's refreshing to be around a family that's *healthy*. I'm tempted to ask if I can be adopted. My mom might get offended though, so I suppose I should just settle for enjoying this moment.

I watch as Grayson picks up a chess piece and moves it. Jasmine, Dahlia's younger sister, is sitting across from him, her brow furrowed in concentration. Apparently Grayson has been teaching her for a few months now, claiming he'll turn her into a prodigy. I don't doubt him. His teaching style incorporates gentle teasing and thorough explanation of each successful move or mistake made. Watching him makes me want to forget everything I know about chess just so he can be the one to teach me.

"He's a good teacher," Dahlia says in a low voice from beside me on the couch. A few of us came inside for a reprieve from the evening humidity, while the others jumped into the pool. Except Maverick, who left a while ago saying he had an early morning opening up his bakery.

Dahlia and Juliette are a part of our indoor camp. Juliette has made herself at home at the opposite end of the sectional, a worn copy of *Emma* in her lap. Her eyes fell shut a few minutes ago, and no one moved to wake her.

I wonder what it would be like to feel that comfortable in a home that wasn't yours. I've never felt that way, besides at my mom's house. Maybe Juliette is naturally trusting, but I don't think so. I think this home—this *family*—has made her feel safe.

"He is," I reply, shifting my gaze back to Grayson. The light is low and warm, casting shadows that make his jawline even more prominent and his normally bright blue eyes look like an inky indigo.

"So, you two..." Dahlia trails off.

"Are just friends," I fill in. "He's doing me a favor. I brought him into my mess and he was kind enough to run with it instead of away from it."

"Sounds like Grayson," she says with a smile. "He's always ready to help. Even before Levi and I got engaged, he treated me like family." She sniffs, her eyes shining.

She fans her face, laughing at herself. "I'm sorry, I get emotional thinking about it. There was a time when Levi wasn't doing well and ... Grayson made sure I knew, so that I could help him."

I look over at Grayson again. He's pointing at various pieces on the board. His voice is low, but I can tell he's explaining the moves Jasmine could make next. There's so much more to him than I thought. I feel guilty for stereotyping and judging him based off of the little I saw at the gym. With each new layer I get introduced to, I have to shift my opinion of who he is.

"Sometimes I wonder–" Dahlia pauses. She looks torn, but continues. "I don't know. I guess I wonder who takes care of him. He's always so happy, and quick to pick up a sword to fight whatever battle his siblings are up against, but I just..." She shakes her head, twisting a ring on her finger. "Listen to me, talking your ear off. I get all psychoanalytic when I'm tired. I'm going to see if Levi is ready to go."

I don't know how to respond, so I stay silent. She pats my leg over the crochet blanket I've cuddled up with, then gets up and walks outside. Soon after she disappears through the back door, it opens once more and Adrian walks in. He must have changed in the cabana outside, because he's completely dry except his hair.

It's still strange to see someone who looks exactly like Grayson walking around. He wears his hair different, and gives out smiles far less often, but besides that, they're copies of each other.

Adrian looks over the back of the couch, a warm smile gracing his face when he sees Juliette sleeping. This is the third time I've seen that expression on him over the hours I've been here, and all three were because of Juliette. A bittersweet longing swells in my chest as he walks around the couch and kneels in front of her, softly brushing her blonde hair away from her face. He kisses her cheek and she stirs.

"Sunshine?" she questions in a sleepy voice.

I learned earlier in the evening that she started calling him Sunshine as a joke, but it stuck. My heart almost burst from how cute I thought it was.

"I'm here, Jules," he says, so low I barely catch it. "Are you ready to go home?"

She murmurs a yes, so he draws her up in his arms. Foolish tears sting the back of my eyes. I look down at my lap, blinking a few times to keep them at bay.

"We'll see y'all later," Adrian says.

"Drive safe," Grayson says in response.

I look up, prepared to say a generic goodbye, when I find Adrian standing above me, Juliette curled up against his chest, her copy of *Emma* held in her arms the way a child holds a stuffed animal.

"It was nice to meet you," I squeak out, feeling intimidated by the intensity of his stare.

He dips his chin. "Take care of my brother on this trip of yours." Most people would phrase this as a question, but the hardness of Adrian's tone sounds more like a command. I simply nod.

"What are you talking about over there?" Grayson asks, but Adrian is already walking away.

I catch Grayson's gaze and muster up a smile, though my emotions are clashing in my head like rocks in a tumbler. What is it about him that has his family thinking he needs someone to take care of him?

"Are you ready to go?" he asks, the gentleness in his tone not unlike Adrian's when he was speaking to Juliette.

You're imagining things, I scold myself. Maybe Grayson does need someone to look out for him, but it can't be me. There's no way someone like him could be satisfied with a woman like me. He's everything I'm not, and I don't see the edges of our puzzle pieces fitting together. He needs an unapologetically adventurous woman.

Not a girl who gets embarrassed easily and spends all her time in fictional worlds.

"Only if you are," I reply. "You can finish your game."

"We finished," Jasmine groans. "He won, again. I don't know why I keep playing."

"You get better every time," Grayson encourages her with a smile. "You said you beat one of your friends last week."

"Yeah, I did. You should have seen his face when I beat him. It was hilarious."

"*Him*?" Grayson questions, a touch of darkness creeping into his tone.

"Oh look at the time, I think I'll ask if Dahlia is ready to go home," Jasmine speaks fast, pushing to her feet.

She starts toward the back door, but Levi and Dahlia come in before she gets there, all snuggled up together. Dahlia's hair and well, *everything* is soaked. She must have gotten pulled into the pool, but by the way she's looking at Levi, she doesn't mind.

"Did you know Jasmine has been playing chess with a *boy*?" Grayson asks as he stands up.

"No," Levi says at the same time Dahlia says "Yes."

"You knew and you didn't tell me?" Levi wears an incredulous look.

"I didn't tell you because I knew you and your brothers would try to kill him. They've hung out a few times at the house, under my supervision," Dahlia says.

"I want to meet him. We need to make sure he's good enough for Jaz," Grayson says, making me smile.

"I agree, I think he needs to meet with all of the brothers. And have a background check done."

"No, *please* no," Jasmine begs. "Dahlia, tell them they can't meet him."

"None of you are meeting him," Dahlia says, then shares a look with Levi. "Okay, *maybe* Levi will meet him, but only for a few minutes."

"I'm never going to have a boyfriend," Jasmine laments.

"Good," Levi and Grayson say in unison.

"You're both the worst," Jasmine says, but I can hear the affection in her tone.

"Yeah, yeah, you love us," Grayson says with a grin. She rolls her eyes and walks away.

"I guess we should get going. I'm hoping riding in the Jeep will dry me off some before I get home," Dahlia laughs.

"Y'all be safe, love you," Grayson says and they respond in kind.

"It was nice getting to know you more," Dahlia says to me on her way out. "I hope we get to hang out again."

"Me too," I say, and it scares me, but I mean it. Could I be friends with Grayson's family without being *with* Grayson? I find my answer in the uneasy feeling in the pit of my stomach. No, I wouldn't be able to have this family without being a real part of it.

One day Grayson is going to find a woman who's everything he could want and more. She'll get to talk books with all of the girls and fall asleep on MJ's couch whenever she gets too tired. She'll get the laughter and inside jokes, the safety and the warmth of Grayson's affection. Jealousy heats my blood at the thought, but I fight it off with the hope that I'll find my own Carter family to marry into one day.

"Ready?" Grayson's voice drags me out of my thoughts, his hand held out in between us. I nod and move the blanket off my lap before letting him pull me up off the couch.

"Thanks," I say in a quiet voice.

He reaches into his pocket then pulls back out the engagement ring. I let him slide it on my finger, my stomach dipping at the gentle touch.

"That's better." His low voice sends tingles down my spine. "Now, how about we get you home? I'm sure you've had your fill of the Carters."

If only that were true. I'm not sure I could *ever* have my fill of them.

"Should we say goodbye to MJ and Sebastian?" I ask.

Grayson shakes his head. "Maddie went upstairs earlier. They're alone in the pool. I've got a feeling we probably shouldn't intrude."

My eyes widen at his implication. "Good point. Let's go."

He chuckles and takes my hand again, walking us through the dimly lit house. To keep from focusing on how good it feels to hold hands with him, I let my gaze wander over the paintings on the walls as we pass them. There are a lot of landscape scenes. Roaring oceans, towering forests, and even a desert with a black storm cloud hovering in the distance. One painting in particular catches my eye, of a backyard sunflower garden. It reminds me of the sunflower painting in Grayson's house. MJ must have painted it for him, which is sweet of her. Maybe sunflowers are her favorite.

"Thanks for coming today," Grayson says as we reach the front door. I step through when he opens it for me.

"Of course, I had a good time. You have a great family."

"They can be too much for some people," Grayson says. He fishes his keys out of his pocket and unlocks the car.

"I think they're too much in a good way. Like too much laughter, or ice cream."

He smiles at my words. "That's a good way of putting it." He opens the passenger door for me and I slide in.

"I think everyone really liked you," he says once he's in the car with me. "Even Adrian, and he doesn't like anybody—well, except Juliette, and family."

"I'm glad," I say with a laugh. "Maybe now they won't be worried about you going to Hawaii with me."

"Yeah, I don't think they're worried about that."

They might not be, but I am. After spending all this time around Grayson, I'm certain that I made a mistake in choosing him to be my fake fiancé. He's *too* good. I'll just have to make sure I hold tight to my boundaries, or else I'll find myself heartbroken at the end of all this, while Grayson moves on to the next woman waiting to take my place.

Chapter Seventeen

Grayson Carter

I set down the video game controller with a sigh before checking the time on my phone. It's past two in the morning, but I can't sleep. When I try to lie down, my mind starts to spin. I feel like I'm trapped in a rip current, and if I stay in bed any longer, I'll go under. So I've been attempting to distract myself with TV shows and video games, but it hasn't done me much good.

My thumb swipes up on my phone and I find myself scrolling through my contacts. I don't want to bother my siblings–or anyone else–with this, but I know I can't distract myself forever. I hover over Adrian's name, since he's the one who knows the most about what I deal with.

A few years ago, I had a panic attack in front of him, and he made sure I got help. He was a good brother, waiting for me in the lobby of my therapist's office those first few visits. But now that I've gotten my anxiety under control, it's felt difficult to talk about those times it slips out of my grip. I don't want him to worry about me, or feel like he needs to stop his life like he did back then. He'll have a wife soon, and they'll build their own family. I can't rely on him forever.

Besides, how am I supposed to tell him that he's a part of the reason I think my anxiety is flaring up so much? Seeing him and Juliette together, then Levi and Dahlia, plus MJ and Bash has made the weight of my loneliness more apparent. All of them are so *happy*. Maddie is growing up. Jasmine will be off to college soon. Everyone is changing and I don't know how to feel about it. I'm always ready for a new adventure, but I'm not invited on this one with them.

I can't ruin their happiness by sharing how I feel. They'd drop everything to make sure I was okay, and they'd share less and less about their lives. I don't want that. It's better to just get through this without them.

My scroll continues until Sloane's name jumps out from my contact list. She's likely asleep, and we spent most of the day together, so she'd wonder why I was calling her. It's not like she's my real fiancée either. I shouldn't bring her into this. I keep scrolling, until I hit the bottom of my contacts. My left leg shakes as restlessness spreads like ants crawling all over me. I shoot up off the couch and start to pace my basement. A list of coping mechanisms runs through my head, but instead of it being comforting to have options it's overwhelming.

I don't want to go through this alone.

I scroll back up to Sloane's name and press call. Maybe she'll be asleep. I realize by the second ring that I might wake her, but just as I'm about to hang up, she answers.

"Gray?" Her voice is soft in my ear.

"Did I wake you? I'm sorry if I did." My words come out in a rush, like a broken fire hydrant.

"Are you okay? You didn't wake me. I can't sleep, so I'm writing." The sound of fingers against a keyboard confirms her words. I close my eyes and ground myself in the melodic clicks.

"I'm okay, just can't sleep either." I hope I don't sound as desperate as I feel.

"Are you a night owl? I am, but you seem like a morning person. Didn't you say you like the sunrise?" With each word she says, the tight band around my chest loosens a little. I begin to feel less alone, and with that, more capable of bringing myself down. I focus on the sound of her typing while taking in deep breaths.

"Gray?"

I blink my eyes open. I forgot I was on the phone. "I'm here, sorry." I rake a shaking hand through my hair. "I'm a morning person, but sometimes I have nights like this, where I can't sleep. Didn't you say you liked the sunrise better than sunset too?"

My breathing starts to even out. The buzzing in my veins dulls. It almost got bad, but this is helping. A voice in my head whispers that I should tell Sloane about what I'm going through, but I don't know if she's ready for that yet. I don't want to scare her away by putting too much on her.

"I do, but I still stay up late," she says, a soft laugh following her words. "I try to have a routine to help me go to sleep, but I end up pulling my laptop into bed with me and working until I can't keep my eyes open. I always feel the most creative when it's dark and quiet."

"Do you get scared while writing the suspense parts at night?"

She shared with Dahlia today about how it's felt writing romantic suspense when that's not her usual genre. I also get her email newsletter each week, so I knew she was writing in a new genre, but she doesn't know that. Another thing I should tell her.

"All the time." She says it so plainly I can't help but laugh. "I figure it's how I pay my dues as a writer, so I can be one of the greats someday."

"You are one of the greats already," I tell her.

"I think that's the sleep deprivation talking."

"You wouldn't believe me even if I said the same thing at noon."

She hums in response.

"You don't give yourself enough credit, Rose."

I sit down on my couch, my body finally still. My eyes fall shut as Sloane continues to type. I don't mind that she's not answering me. It's enough to know she's there. Though I do wish she could see just how amazing she is. I'd love to see her walk into a room as confident as can be.

My limbs start to feel heavy, the adrenaline of my anxiety wearing off and bringing on a wave of sudden exhaustion.

"How many bullets are in a handgun?"

"Hm?" I force my eyes open, trying to stay awake.

"Google says it depends on the kind of gun. What kind of gun would a bodyguard carry?"

I rub my eyes with one hand, a yawn escaping me. "I'm not sure that there's a standard for that," I answer. "Our guys carry Glocks, which are seventeen rounds on average."

"Thank you." She sounds like she's in awe. "I was just talking out loud–I do that sometimes while writing–but I forgot you work in *private security.* I have more questions, but you sound tired. I can ask tomorrow." The bubbling excitement in her voice makes me smile.

"I'm not too tired for you. Ask away, I'm all yours." *In more ways than you realize.*

"You're slurring your words," she says with a giggle. "We can talk tomorrow. I'm not in a rush."

"When's your deadline for this one?" If I recall correctly, it's set to release soon.

"I'm supposed to send it to my editor a week after we get back from Hawaii, but I'm halfway through so–"

"*Halfway?*" My eyebrows fly up. "You only have three weeks until then, and one of those will be on vacation."

"I've done more with less time, don't worry about me." I shake my head in disbelief at her words. "You should get some rest though. I'll text you tomorrow."

"I don't know if I can sleep. I'm in shock from hearing that you plan on writing *half a book* in less than three weeks."

"This is normal, trust me. Now, *go to sleep*, hubby."

My chest warms. "Okay, I'll go, but only because you called me hubby. And we're talking about these deadlines of yours tomorrow."

"Goodnight, Gray," she says through her laughter.

"Goodnight, Rose."

We hang up and I drag myself to bed. I fall asleep as soon as my head hits the pillow, dreaming of hazel eyes and sweet smiles.

"That's your second trip to the espresso machine," Adrian comments from behind me.

"Do you get any work done, or do you just watch me all day?" I pinch the bridge of my nose. "Sorry, that was harsh."

"I've said worse," he replies and I laugh.

I stir a packet of sugar into my double shot of espresso, then pour the steamed milk over the top. One of our employees, Jake, was a barista in college and insisted on having a real machine instead of a pod-based one. It tastes better but requires more work and cleaning. Usually I convince him to make me something, but I didn't have the energy for conversation today.

"You don't usually need coffee, especially a second cup. I expected to come in here and find you bouncing from wall to wall like a ping pong ball."

I clean the steam wand as he talks, then dump out the used espresso grounds before finally turning around to face him. "I didn't sleep much last night," I tell him, then take a sip of my latté. "I was up late talking to Sloane."

The most I can get away with when it comes to Adrian is a lie of omission, so that's what I go for. Hopefully he buys it, because I'm too tired to put up a fight.

"Really? After spending hours together, you stayed up late talking to her?"

I walk past him in order to leave the breakroom. "Wouldn't you do the same for Juliette?"

"I would, but she's my real fiancée. I thought you said you two were just friends?"

My shoulders tense at his words, but I don't let my steps falter. "I did say that."

"Didn't you also say once that friendship makes a great foundation for something?" Adrian's voice takes on a teasing tone as he follows me to my office. "What was it again?"

Marriage. I told him friendship made a good foundation for marriage. And when I said it I didn't once think that he'd ever be able to turn around and use my words against me.

"I liked it better when you were closed off and didn't talk," I grumble as I walk into my office. I shut the door on his laughter, leaving him in the hall.

If only my words about friendship and marriage could apply to Sloane and me. It's easy to be optimistic about the love lives of others. When it comes to mine, my hope waxes and wanes day to day. I sit down at my desk and shake my computer mouse, waking up the monitor. On my screensaver is a widget with a countdown to Hawaii. Hope increases within me once more. If anything could push our relationship from *fake* to *real*, it's this trip.

CHAPTER EIGHTEEN

Sloane Covington

"I changed my mind. I'm okay with Brooke thinking I'm weak. I don't want to go to Hawaii," I tell Grayson as we settle in next to each other on the private plane my family has chartered. Unsurprisingly, everyone else who will be joining us is late. But at least that means we have the plane to ourselves while I melt into a puddle of nerves.

"If you really feel that way, we can walk off the plane right now."

"Seriously? You won't be upset?" I look over at him. His eyes are serene, reminding me of the calm waters found in a tropical lagoon. The kind of waters I might get to see if I don't chicken out of this plane ride.

"Why would I be upset?"

"You'll miss out on a vacation to Hawaii, which was your only reward for doing all of this for me."

He smiles at me and shakes his head. "Sloane, none of this has been a chore for me. I've had fun these past few weeks. We don't have to go to Hawaii. You don't owe me anything."

I look down at my hands. At the engagement ring that I've gotten used to seeing there. Last night, I took it off before doing a face mask with Myla and Simone–I didn't want to get it dirty–and I felt naked without it. That alone should make me want to distance myself from Grayson. Instead, I find myself inching closer and closer to the edge.

How close can I get before I fall? If I slip, what will be at the bottom waiting for me?

"Rose?" Grayson draws me out of my thoughts. "If you want to get off the plane, we should do it before it's too late."

I bite my lip. If we walk off this plane, there won't be anything keeping us together. Sure, we said we'd be engaged until the end of the summer, but there won't be any reason for us to be seen together after Brooke and Topher's wedding. Grayson would be free to move on, like I know he will. And maybe it's selfish, but I don't want to let him go just yet.

"I want to go to Hawaii. I can do this." I punctuate my sentence with a nod.

"Atta girl," he says with a grin. My stomach does a little somersault in response.

Monica steps onto the plane, pushing her designer sunglasses up onto her head. She looks over at us with a plastic smile.

"Good morning, Monica," I say, proud that my voice doesn't shake.

"Sloane, I'm glad you could make it. And you brought your little boyfriend with you."

"My fiancé," I correct. She sniffs, then sashays down the aisle to take a seat at the back of the plane.

One by one, my dad, Brooke, and Topher get on the plane. Each giving an icier greeting than the one before. Then, Topher's parents step aboard. They flash me tight smiles on their way to the back where Monica and my dad are seated. The only perk of their poor hospitality is that they've all chosen to sit as far away from us as the plane will allow.

"I really hope I don't die on this plane," I say, fidgeting in my seat. "It would be awful to die with a group of people who hate me."

"We're not going to die," Grayson says, sounding concerned for me. I don't blame him.

"I hope not. I really want to die like how they did in *The Notebook*, except without her forgetting anything. Just peaceful and happy in my sleep next to my husband."

"I wouldn't have thought you to be so morbid."

"It's not morbid, it's romantic." Grayson gives me a skeptical look. "Well, maybe it's a *little* morbid. But we're in a flying metal death trap. I'm entitled to be a touch macabre."

He chuckles. "Fair enough, but maybe changing the subject would help you feel better? Why don't you tell me about the book you're writing?"

The pilot comes over the intercom before I can respond, telling everyone to buckle their seatbelts. I try to push mine in, but my hands are shaking too much. Grayson gently takes the belt away from me, and clicks it into place. His hand brushes against my hip. I can barely feel it through my clothes, but it sends tingles through me nonetheless.

"Thank you," I whisper.

The plane starts to move, and Grayson places his hand, palm up, on the arm rest between us. I slide my hand into his. He interlocks our fingers.

"I've got you, Rose," he says in a low, soothing voice.

I close my eyes as the plane lifts off the ground, and choose to trust his words, at least for now.

The plane dips, and with it my confidence. We're barely halfway through the *ten hour* flight to Honolulu and we've hit turbulence. For the first hour, Grayson talked me through my nerves by asking me questions about my favorite books. With his help, I was able to calm down enough to pull out my Kindle and read. I actually packed two paperbacks, but you can't read those one-handed, and there's no way I was letting go of Grayson's hand.

He surprisingly had his own Kindle, so we read alongside each other, while his thumb stroked my hand. Which he's still doing now, as I grip it with all the strength I have.

"Gray, I-I can't do this," I whisper. My stomach rolls and I clench my eyes shut. Even though no one is sitting near us, I don't want to appear anxious in front of them. It'll just be more ammo for them to use.

"It's okay, Rose. I'm here, you're not alone." I nod, repeating his words like a mantra in my head. "Let's try something together, okay? We're going to breathe in four counts, hold four, then let it out four counts. Can you do that?"

"I think so." I open my eyes and meet his, grounding myself in the kindness I find there.

He coaches me through the first few rounds of breathing, tapping my hand with his thumb as a way of counting. Soon enough, we're breathing in tandem and I feel my nerves dissipating.

"You're doing great," he says with a gentle smile. "How about we make a bucket list of things we want to do while we're there?"

I nod in answer, maintaining the breathing pattern he showed me. He pulls out his phone, still holding my hand, and starts tapping on the screen with his thumb.

"Any ideas?" he asks.

"I want to see the sunrise and the sunset at least once," I say the first thing that comes to mind.

He nods while he types. "I like that one. How about reading on the beach?"

"That's a given," I reply and he smiles. "I want to drink from a coconut. Oh, and eat a poké bowl."

"Sounds delicious. Do you like snorkeling?"

"I haven't done it since I was probably thirteen, but I think so."

"Then we'll add it to the list."

My muscles start to loosen as my anxiety lessens. I flex my hand in his, but don't let go completely.

"What about you?" I ask him. "Is there anything you want to do?"

"I'm writing some things down," he answers in a nonchalant tone.

"Like?"

"Like snorkeling," he says.

I narrow my eyes at him. "Why aren't you telling me the rest?"

"Because if I did you'd go back to being anxious."

How comforting.

"You have to tell me at some point."

"Hmmm *or* I could surprise you and hope for the best."

"I don't do well with surprises, remember?"

"You liked my last surprise though," he says and I can't help but smile at the memory of our date in his backyard. I wish we were back there, sitting under twinkle lights alone instead of on this death trap with my terrible family and ex-boyfriend. Who have been–much to my surprise–rather quiet this whole trip. Maybe we're getting the silent treatment. One can hope.

"That's true," I acquiesce. "I suppose since you've gotten me through most of this plane ride, I can trust you with a few surprises."

He smiles at me, then lifts my hand to brush a tender kiss across the back of it. My face heats and I look down at my lap. *Grayson Carter just kissed me ... sort of.*

"I promise I won't take that trust for granted."

I want to believe him. A part of me does, but another–admittedly bigger–part is just waiting for everything to come crashing down.

Chapter Nineteen

Grayson Carter

Warm, humid air bathes my skin as we step out onto the tarmac. Sloane's hand is in mine, and even though it has been for over ten hours now, I'm hoping she doesn't let go any time soon. It feels good to be needed. I loved being able to take care of her, as much as I hated how afraid she was during the flight. There was a moment toward the end of it, when her head was resting on my shoulder, that I hoped we'd never land. Sloane would probably hit me if she knew I'd had that thought.

I squint as I scan our general area. A series of black town cars are idling nearby. Our bags are being carried toward them, so I assume they'll be taking us to the resort.

"All that's on the schedule for tonight is to settle in at the resort," Brooke announces to everyone. "Be sure to check your itineraries. All of the events are *mandatory*." Her smile reminds me of a jungle cat baring its teeth.

Murmurs of acknowledgement float up from our group. Brooke grabs Topher and drags him toward the first car. I glance at Sloane, who's watching Brooke and Topher with a wary expression.

"You okay?" I ask in a low voice.

She nods. "I'm wondering if I should have backed out while I had the chance, but other than that, I'm okay."

I let go of her hand to wrap my arm around her shoulders, tucking her into my side as we walk toward the cars.

"If you would have backed out, we wouldn't be able to check everything off our bucket list."

"Speaking of ... I think I should look at the list. See if there are any typos or edits to be made."

"Not happening, wifey."

"But–"

"Nope."

We're almost to the car when I feel her hand travel down my back. She's likely trying to find my phone in my back pocket, but that's not what it feels like.

"Rose, are you feeling me up right now? In front of your *family*?" I ask, trying to sound incredulous.

Her hand springs up as she sputters, "W-what? No! No, I wasn't–I mean I was just–"

I burst into laughter, my shoulders shaking.

"You're the worst," she grumbles.

I'm still laughing when I slide into the town car next to her. Our driver closes the door behind us before getting in the front seat with a simple nod as his greeting.

"Did you expect me to stay silent while you grabbed my butt?" I ask her.

She hits my chest. The driver's eyes flick up to the rear view mirror, then back toward the road.

"Quit saying stuff like that!" she hisses. "People are going to draw conclusions."

"Good," I say with a smirk.

"*Not* good," she groans. "They're going to think I'm incapable of keeping my hands off you."

I lean in close and lower my voice. "I don't mind that reputation."

Her gaze dips down to my mouth. I don't breathe until her hazel eyes raise to meet mine again. She bites her lip and I grip the leather seat to keep from pulling her to me for a searing kiss. Our first kiss won't be in the back of a town car. No matter how tempting her perfect pink mouth is.

I lean back, breaking the moment so it doesn't go too far. Sloane's expression shutters and I regret my actions immediately. She laughs, but it comes out sounding brittle.

"I forgot your Casanova reputation. You're used to this sort of thing."

I frown. "Sloane, I can assure you I am not used to this." I look pointedly at her hand resting on the door, her engagement ring sparkling in the late afternoon sun.

"I meant flirting with women, being all touchy-feely." She waves a hand. I raise a brow.

"I have been called a flirt, but most women aren't allowed to grab my butt," I say drily.

Her face flames red. "I didn't–I wouldn't–" She cuts herself off with a flustered huff. "*Ugh.*" She turns to look out the window, the view of the ocean framing her profile.

Her frustration rolls off her in waves. I'm sure she's tired and cranky from the flight, not to mention the stress of dealing with her family for a week weighing on her. But I can't place why she's so upset. I'm here with *her*. I've never once flirted with another woman in her presence. And she has no way of confirming, but since the day she pulled me into her life, I've avoided all women who aren't my friends or family. All this, for a woman I'm technically not even dating.

I rake a hand through my hair. Before she catches me staring, I avert my eyes, looking out the opposite window. There's a chasm between us and it makes my chest ache. I thought we were having fun, but did I take it too far?

"I'm sorry," Sloane murmurs, drawing my eyes back to her. She adjusts her engagement ring, not looking at me. "I shouldn't fault you for your personality, or for your past."

"It's okay," I tell her, ready to bring back the light to our conversation. Even if it hurts a little that she sees me as some auspicious flirt with no self-control. Sure, I've gone on my fair share of dates, and had some fun conversations, but it's all been in the name of finding *the one*. Dating has never been casual to me. I didn't buy a family home just to squander away my years hopping from woman to woman. I just haven't been able to find my person yet.

"No," she says with a shake of her head. "It's not. I treated you like I had just met you, when I know you more now. You're not two-dimensional. You've got layers, like an onion."

I scrunch my nose up. "Do I have to be an onion? Can't I be something a little sexier? Like a trifle, or a parfait, or one of those really tall chocolate cakes."

She laughs and bumps her shoulder against mine. "*Gray*, you're missing the point." The light is back in her eyes now, making the weight lift off my chest.

"I'm sorry, you were saying I'm an *onion*?" I don't hide the disgust from my tone.

"I was *saying* that I'm sorry, and I'm going to try to do better at seeing you for who you really are, not just who my insecurities tell me you are."

"What were your insecurities saying?" I ask her. She looks down again.

Before either of us can say anything, the car comes to a stop.

"We've arrived," the driver announces. "Welcome to Luana Resort. I hope you enjoy your stay."

"Thank you," I say to him and Sloane murmurs the same as she's opening her door. I get out on the other side. *I guess our conversation will have to wait.*

Our driver unloads our bags from the trunk. I take both mine and Sloane's, ignoring her protests as I haul two backpacks and two suitcases—hers significantly larger than mine—through the resort doors. Brooke struts over to us before I even have time to take in our surroundings.

"Here's the key to your room." She places a key in Sloane's hand. "Don't forget to be downstairs and in the lobby at ten tomorrow morning." She spins around, blonde hair flying.

"Where's my key?" I ask her and she turns around, rolling her eyes like my very existence exasperates her.

"You and Sloane are staying together. No one thought you two would last until the trip, so I didn't book you a room." Her smile is tight, like a rubberband pulled taut. "I spent the *whole flight* making sure there was room for you in all of our excursions and events, but the resort didn't have any more rooms." She says all of this as if it's *my* fault she didn't believe the RSVP Sloane sent in on my behalf.

Sloane looks up at me with wide eyes. I'd laugh at her expression if Brooke wasn't watching us.

"No problem. That just gives me even more time with my beautiful fiancée." I shoot Brooke a wide grin.

"Good. I'll see you both tomorrow."

"At eleven, yes of course," I joke. Brooke's eyes narrow. I hold her gaze with a bright smile. I swear her eye twitches.

"*Ten*," she growls.

"Oh I forgot you said *ten*, my bad. We'll be there." I nod like I'm just now getting it. She turns around with a huff and stomps toward where Topher is stationed at the bar.

The lobby is vast and filled with greenery and color. A row of three glass elevators is to our right, giving everyone a view of the entire resort as they go up to their rooms. There's a large dining area with a tiki bar that has several guests sitting at it already.

"This place is really nice," I say to Sloane as I breathe in the smell of suntan lotion mixed with lemon cleaner. I look at Sloane, who's just staring straight ahead. "Rose, are you all right?"

"*All right*?" She whips her head over to look at me. "No, I am not *all right*. We can't share a room, Grayson."

"I'll sleep on a couch, or the floor." I shrug, because it's no big deal.

She laughs, and it sounds a tinge hysterical.

"I can't believe this is my life," she says under her breath. "Okay, let's go find our room. Where you're going to sleep on the couch or floor." Another hysterical giggle escapes her.

"I'm worried for you," I say as we walk to the elevators.

She nods in understanding. "I'm worried for me too."

CHAPTER TWENTY

Sloane Covington

Is this my karma for writing not one, not two, but *five* books with the 'only one bed' trope? Myla and Simone have poked fun at me countless times about how that trope sneaks its way into most of my books. It's always been a favorite of mine. I mean, how can you top the tension that level of forced proximity brings? Now, I regret writing every single one of those scenes, as well as all of the books I downloaded to my Kindle when I saw the author say they had one. My imagination has endless fodder.

Grayson falls back onto the bed with a sigh. "Don't worry, I won't get too comfortable. I just need a minute."

My heart sinks at his words. He's come all this way to help me, and now he's going to sleep on the floor. There's no couch in our room, just two padded rattan chairs, a matching coffee table, and a king sized bed.

"Maybe..." I begin, hating that I'm already giving in. Grayson pushes up onto his elbows, watching me with curious eyes. "Maybe it wouldn't be that bad if we slept in the same bed. We can create a pillow boundary," I say, feeling my face heat when I think about how many couples that failed for in books I've read.

"A pillow boundary," he repeats my words, amusement lacing his voice.

"If that's okay with you. Or we can alternate who sleeps on the floor," I suggest.

"You're not sleeping on the floor, Rose. I'm a gentleman."

"If I recall correctly, you once said you *weren't* a gentleman," I reply without thinking.

A smirk plays on his lips. His inky black hair is tousled, making him look all the more like the dangerous rogue my heart fears he is.

"My status changes depending on what the moment calls for." His deep, velvety voice combined with the way he's lounging on the bed–the bed we're going to *share*–has my heart fluttering and my skin feeling too hot.

I avoid looking at his agonizingly gorgeous face by letting my gaze bounce around the room. Finally, I spot a way to put distance between us.

"Ice!" I blurt out and lunge for the empty container. "I'm going to get us ice." I snatch my phone off the coffee table next and rush toward the door.

"Do you want me to come with you?"

"No, no I'm fine," I say as I'm pulling open the door. "You stay where you are!" I sound like I'm a cop shouting at a criminal.

I shut the door to the sound of his chuckles and immediately pull out my phone, hitting Simone's contact. I need someone sensible to talk me down, and though it's ten at night there, I know she'll pick up. I quickly walk down the hall to put distance between me and our room.

"Hey, are you okay?" Simone asks upon answering. I already texted her that I landed, so I'm sure she's wondering why I'm calling so soon.

"No," I say and then realize that would make her worry. "I mean, yes, but no."

"I'm going to need you to clarify."

I groan. "I'm sharing a room with Grayson, and I don't think I'm going to survive." Simone snorts at my overdramatic words.

"You'll be fine. It's not like you're sharing a bed." I say nothing. My mind descends into a whirlpool of panic. "*Oh*, you're sharing a bed."

"He offered to sleep on the floor, but I couldn't let him do that after all he's done for me."

I look up right before I run into a wall at the end of the hallway. I look to my left, more rooms. To my right, a window. No ice machine. I turn back around and walk in the opposite direction. I can't very well return without ice. He probably–more like *definitely*–knows I didn't leave the room for the sole purpose of getting ice, but if I return without it I'll look even crazier than I already do. I listen to Simone relaying the information to Myla.

"Myla says you caused this by writing all of those one-bed scenes in your books." Simone's voice is laced with humor.

At least I wasn't the only one with that theory.

"What am I supposed to do?" I whine. "I cannot possibly make it through five nights of sleeping next to Grayson Carter. What if I accidentally break through our pillow boundary? Or sleep talk and say his name? Do you know what five nights of sleep deprivation can do to a person?" With each question, my voice gets higher pitched.

"Take a breath, S." I suck in the lemon-scented air at Simone's command. "You're going to be fine. You're both adults. It's just sharing a bed, nothing more."

Nothing less, either.

"This is all easy for you to say because you are home, safe and sound, with only Roman C Kitten to share your bed."

"Thank you for reminding me of my lack of romance," Simone replies. Her tone is drier than my skin when I forget to apply moisturizer.

I finally find the area with the ice machine. It's a little nook just big enough for someone to hide in. So I do.

"I'm sorry." I sigh. "I just got off a ten hour flight when I despise airplanes. Now I'm sharing a bed with a man who looks like he stepped out of one of your novels."

"Hmmm, who would he be?" Simone asks, instead of attempting to comfort me.

I nestle myself in between the wall and the ice machine. If anyone saw me they'd probably call security, but something about the darkness and low hum of the machine calms me. I push up on my toes and set the container on top of the machine so I don't have to hold it. There's a good chance I'll end up throwing it if my emotions continue to spiral. Then I'd *really* scare someone.

"Prince Castien. With his dark hair and ocean eyes, he's a perfect fit."

I lean my head back against the wall and picture Grayson wearing a crown of pearls and sapphires, like the evil prince from Simone's latest fantasy romance series. The one that everyone fell in love with–me included–so she ended up having him get the girl instead. Grayson would look good in a crown, but that's not saying much. He'd look good in anything.

"Maybe by looks, but he's too innocent and sunny to be a villain."

My mind flashes to Grayson leaning in, smirk on his lips, whispering about how he wouldn't mind people thinking I couldn't keep my hands off him. He may not be villainous, but he's certainly not *innocent*.

"You'd be surprised," I mumble. "You're not helping me, by the way."

"I'm distracting you from your situation."

"By reminding me of how Grayson resembles the character who I said could, and I quote, *kidnap me any day of the week*?"

"Rose." I jump at the sound of Grayson's voice, hitting my knee on the machine I'm wedged up against.

"*Ouch*," I mumble, then look up at him. "Grayson, you're supposed to be in our room."

Simone gasps in my ear.

"I came to check on you," he says with a smirk.

"I'm all good, just having a little girl talk." I direct my next words at Simone. "I'll call you later." I hang up before she can say anything else.

Grayson holds his hand out to me. I take it and let him pull me from my hiding spot.

"Is there a reason you're hiding from me?"

"Hiding?" I force a laugh. "I'm not hiding from you. I like to be in small spaces when I talk on the phone."

"Mhmm." Amusement lines his expression. "For someone who writes fiction, you're not great at spinning a story."

I sigh and look down at my hand, still nestled in his. That's when I notice that he's changed into tan shorts. My eyes travel up. And a white linen button down, with–*of course*–a few buttons undone at the top.

"You changed," I state, then meet his eyes. "Why did you change?"

"Because we're going out, and I would be much too hot walking around the island in sweatpants."

"Where are we going?" I almost whine about wanting to curl up in bed after the long flight, but then I realize that I'd be in bed with *him* ... so I keep those thoughts to myself.

"To check two items off our bucket list." He guides me out of the ice machine nook and down the hall to our room.

"Which two?" I'm keenly aware that this man is being vague because he's mischievous by nature. Like a troll under a bridge. Only, he doesn't look like a troll.

"Get changed and meet me in the lobby," he says as he lets go of my hand, then slips a room key into it.

I put my hands on my hips. "Don't tell me what to do. I'm not doing anything until you tell me where we're going."

He raises a dark brow, eyes gleaming. "I could always kidnap you. Though I'm not sure if it's considered kidnapping if you want it to happen."

My face flames. *He heard everything I said.* I spin to face the door and tap the room key on the handle. It turns green and I push inside.

"I can't go out tonight on account of being too busy dying of embarrassment," I say as I go to shut the door on him. He sticks his foot in to block me.

"What's there to be embarrassed about? I for one think it's cute that you picture me in your head while reading. In fact, I'd love to hear more about this Prince Castien. All I know right now is that he's ridiculously handsome and is prone to kidnapping."

He grins at me through the crack in the door. I glare back at him.

"I changed my mind. You can sleep on the floor. Or better yet, in *the hall.*" I give up on keeping him out and walk further inside our room instead. He follows behind me.

"Come on, Rose, don't be mad at me. I'm only teasing."

"Yes, well your teasing has earned you an evening alone," I huff. I start to open up my backpack so that I have something to do with my hands.

Warm, strong arms wrap around my waist from behind. I squeak, stiffening in my spot.

"I'm sorry for teasing you," he murmurs near my ear. I think I've forgotten how to breathe. "But don't make me watch the sunset alone, please."

He could ask me to jump out of a plane with no parachute right now and I'd say yes. It's unfair how he affects me. Especially when I know I likely don't have the same effect on him.

"Okay," I manage to whisper. "I'll go."

"Thank you," he says, then pulls back. The warmth of his embrace leaves as suddenly as it arrived. "I'll see you downstairs, Princess."

I hum in response, unable to face him. It's only after the door clicks shut that I realize he gave me a new nickname. One I shouldn't like as much as I do.

CHAPTER TWENTY-ONE

Sloane Covington

"No, *no*, absolutely not," I say as our driver pulls up to a karaoke bar.

"You don't have to sing," Grayson tells me as he opens the car door. "But the reviews said there's good food and it's beachfront. We'll get to watch the sunset with entertainment."

"The sunset *is* the entertainment," I say as I slide out of the car after him. "I thought we were going to have a relaxing evening on the beach." I smooth down my pale blue sundress. I'm already nervous just being in the proximity of a microphone.

"We'll have that this week, I promise." He holds out his hand and I reluctantly take it. "But for tonight, I think this could be fun."

"Gray, this isn't me," I explain as he leads me up to the cabana-like building.

The place barely qualifies as a building, what with most of it being out in the open. There's a wooden stage with a TV and two microphones on it. Someone is singing a horrendous version of a song from *Grease* with their eyes closed. I can't help but giggle when the person bursts into laughter in the middle of their serenade. The sunset serves as a backdrop for the whole bar, and it really is a great view. The waves are crashing in the distance while birds fly above.

"How do you know unless you try?" he asks as we walk to a hightop table.

"The same way I know that murder isn't for me."

He lets out a surprised laugh. "That comparison doesn't work in the slightest. Karaoke and murder are not in the same category."

We sit on opposite sides of the table and though we've had many romantic moments over the past few weeks, this feels oddly like a real date.

"Sure they are. The category is: activities I know I don't have any interest partaking in." He smiles and shakes his head at my words. "In all seriousness, I'm not good in the public eye, Gray. You've seen me. I could barely string together a conversation in front of Dahlia and Juliette when I first met them."

"I'm not going to force you to do anything, Rose." He meets my eyes. "If you want to eat and watch the sunset while laughing at everyone who goes up on stage, we can do that. But if there's even a *tiny* part of you that thinks it would be fun, then I think you should do it. And I'll be up there with you, of course."

I bite my lip. The person on stage looks like they're having fun. Their friends are waving their phone lights like they're at a concert, laughing like they don't have a care in the world. No one here is rude, even though the person sounds objectively terrible. I guess everyone here came to a karaoke bar expecting people to do this.

While I'm considering, our waiter comes up. I order a water and Grayson orders the same, as well as an assortment of appetizers.

"The longer I think about it, the sicker I feel," I tell him once the waiter has left. My stomach is rolling at the thought of being in front of all of these people.

"But do you want to do it?"

"The smallest, tiniest, most *miniscule* part of me thinks that it might possibly be kinda sorta fun."

The smile he sends my way is soft and kind. He slides out of his chair and tugs me out of mine. My heart stutters in my chest when he tucks my hair behind my ear. Warmth spreads through me, but it's doused with cold water when the people on stage finish singing. No one walks up to replace them, which means there's an opening.

"I-I don't know if–" I can't get my thoughts in order. Grayson pulls me toward the stage. My feet feel like someone strapped cement blocks to them.

"Have you seen *The Greatest Showman*?" he asks me as he steps up to the computer where you choose the songs.

"Only about a hundred times."

He grins over his shoulder. "I knew I liked you, wifey." He types for a moment. "All right, are you ready? Nevermind, don't answer that." He pulls me on stage and hands me a microphone with an encouraging smile.

There are no stage lights, but I almost wish there were, so that it would be harder to see all of the people staring at me. The tune of *Rewrite The Stars* starts playing and a few people clap at Grayson's choice. I look down at my sandals. *I love this song.* If we were alone in the car I'd belt this out with him. Who am I kidding? Even then, it would take some coaxing for me to do more than just mouth along.

Grayson takes my hand and pulls me to him as he starts to sing the first verse. The crowd cheers and whoops. His hand slides up my arm and over my shoulder, coming to rest under my jaw. I'm mesmerized as he sings better than a man who looks like he does should be allowed to. His thumb caresses my cheek. I try not to let the action go to my head. It quickly does, burning itself into my neural pathways so I'll be doomed to relive the perfection on every sleepless night.

The next verse is mine and I lift the microphone to my lips, practically whispering the words. Grayson doesn't move from where he's holding me close. His bright blue eyes stay locked on mine. With each caress of his thumb, my fear is uprooted and thrown to the side like weeds in a garden. I'm left to bloom beneath the sun of his smile. Soon enough, the whole crowd fades away. It's just me and him singing to each other. And though I'm certain I sound terrible, the way he's looking at me makes me feel like I'm capable of winning a Grammy.

The song picks up as we sing in tandem. He takes my hand and steps back, spinning my arm over my head before twirling me into his chest. When he spins me back out, my dress flares around me and the crowd goes wild, but it barely registers because all I care about is him. The salty air whips around us. His skin is golden in the fading light and his hand is warm in mine. I want to capture this moment, like fireflies in a jar, and hold on to it forever.

My voice grows louder and louder until I'm singing the way I do when I'm alone and think no one can hear me. Grayson lets me twirl him, ducking his tall frame beneath my outstretched arm. I can barely keep up with the lyrics because I'm giggling so much. He slowly pulls me to him and dips me back right as the song is ending. His arms wrapped around me is a heady feeling. I come up giddy and breathless and *alive*.

"Ladies and gentlemen," Grayson booms into the microphone. "Give it up for my future wife, Sloane Rose!" He steps to the side and holds my hand up before guiding us into a bow. The sound of applause fills my ears. I can't stop smiling. We bow twice more, as if we're accomplished thespians. The crowd behaves as if they believe us.

I place the microphone back on the stand. The adrenaline coursing through me makes my hands shake. As soon as we're off the stage, Grayson picks me up and spins me around.

"That was amazing!" He sets me on my feet and cradles my face in his hands. "*You* were amazing, Rose. I'm so proud of you."

Something cracks open inside of me at his words. My eyes burn with unshed tears.

"All I did was sing karaoke," I whisper around the emotion lodged in my throat.

"All you did–are you kidding me?" He wraps me up in a hug that I could live in. "You conquered a fear. That takes guts."

"I wouldn't have done it without you."

"So? That doesn't diminish what you did. Everyone needs a push every now and again."

I don't say anything more. I don't think I can without bursting into tears. My heart feels upended. Grayson's words and actions don't fit in with my dad's, or Monica's, or even my own. His treatment of me is so different–so kind–that I'm not sure where it's supposed to reside in my heart.

He pulls back and looks down at me. I blink back my tears, then stretch my lips into a smile. I don't want to ruin this moment.

"Thank you for going up there with me, Gray."

"You're welcome, Princess."

I roll my eyes while he laughs. "You just had to go and ruin the moment."

"What? You don't like your new nickname?"

I huff and pull away from him to head back to our table. The appetizers Grayson ordered are waiting for us, along with our waters. Condensation drips down the abandoned glasses, but our food is still steaming.

"That's not even the nickname he calls her in the book," I say as I slide into my seat.

"What does he call her?"

I shoot him a flat look. "I'm not telling you."

"That's okay, I don't like spoilers anyway and I downloaded the whole series to my Kindle while you were getting ready."

My mouth falls open in shock. He attempts to stick a French fry in it. I swat his hand away, trying not to smile as he laughs.

"I can't believe you bought Simone's books," I say as I reach for a fried pickle.

"I planned on reading them one day. They just got bumped up my TBR when I heard of your adoration of a certain evil prince."

I ignore his teasing and focus on his first sentence. "Why were you going to read her books? Had you heard of them before we met?"

He takes a drink of water. "She's your friend. Any friend of my betrothed's is worthy of my support." He shoots me a playful grin before digging into a pile of nachos.

Though he's been teasing me, it's clear that he genuinely intended to read Simone's books.

"And Myla's?" I ask. He nods while he finishes chewing.

"I bought her latest release, but Dahlia stole it from my house before I could read it."

I grab a French fry and dip it in the pineapple sriracha ketchup next to the basket while I think. Is it possible that Grayson cares for me on a level deeper than I thought? I sneak a glance at him. He's watching a trio of friends belt out a Taylor Swift song with a smile on his face. I can't help but smile too, which is a trend around him, I realize. When his head turns, our eyes catch. His ever-present grin widens and a little seed of hope floats through me, like dandelion fluff in the wind.

"What?" he asks when I hold my stare.

"Do you think we sounded that awful?" I ask and he shakes his head.

"No, I think we were incredible."

Me too.

CHAPTER TWENTY-TWO

Grayson Carter

Sloane is in the shower. The *shower*. My earlier insistence that it wouldn't be a big deal to share a room with her was wrong. So very wrong. I'm not sure I can bear five nights of the steam carrying the scent of her tropical soap to me while I sit here pretending to read. Or her pretty blush when she asked if it was alright that she got a shower before me. I couldn't even tease her. The words got stuck in my throat.

It's been forty minutes since she disappeared behind the bathroom door with an armful of her belongings. I don't fault her for wanting a long shower after our flight and being out at the karaoke bar. But I do wish she would finish soon so that my mind could rest. Though I suppose it won't have time to rest, it will just move on to the next problem at hand: sharing a bed with her.

My phone buzzes on the coffee table and I snatch it up, grateful for the distraction. The text on the screen when I unlock it makes my brows furrow.

Drew: Hey man, does your company by chance do any private investigating?

Drew is a family friend I grew up with. He and his little sister Evie spent a lot of time over at our house, especially during and after their parents' messy divorce. We don't see him as often now, with Drew having his own family. And we see Evie even less, since she's living in New York working as a photographer and, last I heard, married with a baby on the way too.

Grayson: No, we don't. Is everything okay?

Drew: I'm worried about Evie, but I'm probably just overreacting.

I frown. Drew has always been overprotective, but never to the length that he'd hire someone to investigate Evie. I've also known them to be close, so I don't see why he'd need to check on her in this way. I exit out of the text thread and pull up one with Maverick. Mav is closer to them, since he and Drew played football together. Maybe he'll know what's going on.

Grayson: Hey, do you know why Drew is asking me about hiring a PI to check on Evie? Is she alright?

I tap my fingers on the arm of the rattan chair I'm sitting in. The sound of running water stops. Sloane must be done with her shower.

Maverick: She's been more and more distant lately. I'm concerned too. I told him we should just go to NYC and check on her in person. But he said the last time he did that Evie blew up on him.

I sigh and rake a hand through my hair. Evie has always been on the wild side. We used to joke that her last name–Wilder–suited her perfectly. So when she jetted off to New York, I didn't bat an eye. When Drew told us she married some male model she hadn't known long, it didn't surprise me. What *did* catch me off guard was when shortly after that, she announced she was pregnant. She always talked about seeing the world before she had kids, but that was when she was in college. Maybe she changed her mind, or her husband swayed her. Either way, it's probably nothing to be concerned about.

Grayson: Maybe she's just busy with work. You know her job is fast-paced. There's a chance she's trying to get as much work in as possible before the baby gets here.

Maverick: Maybe, or maybe her husband is keeping her from talking to her loved ones.

My eyebrows shoot up at his bold statement.

Grayson: Do you really think so?

Maverick: I don't know what to think anymore. All I know is she isn't acting like the Evie I knew. As wild as she was, she wouldn't ignore her brother like this.

I don't know Evie like Maverick does, so I can't say whether he's right or not. Even if I could say he's wrong, I wouldn't. Maverick cares too much about the Wilders to see reason. He won't give up or pull back until he can see with his own eyes that Evie is safe and sound. His protective nature is a good quality; I only hope it doesn't land him in jail. I know if it came to it, he'd fight on Evie's behalf.

The sound of the bathroom door opening makes my head snap up. Sloane pads into the room and sets her clothes in a pile beside her suitcase. Her skin is flushed pink, looking warm and soft in the dim light. Her hair is down her back in a wet braid, making the pale blue silk of her pajama top turn navy.

"Sorry I took so long," she says as she walks over to the nightstand where her phone is charging. "I needed it after the long day."

"Don't be sorry, I don't mind."

She looks up from checking her phone and smiles. "You're a good fiancé, Gray." The lack of the word *fake* in her sentence makes my heart skip a beat in my chest.

"You make it easy, Rose." I stand up and stretch. Her eyes follow my movements like she can't help it. I wish she wouldn't look at me like this when we have to share a bed. At the same time, it gives me hope that this summer won't be the end of us.

I gather what I need for my shower and head to the bathroom. As soon as I enter, I'm overwhelmed by everything *Sloane*. The scent of coconut lingers in the warm air, her toiletry bag sits open on the counter, her lavender hair brush laid beside it. There's a pink loofa hanging from the handle that turns on the shower. Her towel drying on a hook.

I turn on the shower and spot a line of mini soaps and products sitting on a shelf. I place mine on the shelf below it, trying to ignore how perfect it all looks. There's an air of domesticity to it that feels bittersweet. If only this were a real engagement, then I'd be able to think of this moment as a glimpse of the future. Not merely a picture of what I wish I could have.

My shower goes by in a blur of what-ifs. *What if Sloane was mine? What if she has feelings for me too? What if the attraction that feels evident between us could blossom into something more substantial?* By the time I'm finished getting ready for bed, I've exhausted all avenues of thought and myself.

I walk back into our room. All of the lights are out except the lamp on my side of the bed. Sloane's face is softly illuminated by the glow of her Kindle. She's propped herself up on a mound of pillows, with a line of them on her right side, all the way down the middle of the bed.

"Will it bother you if I read for a little while?" she asks as I walk over to the nightstand. I hook my phone up to the charger, then take a sip of the water bottle I set there earlier.

"You're not tired?" I ask instead of answering.

She gives me a sheepish look. "I am, but I got to a really good part in this book before I had my plane freak out."

I slide into bed, tucking the pillow up under my neck as I roll over on my left side to face her. Even with the pillow boundary, this feels all too intimate.

"I understand. Last week I stayed up way too late because the book I'm buddy-reading with Maddie was getting good."

She looks down at me from where she's propped up, her expression tender. "I think it's sweet that you read with her."

"It's fun for both of us," I say with a shrug of my shoulder.

"You love her a lot," she says softly.

I smile. "Of course. She's family, and family is everything to me."

Sloane returns my smile, but there's something in her eyes I can't read. "You're a good uncle."

"If you keep complimenting me, you're going to give me a big head," I joke.

"It's true." Her voice is almost a whisper, but it hits me hard, reverberating through the empty spaces in my heart. "You're *good*, Grayson Carter. The very definition of it."

I swallow down the emotion rising within me. Her words are so simple, but I'm not sure anything has affected me so deeply. I've spent the past few years wondering if my loneliness was because there was something wrong with me. But here she is, whispering into my very soul, contrasting my deepest insecurity with a mere sentence.

"Thank you," I rasp out, then avert my eyes and pull the blankets further up over me. I'm not sure I can handle anymore of her unbridled kindness. I might say something I shouldn't, something she's not ready for. "I should get some sleep. Goodnight, Rose."

"Goodnight, Gray."

She turns her attention back to her book. I watch her for a moment, unable to help myself. Her lips are turned up at the edges in a soft smile. She holds her Kindle with one hand, toying with the edge of her braid with the other. A little gasp escapes her. She looks over at me, likely worried that she's disturbed me. I just smile at her.

"Sorry," she whispers to me and I can see it. I can see this exact moment years from now. Her reading in bed, little gasps and sighs echoing in the night. I'd wake up and tease her about staying up too late. Then I'd pull her close and make her forget all about the book that so enthralled her. Her gasps and sighs would be due to me. The image is so achingly perfect that I almost can't reassure her that it's okay. Because it feels like it's not. This is a cruel form of torture, one she's utterly unaware of her role in.

"It's okay," I manage to grate out.

She turns back to the book once more, biting her lip. I squeeze my eyes shut and tell myself not to open them again until tomorrow morning. Sleep will save me tonight, if I can avoid dreaming of her. She gasps again and my stomach flips. *Outlook not good.*

CHAPTER TWENTY-THREE

Sloane Covington

I open the itinerary on my phone while sitting across from Grayson at breakfast. Dread settles in my stomach like cement.

"We're going to be apart today," I tell him. He frowns while cutting into his waffle.

While getting ready this morning, we both admitted to ignoring the itinerary. Grayson ignored it because he likes surprises. I avoided it because I planned on not attending any of the activities except the wedding. Then Brooke emphasized how everything was *mandatory* and since my dad is footing the bill with a 'whatever Brooke wants' attitude, I feel like I have to participate.

"What's on the agenda?"

He reaches for the syrup, his muscular forearm on display. It's disconcerting in the most frustrating way how gorgeous he is. His inky black hair has a slight wave to it today, and I know for a fact he didn't do anything but wake up and run his hands through it a few times. I know this because I watched him do it while refusing to get out of bed. I could have stayed under the covers all morning, breathing in the way his citrus scent mixed with my coconut one.

Soft morning light filters in through the nearby window and bathes his lightly tanned skin in a golden haze. He's wearing what apparently is his summer uniform–shorts and a linen button down–and I still haven't gotten used to the few buttons he leaves undone. Suddenly I want to write a summer romance, one where the heroine gets to indulge herself in a way I never will, pressing her lips to the triangle of exposed skin...

"Rose?" I blink and look up from his chest, right at Grayson's smirking lips. "I know you're going to miss me today, but you don't have to stare. We have all week together."

My face flames. "I-I wasn't," I stutter, looking down at the yogurt parfait. "The guys are playing golf today," I quickly change the subject. "While the girls go to the spa. We'll meet up at the beach for a catered picnic lunch at one."

Grayson doesn't say anything right away. I chance a look up at him. He's not smirking anymore, instead his eyebrows are pulled together in worry.

"I hate that you'll be alone with your stepmom and Brooke for all that time."

I shrug. "I'm more worried about you than me. I'm used to their passive aggressive digs."

"Don't worry about me, wifey, I'm capable of withstanding more than you think." He winks. "And if you recall, I know how to have a good time on a golf course."

"Now I'm more worried for them than you." I laugh. "My dad is very much a fan of golf course etiquette."

Grayson's lips turn up in a mischievous grin. "I have *so* many ideas on how to ruin today."

"You're quite villainous this morning," I say as I reach for my coffee.

"Well, my future wife does have a weakness for morally grey men."

I smile over the rim of my mug. "Within the pages of a book, Gray. Not in real life."

"So you don't want me to pretend I don't know anything about golf until everyone there but me is severely annoyed?"

"It's tempting..." I trail off, watching his blue eyes sparkle with amusement. "But it would probably make our situation worse."

"*Fine.*" He lets out an overly dramatic sigh. "I'll behave."

"I'm not convinced you know how," I quip.

"Mmm," he hums as he takes a sip of his coffee. "My ability depends on the situation." His eyes meet mine. "And who I'm with."

Warmth pools in my abdomen. "And when you're with me?" I dare to breathe out the question. Maybe his boldness is wearing off on me after all.

He opens his mouth to respond, then stops. His face falls as he gestures over my shoulder. I turn in my seat and find Brooke storming toward me.

"Why have you not been answering your phone?" she snaps as soon as she's within earshot. A few guests shoot surprised looks her way.

"Good morning, Brooke," Grayson says in a calm tone. Her head whips over to him just long enough to glare, before swiveling back to me.

"I have been calling for twenty minutes now." She holds up her phone and shakes it.

I frown and pick my phone up from the table, realizing upon unlocking it that I never took it off *do not disturb* when I woke up.

"Sorry, Brooke, I had my notifications off."

She crosses her arms with an angry huff. "Our reservation got moved up and we're now fifteen minutes late because of *you*."

I sigh and start to stand, but Grayson places a hand over mine. "You haven't finished eating."

I meet his gaze. "It's okay," I say but he shakes his head.

"Brooke, you told us to meet you at ten. You can't change the plans last minute and expect Sloane to abandon her food."

Brooke blinks. It's as if she's malfunctioned. "*I'm sorry?*" she seethes.

"An apology is a great place to start," Grayson says and my mouth falls open.

Brooke's face mirrors my shock, but there's a layer of pure rage on top. My stomach churns. Grayson's kind gesture might be for nothing. I'm not sure I'll be able to eat.

"Meet us at the spa. The reservation is under Covington. Don't take too long," she grits out before turning and stomping away.

"You didn't have to do that," I tell Grayson once she's far enough away.

"Of course I did. I won't sit back and watch her treat you that way."

Not for the first time around him, my eyes sting with happy tears. I blink them back.

"Thank you," I say quietly while stirring my parfait around. "No one has ever done that for me before."

"This is the bare minimum of what you should expect," Grayson says, his gruff tone drawing my eyes up. "You deserve so much more than you think you do, Rose."

He must be determined to make me cry. I bite the inside of my cheek to stave off the tears. My instinct is to reject his words, to tell myself that he's just being nice. But for once I push back against that instinct, instead letting his words sink in. It's uncomfortable to consider that he could be right when I've spent most of my life bending under the wills of others. Maybe by the end of our summer together, I'll believe him.

Under other circumstances, I'd probably love this experience. The air smells of lavender and eucalyptus, and soft instrumental music plays over the speakers. Yes, if I was alone, or even with Myla and Simone, this would be wonderful.

Instead, I'm clenching my jaw so hard I'm worried I might crack a tooth. Monica, Brooke, and Topher's Mom Vicky are lying down on tables next to me. We're all getting facials, but instead of a silent peaceful experience, Brooke has been talking *nonstop* about the wedding and the month long honeymoon that will follow. This wouldn't be so bad, if it wasn't for her attempting to turn everything into a dig against me.

"Topher is so excited to travel," Brooke circles back around to the honeymoon topic. "He didn't have a chance to travel much in the last year, and he told me he missed it so much."

The esthetician smooths another cream over my face with a soft brush. I inhale the soothing scents through my nose and try to calm myself. Brooke is clearly trying to say that Topher didn't travel much in the last year because we were together, and I happen to hate planes. But in reality, he never took a vacation from work. I think that's how our relationship managed to hold on as long as it did. He was working day and night for his dad, so it left little time for us. Even just thinking of Topher and me as an *us* has bile rising in my throat.

"How much longer?" I ask the girl working on me, Molly, in a low voice.

"Thirty more minutes," she answers in a sympathetic tone. You know it's bad when a complete stranger can recognize what's going on.

My sigh is as heavy as Brooke's hints. This is going to be a long morning.

"What about you, Sloane?" Vicky's question catches me off guard. "Have you and Grayson set a date yet?"

Vicky was always nice to me. She's never put me down like Monica and Brooke, but it still makes me nervous to have her asking me questions when I turned down her son not long ago.

"We haven't set an exact date," I answer in a quiet voice. "We'd like to get married in the spring, though."

"Spring weddings are always so beautiful," Vicky replies, making me smile. Maybe we've hit a turning point in the conversation. Surely Brooke can't find anything to say about the season.

"I hope it doesn't rain," Brooke interjects in a tone that implies she hopes just that.

"I think rain is kind of romantic," I reply truthfully.

"I heard it's good luck if it rains on your wedding day," Molly says as she uses a warm towel to wipe away whatever treatment she just put on me. I opted for a hydrating facial, because it seemed the least complicated. Brooke tried to get me to do a chemical peel, but I'm well aware that I wouldn't even be able to go out in the sun after without harming my skin. I think that's exactly why she tried to push it on me.

"Who cares about luck if your whole day is ruined? The wedding is the most important part."

I bite back my retort, deciding to choose my battles wisely. I've dreamt about my wedding plenty, but even if I got married on the courthouse steps in shorts and a t-shirt, it wouldn't matter to me as much as my marriage being full of love. *That's* the most important part.

"Yes, exactly," Monica chimes in. "Those of us who care about the image we put forth into the world understand that big events such as this one are important to look our best for."

I scowl. Maybe the facial will help the wrinkles I'm sure to get from being around these women.

"I suppose I wouldn't care as much if I wasn't a Covington," Brooke muses.

"I'm a Covington and I don't care," I mumble as Molly massages a serum into my skin.

"There's having the last name, and then there's embodying it. Don't you think, Mom?" Brooke asks. I resist the urge to throw one of the dermaplaning scalpels at her head.

"Oh yes, darling. There's a certain way a true Covington carries themselves. They're confident and don't shrink in public." I clench my jaw tight. "They also have impeccable style and are never caught in loungewear outside of the home."

She says *loungewear* like someone else might say *felony*. It's only her intense dramatism that keeps me from feeling too terrible about myself. Even at my most confident, it's hard not to second guess myself around the other Covingtons.

The conversation drifts back to Brooke and Topher's wedding. She goes into detail about how her hair will be done for the big day. I try to tune her out, letting my mind drift to sweeter, brighter things. Memories of Grayson spinning me around in the karaoke bar, the way the morning light hit his face in bed, and the conversation at breakfast come to mind. I find myself smiling even as Brooke throws barbs my way.

I miss him. The thought settles like a stone in my stomach. I shouldn't miss him after being apart for an hour. We're not a real couple. And yet, I find myself eager to see him again. Not because I want to be away from these women–though that's certainly true–but because being around him makes everything better. Makes *me* better. I press a hand to my fluttering stomach. *This is not good.*

CHAPTER TWENTY-FOUR

Sloane Covington

The waves tickle my ankles, making me smile. After a long morning of listening to Brooke and Monica alternate between insulting me and complimenting themselves, it feels good to have a moment alone. As soon as we came down to the beach, I rushed toward the water to let it soothe my worries.

I drink in the salty air and tilt my face up toward the afternoon sun. I'll have to go back up to the group soon for lunch, but for now I'm going to soak in this peaceful moment. The breeze toys with the hem of my swimsuit coverup and swirls through my hair. I watch the water pull back and wiggle my toes in the gritty sand as I wait for it to return.

Warm, strong arms wrap around me from behind. I smile, immediately knowing that it's Grayson. I turn around in his arms. He smiles down at me, his blue eyes bright.

"I'm so glad you're here," I admit to him.

"Was it that bad?" he asks, while tucking my windswept hair behind my ear. I feel the eyes of the others on us, and I'm sure he does too, but when he does things like that I can't help but wonder why.

"I'd have rather been on an airplane," I say and he cringes.

"That's rough. My morning wasn't so bad; I beat everyone at golf. I think Topher wants to run me over with a golf cart."

My smile grows at his words. "I'm sure my dad wasn't happy he lost. I think most people lose on purpose around him."

"They'd have to, because there's no way he's beating anyone with skill." I burst into laughter, my head falling forward on his chest.

"I wish I could have seen his face when you won."

"You should still be able to. He's not dropped his sour look since we left. I think the rest of our afternoon is bound to be at least a little tense." He runs a hand up and down my back. I let my head rest against his chest, using the fact that we're in public as an excuse.

"At least we're together now, though."

"Yes, we're together now." He holds me tighter. "I hate that your family is like this, Rose. I wish I could change it all for you."

My heart squeezes. I've wished and prayed more times than I can count that my family could be different. No man has ever cared enough about me to share my heart's desire, until now.

"It's only this part of my family," I try to reassure him. "My mom and stepdad are wonderful, and my mom's mom, my nana, is sweet. You'd like them. I didn't tell them about us, because I didn't want to lie to my mom or upset her by telling her the truth. Maybe at the end of summer I can introduce you as my friend." The word *friend* tastes bitter in my mouth. But that's what we'll be at the end of all this. Just friends.

"I'd really like that," he says.

I pull back to look up at him. "We should probably go back before they have another thing to berate me about."

He sighs, but nods and slowly steps back. My arms drop from around him, but his hand finds mine right away, soothing my disappointment. We head back up the beach to the tent everyone is lounging under. Grayson's hand in mine boosts me and gives me the strength to face this uncomfortable situation head on. I pull back my shoulders and paste on a smile. I won't let them get to me this time.

"Just admit that you're bored," I say, turning my head to look at Grayson. We're lounging on a pair of beach chairs, reading. We've been reading for an hour now and while I've enjoyed every minute of it, I know Grayson must be itching for adventure.

"I'm not bored, Rose." He sighs. "I'm quite enjoying Simone's book."

"If you were at the beach with your family, you wouldn't be reading."

He gives me an exasperated look. "You are correct. If my brothers were here, we'd probably be playing some sort of sport. But I'm here with you and perfectly content with reading on the beach."

"You don't wish you were doing something else?" I press.

"The only thing I would change is the presence of your family." He winces, glancing over his shoulder at where Brooke, Monica, and Vicky are tanning on chairs nearby. All of the men went up to the tiki bar to drink and watch sports, leaving the women and us here on the beach. Grayson and I dragged our chairs a good distance away, but not so far that they'd notice and comment. After the painfully tense lunch we had, all the way across the beach isn't enough distance for me.

My dad interrogated Grayson about his work, and when he came up short on ways to talk down about it, he turned his attention to me. Grayson stood up for me, but I made sure to keep him from saying too much. I don't want my family's wrath unleashed on him. He's already been through enough.

"That was harsh, I'm sorry," he says and I shrug.

"It's okay, I feel the same way." I tuck my Kindle into my beach bag and sit up fully on the lounge chair. "Let's do something."

His eyebrows raise over his black aviators. "What do you want to do?"

Anything that will make me feel like I'm not holding you back. I bite my lip.

"Why don't we go down to the water? It would be nice to cool off."

"We can do that, but you should know I'm happy here with you." He's only ever been sincere, but it's still hard to trust his words. I don't know how he could be happy with someone like me. He's the kind of man who adds karaoke bars to bucket lists, while I put watching the sunrise.

"I want to go for a swim," I tell him in lieu of a direct response.

"Okay, then let's go swim." He puts his Kindle in the bag next to mine. It shouldn't be romantic to see them together, but it is.

I watch—mesmerized—as he stands up and tugs his shirt over his head. My mouth goes dry. His muscles look as though they were carved out of stone. I forgot how often he was at the gym, but I won't be able to forget now. Not with his hard work on display right before my eyes. How am I supposed to pull off my coverup when he looks like *that*? I've never been terribly insecure about my body, but his perfection has me feeling more shy than usual.

Before he can catch me staring, I stand up and avoid looking at him as I pull the white gauzy dress over my head. I wore one of my favorite swimsuits today. It's dark green, with high waisted bottoms and a halter neck top with scallop trim. I take a deep breath, prepare myself for whatever his reaction might be, and lift my head.

Grayson is on his knees in the sand, bowing down repeatedly. That is not what I expected to see, to say the least.

"What on earth are you doing?" I ask him.

He pauses, arms raised above his head. "The only thing I can before such magnificence: bow down."

"You are ridiculous." I'm torn between melting and dying of laughter at his response. "Get up before people start to stare," I say, unable to keep from giggling.

I look around and see a few people already watching us. I cross the distance between me and Grayson and start to pull up on one of his shoulders.

"People are *watching*," I say and he just grins up at me from his place on his knees.

"Okay, I'll stop." He grabs my hand and starts to toy with my engagement ring. "But at least let me propose to you all over again. The occasion calls for it."

I hit his shoulder, my face feeling hot. "You're being dramatic."

His eyes meet mine, heat flickering within them. "I can assure you I'm not." I'm enthralled, incapable of looking away from him.

"You are without a doubt the most beautiful woman on this beach, Rose."

I take a step back, pulling my hand from his. My heart can't handle the full force of his compliments. After all his kind gestures, I might risk it all and open myself up to heartbreak. *This is just how he is*, I try to tell myself. But when I look into his eyes I can't help but wonder if that's true. Whatever the answer, I'm not equipped to deal with it right now.

"Race you to the water," I blurt out, then take off, kicking up sand as I go.

He catches up to me halfway to the shoreline. I squeal when he lifts me in the air. His arms are warm and strong around my bare waist. He runs into the waves and throws me in. I come up gasping and giggling, my hair floating in the water around me.

"I can't believe you threw me in!" I splash him as he swims closer.

"You're the one who challenged me to a race," he says, unaffected by my splashing. He catches my hands mid-splash and draws me to him. "Carters play to win." His silky voice makes me shiver.

"You could have won without picking me up."

"Not the game I'm playing." His hands lightly hold my waist as the waves buoy us. I'm not tall enough to stand, but since he's holding me I don't have to tread water.

"Well, you seem to have won both games. I suppose that means you get a prize."

"Yeah?" His voice is husky. The look in his eyes almost changes my mind. *Almost*.

"Yeah," I whisper and lean in ever so slightly, before shoving down on his shoulders to push him under the waves. He loses his grip on me, so he doesn't drag me under with him.

He comes up sputtering, while I laugh.

"You're going to pay for that." The playful glint in his eyes has me pushing away from him.

I don't get very far before he catches me and lifts me up to throw me once more. We spend the rest of the afternoon like that, laughing and dunking each other beneath the waves. When we start to get too tired to keep going, we walk back up to our chairs.

Grayson wraps a towel around my shoulders before grabbing one for himself. I snuggle into the sun-warmed fabric and let out a contented sigh. My eyelids are heavy, my sides ache from laughing, and my lips taste of salt. *I wish every day was like this.*

Grayson scrubs a towel against his head to dry his hair. Rivulets of water stream down his abdomen. The sun has kissed his skin, turning it golden in the afternoon light. He drags the towel across his chest next. My eyes lift to his face, catching the boyish grin he throws my way.

"What do you think about getting dinner, then having ice cream and watching the sunset?"

I think you're perfect and if I had more courage, I'd tell you I want this to be real.

"I think that sounds like a great night."

CHAPTER TWENTY-FIVE

Grayson Carter

I've always loved the beach. The briny air, the sound of the crashing waves, the way that everything seems brighter and more alive even on the bleakest of days. But even if I didn't, I'd have to love it after today. Even if I hated sand and the way it comes home with you no matter how diligent you are in brushing it away. Even if seagulls stole my food every time I so much as stepped foot on the shoreline. Even if the sun was always too bright and my skin blistered beneath it. I'd still love it, because of Sloane.

She lifts a spoonful of butter pecan ice cream to her lips and I watch—utterly enchanted by the small movement. Her hair is loose and wild down her back, the salt air making it mimic the ocean waves. She's wearing an oversized white t-shirt that hangs off her sunkissed shoulder. I'd give anything and everything to press a kiss to the exposed skin there. There's a tanline from her swimsuit that I want to map out beneath my fingertips, beneath my lips. She hums after her bite of ice cream and heat pools within me. I wonder if I could elicit the same sound from her.

"This sunset might change my mind about loving sunrises more," she says as she gazes out at the fiery stretch of sky before us. Golden yellow, orange, and burning red strokes paint the horizon. Wisps of cotton candy pink clouds break up the canvas, making for a stunning view. Sloane pulls her phone out of the pocket of her faded denim shorts and snaps a picture.

"Wait," I say as she goes to put her phone away. "Let's take one together."

I set my cup of mint chocolate chip ice cream beside me in the sand, then take her phone from her. After changing it to the front-facing camera, I wrap an arm around her and pull her into my side. She smiles and I do too. I take the picture, then click the photo to see how it turned out. My heart skips in my chest. This is the kind of photo I'd frame and put on my desk. One of my employees would walk in and ask about the picture. I'd smile and tell them of the time I went to Hawaii with my fiancée. They'd nod in a polite way, then move on with their day. Meanwhile I'd be brought back to this beach, taste the ice cream on my lips, see the wind toy with Sloane's hair the way I wish I could.

"Mind if I send this to myself?" I ask her after a moment. She nods her approval and I click the send button. But when I type in the letter *G*, my name doesn't appear. "Do you not have my number saved?" I ask her, my tone incredulous.

She laughs softly, reaching over to delete the *G* and replace it with an *H*. Right below someone named Hannah is a contact that steals my breath from my lungs. *Hubby*. With a ring emoji and a turquoise heart beside it.

"I changed it after the beach today," she says, her voice so low that I barely hear it over the wind and waves.

I press send without a word, then turn to look into her eyes. There's trepidation growing in her hazel irises. The emerald flecks like buds of apprehension springing up from rich brown soil. Words rise to the tip of my tongue, then fall back like the tide. What could I say that would lessen her fear when I don't know why she's afraid?

"Do you want to go put our feet in the water?"

Her lips turn up in a faint smile at my question. "I'd like that."

I like you. I might even be falling in love with you.

We walk to the edge of the sea. The water laps at our ankles, cooler in the evening than it was when we were laughing amongst the waves earlier today. I watch as Sloane tips her spoon upside down; she places it on her tongue and my world flips. I've never felt so utterly desperate and gone for a woman in my life. It makes me feel jittery and off balance. I can't tell if the feeling is good, or if it's my body telling me I'm risking too much. When Sloane glances over and smiles at me, I find that I don't care about the risk. If falling for her is jumping out of a plane, I don't even need a parachute, just let me get a running start.

The next morning I'm no less desperate than the night before. Sloane is wearing a pair of athletic shorts and a black tank top. Her white swimsuit straps are showing, standing out against her tan skin. She smells of coconuts and freshly grated limes. Her scent haunted me all night as she slept on the other side of a mountain of pillows. When I woke up and saw her sleeping in the morning light, I wanted to tear down that pillow boundary and kiss her for hours. But instead, I woke her so we could get ready for a hike with her family.

Her ponytail brushes against my arm as she leans against me. She's gazing longingly out the window of the shuttle we just boarded. There's another couple at the front near the driver, but none of our party is on here, even though we were scheduled to meet here ten minutes ago.

"We'll spend all day on the beach tomorrow," I tell her and she looks up at me with a smile. "The only thing on the itinerary is the rehearsal dinner that night, so we'll have plenty of time. We can hunt down a coconut for you to drink out of too."

Her smile grows. "What about the rest of our bucket list? I know snorkeling is on there. And watching the sun rise." Along with a few other things she doesn't know about, one of which we might be able to do today if my trail research is correct.

"I'm not sure if we'll check everything off, if I'm honest."

"Next time," she says and lays her head on my shoulder. I spot a bird soaring over the shore and feel as though my hope is attached to it.

"Next time," I echo softly.

Sloane's phone lights up in her lap. She unlocks it, then sits up, her eyes wide.

"There's a problem with Brooke's dress," she says as she reads. "Monica and Vicky are consoling her while they try to find a seamstress. They aren't coming, and neither is anyone else."

"It would be wrong to be happy about this," I say and Sloane bites her berry-stained lip.

"Yes, very wrong. She's probably stressed beyond belief."

"At the same time, she's marrying your ex and is kind of..."

"The worst?" Sloane fills in. I nod.

"In that case, I'm so happy I wish I had a bottle of champagne to pop in celebration," I say and Sloane giggles.

"I'd like to toast whoever messed the dress up in the first place."

My eyebrows raise and I grin at her. "Someone is feeling villainous this morning."

"I'm merely the victim rejoicing over the villain's demise."

My smile dims at hearing her call herself a victim. I grab her hand and place a soft kiss on the back of it.

"You're no victim, Rose. You're the heroine who defeats the villain. A warrior princess who stands up for what's right," I say as I recall what I read of Simone's book yesterday. While I started it just to find out what nickname to tease Sloane with, I quickly got sucked in. I see so much of Sloane in the main character—a beautiful princess who fights for her kingdom—that I want to ask Simone if she based it off her friend.

"I don't—" Her words are cut off as the shuttle lurches forward. In the midst of our conversation, I'd forgotten where we were.

"Do you want me to tell the driver to stop?" I ask her.

She hesitates, then answers. "Hiking the island sounds a lot more fun now that we'll be on our own."

I nod in agreement. "I'm glad you think so, because I planned on checking something off our bucket list on this hike."

"I don't suppose the item is to look at a waterfall?"

I chuckle. "No, no it is not. We can add that though, if you'd like."

"I'm not built for all of this adventure." She sighs.

I squeeze her shoulder. "Are you sure about that? You've had your fair share of wild moments over the course of our time together."

"Those were anomalies. I was made for snuggling up under blankets and browsing libraries. There's not an adventurous bone in my body."

"Really?" I question as I slide my hand down her back and over to her waist. "Not even right here?" I tickle around her ribs and she gasps, pushing against me while laughing.

"Stop!" she says through giggles. I reach my other hand over to tickle her other side.

"What about right here? I think there has to be at least a little adventure in here." She pushes at my hands, her eyes squeezed shut as she laughs and gasps for breath.

"Mercy," she begs. I laugh and slow my movements to a stop. Then I pull her back against my side and squeeze her. She catches her breath while laying her head against my chest.

"I think you'll see you're more adventurous than you believe." I rub circles on her bare shoulder.

"I don't know how you could think that."

"Just trust me."

"I'll try," she whispers, and it feels like she's talking about more than a bucket list.

CHAPTER TWENTY-SIX

Sloane Covington

"How did you propose?" Stephanie–one half of the couple we're hiking with–asks Grayson.

When we stepped off the bus, Grayson introduced himself to Stephanie and her husband Mark. I would have never introduced us, instead opting to walk at an awkward pace so that I didn't run into them or anyone else. Thanks to Grayson's extroverted nature, we're saved from that. After his greeting, Stephanie suggested we walk together, so now we get to chat with a sweet couple while we hike through gorgeous scenery.

The air is humid, but not too hot since we're under the cover of trees. All of the foliage is bright, in varying shades of green with pops of color from different flowers. The trail has been fairly easy, a winding dirt path with the occasional rock to scale. All of the exertion is worth it though, with how beautiful it is out here.

"I set up a picnic in my backyard," Grayson replies, not at all doing justice to how beautiful and sweet that moment was. Even if it was a fake proposal.

"He set up twinkle lights too," I add. Grayson places his hand on the small of my back as we walk up a particularly precarious part of the trail. "It was the most romantic thing anyone has ever done for me."

I glance over at Grayson to find him wearing a bright smile. My stomach must be training to be a gymnast because it won't stop flipping. Every little touch, every smile, every word from Grayson makes me feel all fluttery inside.

"That's so sweet," Stephanie gushes. "Mark proposed at my favorite restaurant. It's a pizza place and they spelled the question out in pepperoni." She laughs.

Mark wraps an arm around her as they walk ahead of us on the trail. Stephanie told us earlier that this was their third anniversary, and their fourth time coming to Hawaii, the first being for their honeymoon. They want to come back every year, even when they have kids. Which will be soon, considering the adorable baby bump Stephanie is sporting.

"That's really cute," I tell her. She shoots me a smile over her shoulder. "What was your wedding like?"

"We got married in a pasture near my parents' house. It was all very casual, which we loved. The pizza place catered our dinner and I wore sneakers under my wedding dress," Stephanie answers.

"You can't beat pizza and beer at your wedding reception," Mark adds with a chuckle. "What about you two? Have you started planning yet?"

"Not yet," Grayson replies for us. "We're taking things slow."

We pause to take in a small but beautiful waterfall. The lush green trees combined with the rushing water make for an idyllic resting spot. Grayson hands me a water bottle and I give him a grateful smile before tipping it back. Over the course of our hike so far, we've taken to stopping at little spots like these. The first time we stopped, Mark gave us a grateful look. I think he's not so sure about Stephanie hiking all this way while six months pregnant.

"I'm sure you've dreamed about your big day though," Stephanie says before taking a sip of her own water.

I nod. "I think I'd like something simple, but elegant. An intimate ceremony with lots of flowers."

"Nothing to do with books?" Grayson asks. If Stephanie thinks it's odd that he doesn't already know, she doesn't say so.

"Myla and Simone said they'd make sure my bridal shower was very bookish." I smile, even as a pang of homesickness shoots through me. I've texted them, but it's not the same as spending every day together. "And I think it would be fun for our invitations to look like little books. If that's even possible."

Grayson gives me a look I don't understand at first. It's affectionate, but surprised. I comb back over my words, then realize I said *our* invitations. As if this were real. But it was just because we're in front of Stephanie and Mark. I wouldn't have said it if we were alone. I think.

"I think Juliette could work her design magic on that," Grayson says. I forgot that Juliette designed invitations and stationery. "I'll make sure all your dreams come true, Rose."

The way he speaks sounds like he's serious. Like we're not just playing pretend in front of these two strangers.

"You two are the cutest!" Stephanie says before clapping her hands together. "Now is everyone ready to keep going? I'm dying to get to my favorite waterfall. It's *stunning*."

"I'm ready." Grayson puts our water bottles back in his backpack, then reaches his hand out.

"Me too." I take his hand and we head further down the trail.

More small talk peppers our trek, and with Grayson by my side I don't feel awkward. His presence calms me and keeps me from stumbling over my words too much.

"It's just up ahead!" Stephanie calls over her shoulder as she picks up speed. A harried Mark follows her, hands out around her like she might tip over at any second.

Stephanie's excitement is infectious, and I find myself tugging Grayson to keep up with her. He chuckles but follows along happily. When we reach Stephanie, I gasp. Before us is a roaring waterfall surrounded by large rocks and vibrant greenery. I look down over the edge to find a pool of water cradled between the rocks. It's cooler by the water, and a welcome relief after our humid hike.

"This place is popular for cliff jumping," Mark tells us. My heart drops to my stomach.

I turn to Grayson and when I see the mischief glinting in his eyes I speak. "No."

"Come on, wifey, hear me out."

"Hear you out? No way! Do you know how far down that is?"

"It's a thirty foot drop," Mark supplies. Grayson's smile tightens. I'd laugh if I wasn't terrified out of my mind.

"It's so fun though," Stephanie chimes in. "If I wasn't pregnant, I would have jumped the second I got up here."

"She's an adrenaline junkie." Mark laughs. "Do you want us to carry your stuff while you jump? The trail makes its way down to the water, so we can meet you there."

"That would be great," Grayson replies, handing him the backpack with our cellphones, water, and a few snacks. I gape at him.

"I'm not jumping, Gray."

Stephanie and Mark exchange a look, then start down the trail, murmuring a *see you at the bottom*. They likely think we're going to fight, but we're not. We'll simply be walking with them after our *conversation*.

"Rose, listen to me." Grayson places his hands on my shoulders. "You don't have to do this."

"Of course I don't."

He shakes his head, a smile on his lips. "I just mean that this is your choice. You shouldn't make it because of me, or our bucket list. But you also shouldn't decide based on fear."

"There is such a thing as healthy fear."

"There is, but I promise this is safe. I did a lot of research, and you heard Stephanie, she's done it before."

I look over the edge. Swallow. Look back at Grayson. He softly rubs my shoulders.

"If you don't want to, we can catch up with Stephanie and Mark and go swimming once we reach the bottom. I won't think any less of you, and we'll still have fun." He looks into my eyes. "But if there's a small part of you that wants to do this, I think you should."

I take a deep breath in, then let it out. My heart is beating wildly in my chest. But I'd be lying to myself if I denied wanting to jump. Even though my body is screaming at me to walk down the trail, there's a tiny voice that wants to know what would happen if I just *took a chance*.

"It's my choice?"

"Your choice. You're the author of your story." His mouth quirks up at the corner from his cheesy line. "What happens next?"

I'm the author. For once in my life I'm going to make a decision based on what *I* want. I close my eyes. After another steadying breath, I've confirmed my choice.

"We jump."

"That's my girl." He grins down at me, then takes a step toward the cliffside. He holds his hand out, palm up, like so many times before. I slide my hand into his and join him.

"Can you count down?" I ask, already second guessing myself.

"Three..."

Every muscle in my body is taut. *How do people do this all the time?*

"Two..."

Anxiety twists me into knots. *What was I thinking?*

"One!"

Grayson pulls me forward. I let out a scream as we jump. Warm air and the cool spray of water whips around me. I suck in a breath as my feet hit the water and plunge into the cold depths. My hand gets ripped away from Grayson on impact. The roar of the waterfall is muffled beneath the surface. My body is buzzing with adrenaline as I swim upward. I gasp for air when my head pokes out of the water.

Grayson's head pops up a few feet away from me. He whips around, relief coloring his features when he sees me, soon replaced by pure elation.

"You did it!" He cheers and crosses the water to me, wrapping me in a hug. We both have to tread to keep afloat though, so our hug doesn't last long.

"That was amazing," I yell over the sound of the falls. His boyish grin makes my heart skip. I'm going to need a defibrillator if he keeps making me feel this way. He grabs my hand and swims us over to a place where he can stand but I can't, before drawing me into his arms again.

"Are you happy you did it?"

"I am," I admit. "But that doesn't mean I'll want to do everything else on our list." He laughs.

"We'll only do what you want to, I promise." I believe him. I think that's what made me jump. He's never pressured me, just nudged me gently out of my comfort zone. I feel like I'm the one in control for once, and the notion is addictive and energizing.

I study Grayson's face, wanting to commit this moment to memory. We're shadowed by the rocks and foliage surrounding us. The water is chilly, but his arms are warm around me. Pitch black strands of hair hang in front of his tropical blue eyes. I reach up and brush the pieces back softly. Grayson's grip tightens around my waist.

"*Rose.*" The name falls from his lips like a plea for mercy.

I meet his eyes once more, watching as water droplets fall from dark lashes. They trace a path down his cheek to full lips. Lips that are parted in anticipation. Desire curls around me like a silk ribbon. The same voice that told me *jump* is now saying *kiss him*. I look into Grayson's eyes again and feel his gaze whisper, *You're the author, what happens next?*

I lean in, hovering like a pen over a blank page. Grayson doesn't move, doesn't say a word. Warm air bathes my skin as he shudders a breath. The first brush of my lips is dipped in the ink of uncertainty. *Is this okay?* my kiss asks. *Do you want me?* Grayson's hand slides up to cradle my head. His mouth slants against mine, answering *yes* with a surety that turns me molten.

Our kiss is gentle at first. Languid and soft like a spring breeze. But with each caress of his lips I find myself wanting more. I fist his damp shirt in my hands. He responds in kind, his grip tightening around my waist like he's afraid I might drift away. I hook a leg around his waist and a low sound of appreciation escapes him. The sound makes desire pool deep within me like warm honey. He grabs my other leg and lifts it so I'm wrapped around him.

I rake my hands through his silky hair. His fingertips press into the back of my thighs beneath the water. The searing touch chases away the cold. He deepens the kiss and at the first taste of him all my thoughts dissolve like paper in water. All that I can comprehend is him. His touch. His lips. His tongue.

He pulls back and I can't help the sound of protest that escapes me. His smirk is a flash of light in the shadows before he's kissing up my jaw.

"*Gray,*" I whisper, entirely undone. My head falls back, giving him further access to my neck. He takes my invitation, tracing a line with his lips from below my ear all the way down to where my neck meets my shoulder. His teeth graze the sensitive spot and I gasp.

"You're beautiful," he murmurs against my skin. "So, so beautiful, Rose."

He draws my mouth back to his for another decadent kiss. I'm about to go on my own exploration to satisfy my desire to know what the light stubble along his jaw would feel like beneath my lips, when a voice intrudes on our shared bliss.

"How's the water?" Stephanie yells. I pull back from Grayson in a flash of movement, letting my legs drop from around his waist. He doesn't let me go though, just settles his hands above my hips and squeezes.

"Perfect," Grayson shouts back, then lowers his voice. "*Perfect*," he whispers to me.

Chapter Twenty-Seven

Grayson Carter

I watch Sloane bask in the dappled sunlight. Her eyes are closed and there's a faint smile on her lips. Waves of brown hair fan out around her, standing out against the pale blue towel we laid on the ground. After our kiss, we didn't stay in the water long. It was quite cold, and neither of us wanted to be around company. Stephanie and Mark are still in the water, their laughter echoing over to where we've camped out in a patch of sun.

We haven't spoken much at all. While at first I assumed it was because Sloane was in the same blissful state as me, now I'm worried she's pulling back. Her smile gives me hope that I'm wrong.

"What are you thinking about?" I finally ask the question that's been on the tip of my tongue.

She blinks her eyes open, turning her head to look at me. The unguarded affection in her gaze surprises me in the best way. The desire to kiss her again overwhelms me, but I hold back in order to hear the answer to my question.

"I'm thinking of how I could fall asleep right here amongst the greenery," she says and I smile at her. "And of how beautiful it is here. I wish we weren't leaving soon." She pauses. A pretty blush blooms on her cheekbones. "But mostly I'm thinking of how even though I've read hundreds of kiss scenes, and even written my own ... the kiss we shared beats them all."

Words fail me. Nothing seems acceptable to say in response to what she just shared. I push up off my towel and move so I'm hovering over her. One of her hands reaches up. She brushes my jawline with her fingertips, sending tingles cascading down my spine. I hold myself up with one hand and take hers with the other, pressing a soft kiss to the center of her palm, then place her hand against my chest. *It's yours*, I think as I stare into her honeyed hazel eyes. *My heart is yours, if you want it.*

Her fingers clench the still-damp fabric of my t-shirt. She tugs me toward her and I don't waste any time fulfilling the desire written all over her face. We kiss and she tastes like fresh spring water. Her hands slide up my chest to the back of my neck, toying with the hair at my nape. My arms almost buckle when she hums into the kiss.

Needing to have her closer, I roll onto my back and pull her with me. She gasps, but then immediately kisses me again. Our bodies press together, the cool dampness of our clothes burned away by the scorching passion within each touch. I tangle a hand into her hair and wrap my other arm around her waist. Every soft curve of hers fits perfectly against me.

Emotion burns within me as I realize just how perfect she is. She's the sun-warmed towel waiting for you when you get out of the water. A chocolate chip cookie right out of the oven. The kind of book you read over and over again because it never gets old. She's comfort and adventure intertwined in the most achingly beautiful package.

She pulls back, her eyes wide and dazed in a way that sends fire through my veins. Her lips turn up in a secret smile as she brushes my hair back.

"What?" I rasp out.

"You flirt and tease and are someone to everyone." I wince at her words. "But this you," she whispers, running her fingernails over my scalp. My eyes close in pleasure. "This you is all mine." I hear the hesitation in her voice. She wants to believe what she's saying, but she's not quite there yet.

I open my eyes to look into hers. "Yes, Rose. Yours and yours alone."

A smile melts over her. I reach up and brush her bottom lip with my thumb.

"What about this smile?" I ask her. "Can it be mine?"

She kisses the pad of my thumb, then nods. I slide my hand under her jaw, about to pull her lips to mine again, when I hear the voices of our hiking companions.

"I think they're over here. Do you think something terrible happened? We yelled for them a few times." Stephanie's voice rings out.

"No, I think they're probably just having some alone time, Steph," Mark answers.

"Oh, *alone time*."

Sloane giggles as she rolls off of me, back onto her towel. We both sit up right as Mark and Stephanie come into view. They're both drenched, with towels wrapped around their shoulders.

"Are you two ready to head back?" Stephanie asks.

"I think so," I answer, but look to Sloane. She nods, still wearing a smile. My smile.

"Do you want to wait for your clothes to dry off some? We don't mind waiting, or we can split up from here," Sloane says as she pushes up to her feet. I follow suit, grabbing my towel and shaking the dirt out.

"No, we're okay. It's not much longer to the shuttle pick up spot at the end of this trail," Stephanie says.

"Alright, then let's head out," I say as I shake Sloane's towel out for her. Both of them go in the backpack. "Do you want any water or a granola bar before I close this up?" I ask Sloane.

"No, I'm good. But I will want some food when we get back." She looks down at her damp clothes. "After a shower and a new outfit, that is."

"Sounds like a plan." I sling the pack over my shoulder then hold out my hand. She takes it, immediately intertwining our fingers like we've done this for years. Maybe one day we'll be able to say we have.

"Are you sure there's nothing but fruit in that drink, Bubbles?" I ask with a raised brow.

After a quick shower and outfit change, we grabbed lunch at the resort's restaurant. Now, we're sitting at a table by the pool, drinking fresh fruit smoothies from the tiki bar. I'm not sure if I'll ever stop smiling, and it seems Sloane feels the same with how much she's giggling. All I want to do is hear her laugh like this for the rest of my life. I'd give up everything. My house in the suburbs, my half of the company, my car. Drain my bank account, as long as I get to see her eyes light up across from me from now til the day I die.

"It's just a *smoothie*, Gray." She attempts to take another sip, but she's giggling so much that she misses the straw. I give her a look.

"I know I'm ridiculously funny, but even so..." I trail off. She rolls her eyes, still wearing a smile.

"There's not a drop of alcohol in this. I don't want to be *Bubbles* ever again. She made bad choices."

I recall that moment under the sprinklers and stars. Sloane looking up at me through damp lashes. Her whispered confession of wanting to be kissed in the rain.

"I disagree," I say, holding her gaze. "I quite liked her decisions."

She blushes and looks down while stirring her strawberry banana smoothie. I take a sip of my own mango smoothie, the one she scrunched her nose at when I ordered because hers is *clearly the superior choice*.

"Did you want to kiss me that night on the golf course?" she asks, still looking down.

"I've wanted to kiss you since the first time I saw you."

Her head pops up, surprise sparkling in her hazel eyes.

"Don't look so shocked, Rose. I've been flirting with you from the beginning."

She bites her lip. "There's a difference between harmless flirting and..."

"True desire?" I fill in. She ducks her head, blushing. "You're right. But since the moment we spoke I've known this was different. It *killed* me when you said you had a boyfriend. I had to hold myself back every time I saw you in the gym. All I wanted to do was ask you if you had broken up with him yet."

"So when I pulled you into my scheme and made you my fake fiancé..."

I grin. "Second best day of my life, next to today."

Her look is admonishing at first, but it quickly softens into something sweeter.

"It's been real for you this whole time?" she asks, vulnerability peeking through her tone.

"Yes," I answer without hesitation. She silently twists her engagement ring. "I don't expect us to stay engaged, but I would like the chance to date you. To spoil you and cherish you until you're ready for that step."

She slowly lifts her gaze. "I'd really like that. I have to confess I'm not used to this, to the way you are with me. Topher was ..." She swallows, then changes direction. "I was so foolish for staying with him as long as I did. We saw each other so little that our relationship was less real than the fake one I had with you." She lets out a bitter laugh, shaking her head. "I avoided him, and I know he did the same to me. We both just wanted to please our parents. Which I've recently realized is a hopeless endeavor. I'll never be good enough for my dad and Monica."

I reach across the table and take her hand in mine. "You can't be good enough for them, because what they want isn't *good*, Rose. Don't hurt yourself bending over backwards for people who are going to be unhappy no matter what you do."

The smile she gives me is weary, but sincere. She squeezes my hand tight.

"Thank you, Gray." She takes a deep breath. Her eyes are glassy and anger burns through me toward the ones who've caused her pain. "I've been trying to stand up for myself for years. I was on the verge of giving up when I met you. Now I've flown in an airplane, sang on stage, and jumped off a cliff." She laughs like she can't believe it. "I don't know if I've ever believed in myself enough to be able to stand my ground in front of my family. But now I do, because of you."

"You did all of those things on your own, Rose. The only thing I'll take credit for is holding your hand through them."

"When you're not being incorrigibly cocky, you're actually quite humble."

I laugh, the weight of the moment lifting off of us. "It's a hard balance to strike. How could I not be at least a *little* vain with a face like this?"

She presses her lips together to hide a smile. "I was complimenting you, but then you had to go and ruin it by *talking*."

"I'm sorry," I say as I lift her hand to my lips and press a soft kiss to her knuckles. "Would you prefer if I communicated in other ways?"

Her eyes burn through me like a shot of whiskey. I want to get drunk on the desire within them.

She leans in, then whispers, "I've always thought talking was overrated."

This woman is going to be the death of me, but at least I'll die happy.

CHAPTER TWENTY-EIGHT

Sloane Covington

There was a breach of the pillow boundary last night. Someone–*me*–moved a few pillows out of the way to be able to cuddle.
Grayson immediately pulled me to him without a word, but his
merciful silence has run out now that he's awake.

"It's rather interesting how the pillow wall has worked the past
few nights, but not last night. Do you know why that might be?"

I hide my face in his chest, refusing to look at the smirk I know
he's wearing.

"The pillows must have gotten kicked off the bed," I say in my
most convincing voice.

"That would be a valid theory, if the pillows by our feet weren't
still on the bed."

"You moved them?" I try.

"You're cute even when you're lying," he says and I smile. "Since I was about ten seconds away from moving the pillows myself, I suppose I'll stop teasing you."

"Until you find something else to torture me about."

"Exactly." I laugh against his chest. He starts to run his fingers through my hair, making me hum. "What do you want to do today, beautiful?"

"Look for houses in Hawaii?" I murmur into his t-shirt.

He chuckles. "What about something more realistic?"

"I don't want to leave." I sigh. "Tonight is the rehearsal dinner, and tomorrow is the wedding. Both of those things are giant storm clouds hanging over us. And then we have to go home, back to the real world. I just want to stay in our happy tropical bubble."

"Me too, Rose," Grayson says, kissing the crown of my head. "But we can bring our bubble with us." His voice sounds a little off, but I chalk it up to him just waking up.

"I guess you're right." Insecurity flares in my chest. "Yesterday was so perfect without having to see my family. I just don't want them to ruin anything. All of this is so new, it feels like we're swimming with sharks the day after we got our diver's certification."

"We'll be okay." He doesn't sound as sure as usual, but then his voice brightens. "Let's not spoil what we have right now with thoughts of what's to come. Why don't you go get ready for the day and I'll look up where we can find fresh coconuts?"

"Sounds perfect." I grin then press a chaste kiss to his lips. It takes far too much willpower to leave his arms and gather up my stuff to get ready, but I know we have plenty of time together. I smile at myself in the bathroom mirror. I shouldn't worry about us. We'll be okay, just like Grayson said.

I took a little longer to get ready than I normally would for what will probably be just a day spent at the beach. But I wanted to feel extra beautiful, so I applied some light makeup and put oil in my hair to tame the frizz. I'll probably have to do everything all over again before the rehearsal dinner tonight, but that's okay. It'll be worth it when I hear whatever outrageously flirty line Grayson has for me.

After spritzing on my favorite summer perfume, I walk out into the suite with a smile. My smile immediately falls though when I see Grayson curled up on the bed, shaking. I rush over to him and sit down on the edge of the bed.

"Gray, what's wrong? Are you in pain?" The only response I receive is a shake of his head. Panic shoots through me like a geyser. His eyes are squeezed shut and his chest is heaving.

I'm almost paralyzed by fear of what could be happening when the thought hits me. *He's having a panic attack.* Simone told me once about how she used to get them, what she went through, but I don't remember how she coped.

I grab Grayson's hand. His grip instantly becomes akin to a vise. Our joined hands remind me of our flight together where he helped me through my own anxiety.

"Gray." I keep my voice low, brushing his hair out of his face. "I need you to breathe with me. Let's do the four counts thing, okay?"

I continue brushing my fingers through his hair, hoping that I'm soothing him and not making anything worse. Tears spring to my eyes and I blink them away. I need to stay calm.

"Breathe in," I murmur, then whisper the counts to him. "Hold." Four more counts. "Out," I say as I start to run my thumb over the back of his hand.

I coach him through the pattern until his breathing has evened out. My tears begin to fall freely now, and I have to swipe one off his forehead when it falls.

"I'm sorry," he rasps. I shake my head even though he can't see me.

"Don't be sorry, there's nothing to be sorry about." My hand shakes as it sifts through his hair, but I don't stop.

"It hasn't happened in a long time," he says, but I shush him in a gentle tone.

"You don't have to tell me right now, it's okay."

I close my eyes and focus on the sound of his breathing. The fear of him being hurt slowly dissipates, fading from a sharp pang to a dull ache. I would have never thought someone like Grayson would struggle with anxiety. He seems so happy and free. I have to bite the inside of my cheek to keep from crying more. He's the one hurting, not me. And yet my heart breaks for him. It was awful seeing him like that. Knowing that it's happened more than once is almost too much for me to bear. I want to make everything better, to ensure he never feels this way again.

"Rose, I want to talk to you about this." His voice sounds a little more even, but I'm still worried.

"We can wait if you need more time," I respond in a soft voice.

"It's okay, I need to get this off my chest." He takes a deep breath. "After my mom died when I was twenty, I started to struggle with anxiety, but it was manageable. I distracted myself as much as I could. It worked for a while. But a few years back it got really bad.

I-I had an attack in front of Adrian." His voice cracks. "He made me get help. I thought it was under control, but lately when I start to think about the future, if I don't catch myself I end up spiraling."

"Oh, Gray, I'm so sorry. I brought up the future. This is my fault."

"No, no don't put this on yourself." He sits up, wiping his face on the sleeve of his shirt. "You couldn't have known. Adrian is the only one who knows everything, and even he doesn't know that it's been rough lately."

"Is there a reason you haven't told anyone?" I ask, as carefully as possible. I don't want to press him, but I also don't want him to be struggling and need someone.

He sighs. "I haven't wanted to tell my family because a lot of my anxiety is tied up in all of us growing up and them starting their own families. I didn't want them to take on any guilt and give me special treatment when this is just a part of life."

"If I'm overstepping, please tell me, but I think you should talk to your family. Dahlia mentioned being worried about you when we were at MJ's. Maybe they know more than you think and would feel better knowing everything."

He scrubs his face with his hands, letting out a little laugh.

"I guess I shouldn't be surprised people are noticing. Secrets don't stay hidden for long in the Carter family. You're right, I'll talk to them once we're back home."

I take his hand once more and give him an encouraging smile. "If you need moral support, I can be there when you tell them. If you want."

"You'd do that for me?" His eyes shine with raw gratitude.

"Of course I would. How many times have you stood with me when I've walked through anxiety? And even if you hadn't, I care about you, Gray. I want you to be happy and healthy."

He pulls me into his arms, leaning back against the headboard. His lips press against the crown of my head.

"I don't know what I would have done without you helping me."

"You don't have to know because I'm here, and I'm not going anywhere." I press closer to him.

"Thank you," he whispers.

I don't say a word, just close my eyes and focus on his heartbeat. We sit there together in the quiet for some time, adjusting to our new layer of shared vulnerability.

It occurs to me how much I didn't know about Grayson when we first met. I thought I knew him. A heartbreaker with a silver tongue. As cheesy as it is, I judged the book by the cover. And while I am a sucker for a pretty cover, I know it's the content that matters most. A cover can't change you, can't reveal something new to you about life and the world we live in. Only reading the full story can.

This moment was another chapter in Grayson's story. A new revelation of who he is that isn't perfect. It's messy and raw, but it's *real*. And I'd rather have this than the shiny facade any day of the week.

CHAPTER TWENTY-NINE

Grayson Carter

I'm in love with Sloane. From the moment I opened that first book of hers, I've been falling. There was something about the way her words came alive. How she took ink and paper and made a world that drew me in and made me forget my surroundings. Getting to know her in person has felt like perpetual déjà vu. Her mannerisms, her vocabulary, even the cadence of her voice calls back to each of her books in some way. It makes me want to go back and reread everything she's ever written just to see what connections I can make.

But while reading her writing was the first step on the path to loving her, this morning made me sprint for the finish line. All my life, I've hidden away the darkest parts of me so that no one else would have to deal with them. People don't want the outgoing, funny guy to be sad in front of them. It's like they don't understand I'm more than that initial first impression. It makes for an uncomfortable interaction and stilted relationship. I've learned over the years that it's easier to deal with my problems on my own in order to avoid that awkwardness. Having a panic attack in front of Sloane was one of my greatest fears come to fruition, which likely only exacerbated the attack itself. But she didn't pull back when it got dark. No, she walked in with a flashlight and kept me company until morning. That was when I knew I loved her.

"I got it!" Sloane walks toward me, holding a green coconut with a straw sticking out of it above her head like it's Simba from *The Lion King*. "Another bucket list item complete." She grins and takes a sip. Then scrunches her nose up.

I chuckle at her reaction. "You don't like it, do you?"

She morphs her disgusted expression into a smile. "I love it!"

"Rose." I give her a look that says *really?*

"Gray." She smiles, the picture of innocence.

"It's okay if you don't like it. You don't have to pretend."

Her smile falls. "We went out of our way to get one *and* you paid for it."

"So?" I shrug. "It was for the bucket list. We checked it off, which was worth the money and time."

"Do you want some? Maybe you'll like it and then I won't feel as bad."

She hands it to me and I take a sip. Then I dig deep and use all of the training I've had over the years about schooling my facial expression and body language in order to not let my face betray how terrible this is. My sister MJ drinks coconut water daily. She has a whole mini fridge of just those in her house, and Sebastian is even sponsored by it now because he once carried a bottle to the podium during a press conference. This can't be what hers tastes like, because this is *atrocious*.

"I like it," I say with a smile.

"You're lying," she accuses me with a point of her finger. "We've spent too much time together now, *hubby*. I can tell when you're lying."

"How could you tell? I thought I did a pretty good job hiding it."

A grin overtakes her face. "I had no idea. But I figured you'd tell me if I accused you."

"Just for that, I shouldn't take you to our next bucket list stop."

"Fine by me. All of the ones you added terrify me." She laughs.

"It would be pretty strange if an author had a phobia of bookstores."

Her eyes widen. She throws her arms around me, almost making me drop the coconut drink–wouldn't be much of a loss if I did. "You are the best real-boyfriend-fake-fiancé ever!"

I laugh and wrap an arm around her waist. Her head tilts back and her hazel eyes meet mine. The tender affection found in them steals my breath. I dip my head and press my lips to hers. It feels as though every cell, every atom within me is rising up to greet her. When she hums into the kiss I feel it in my very marrow that this is where I belong.

She pulls back, looking as dazed as I feel. I consider confessing my love right here and now, but I want the moment to be perfect. I'm usually all for spontaneity, but not when it comes to something like this.

"Come on," I say with a soft smile. "If we don't get to the bookstore soon, I'm liable to delete it off the list and replace it with kissing you from now until the rehearsal dinner tonight."

Her expression turns playful. "Are you sure the list just says *go to a bookstore?* Because I think it says *make out in one.*"

Heat pools in my abdomen. I steal another kiss from her, then murmur against her lips, "I like the way you think, future Mrs. Carter." Her blush when I pull away makes it feel like the sun is shining right on my soul. I know she said our engagement is still fake, but a part of me hopes that maybe she'll change her mind sooner rather than later...

I roll up the cuffs of my white dress shirt, listening to Sloane hum along to a Taylor Swift song as she gets dressed in the bathroom. After spending a few hours in the bookstore *browsing*, we stumbled out into the daylight with mussed hair and swollen lips. The mere sight of Sloane looking so undone almost made me drop to my knees and propose again. I have an inkling that's going to be a recurring theme in our relationship.

She's *too* gorgeous. We picked up some sandwiches and went down to the beach after our time at the bookstore, and every time I looked at her I thought I'd wandered into the desert and she was a mirage. I've never been the writing type, but a man could wax poetic about Sloane's beauty. If Shakespeare stumbled across her in his time, he would have written a thousand plays with her likeness as his sole muse.

When you combine her looks with her kindness and wit, it's easy to see why I'm hopelessly in love with her. It took every ounce of restraint in my body to keep from just blurting it out. Especially during the handful of times she looked at me in a way that made me wonder if she was feeling the same. I can only hope by the time I'm ready to confess, that she either shares my sentiment or at least isn't scared off by it.

"Gray, which shoes do you think go best with my dress?" Sloane's voice comes from behind me. I finish rolling both my sleeves then turn around.

All coherent thought tumbles out of my head at the sight of her. She's holding up two different shoes, but I can't even give her an opinion on them because...

"Your dress," I rasp out. "It has sunflowers on it." My eyes rove over her, taking in every single flower dotting the fabric. She's wearing a sage green wrap dress, with clusters of sunflowers and daisies scattered over it. Tears burn my eyes for the second time today, but I don't bother holding them back.

"Oh, yeah, aren't they pretty?" She twirls, the skirt of her dress flaring out around her. "I saw it in the store and knew I had to have it. I almost don't want to wear it tonight since it's for Brooke–" She cuts herself off. "Are you okay?"

The shoes drop out of her hands and she crosses the room to me. Her palms press against my now-damp cheeks. Worry furrows her brows.

"I'm fine," I say with a laugh. "Only a little concerned you'll get tired of the waterworks."

She rolls her eyes and begins wiping away my tears with her thumbs. I place my hands on her waist.

"If you're okay, then why are you crying?"

"Sunflowers were my mom's favorite." She stills, her eyes meeting mine. "After she died, my siblings and I all hung on to that detail to honor and remember her."

"The sunflower paintings in your house." Realization lights in her eyes. "Those are for her."

I nod. "MJ paints and draws them often. Since she doesn't sell any of her art, I took a few off her hands when I bought my house so I could have a piece of my mom with me."

She looks down at her dress, then back up at me. "I can wear something different, if it's too much for you."

"No, no." I pull her against my chest. "I love that you chose the dress without knowing. And while sometimes seeing the flowers makes me emotional, it's in a good way. She would have loved this dress." I press a kiss to the top of her head. "She would have loved *you*."

Sloane's grip tightens around me. "Do you really think so?" Her voice is barely above a whisper.

"I know so. I wish you could have met her."

My throat starts to feel thick with emotion. There's not a day that goes by that I don't miss her. It's been over a decade and I still find myself wishing I could just pick up the phone and call her. I know all my siblings, and my dad, feel the same. And even though it's been a long time since she's passed, I know without a doubt she would have approved of Sloane. She probably would have laughed at the story of our fake engagement while simultaneously meddling to make our relationship real.

"Me too." Sloane's soft words give me the urge yet again to confess my feelings. But we have to leave for the rehearsal dinner soon, and

I don't want our special moment to be followed up by seeing her ex and her terrible family.

"All right," I say as I pull back. "Enough tears for tonight. We have to prepare for battle."

She laughs. "Battle?"

I nod, putting on a somber expression. "We're walking into a war zone, but I think if we stick together we'll make it out."

"You went from telling me you could make any event fun to comparing tonight to war. My confidence is waning," she jokes, but I see the fear creeping into her eyes.

"The battle will be won by us having the time of our lives and rubbing it in their miserable faces."

"I don't know if tonight could even come close to yesterday at the waterfall. *That* was the time of my life."

My blood heats as I recall the kisses we shared. Her body pressed to mine, my fingertips tangled in her damp waves.

"You're right," I reply in a low voice. "Nothing can beat yesterday." I tip her chin up and press a lingering kiss to her soft lips. "But I think we can manage to have a good time."

"Mmm or we could skip tonight altogether." She brushes her lips against mine.

"Don't tempt me, Rose."

She sighs against my mouth, giving me one last kiss before stepping back. "If my dad wouldn't have paid for this whole trip, I really wouldn't go."

"I know, but it's okay. All we have to do is get through tonight, then the wedding tomorrow afternoon, and you won't have to see them again for a long, long time."

"The longer the better," she says, making me chuckle. "Now, what's your opinion on the shoes?"

She picks them up again. The question is so *domestic*. It warms my chest to think that one day in the future–maybe in my little house in the suburbs–she'll be posing this same question before date night. I smile bigger than a man making a decision about shoes should.

"The one on the right," I answer, then go grab my own shoes out of my suitcase.

As I lace up my brown oxfords, I try to come up with a list of ways that I can make tonight more bearable for Sloane. While I know one dinner won't ruin the past two days, it would taint the memory of this trip. The last thing I want is for Sloane to look back on our first kiss and be reminded of Topher and Brooke.

"Ready to go?" I ask when Sloane finishes putting in her earrings.

She takes in a deep breath, then lets it out. "As ready as I'll ever be."

CHAPTER THIRTY

Sloane Covington

Grayson wasn't wrong about tonight being a battle. From the moment we stepped onto the beach, we've been under attack. Monica admonished us for being late–we weren't–and Brooke said my dress had too much white in it so I must be trying to upstage her. My dress is *green*. There are a few white daisies on it, but nothing that would take away from the blinding snow white gown she's wearing.

Thankfully they didn't talk to us for long before they moved on to the other guests they flew out for today's and tomorrow's festivities. Grayson holds my hand as Topher and Brooke go through the motions of their wedding ceremony. Multiple photographers are taking photos and if this were a rehearsal for people I liked, it would be a beautiful moment. The sun is beginning to set in the distance, turning everything a hazy pink color.

Topher and Brooke share a stiff kiss. It could be my eyes playing tricks on me, but I swear Brooke wipes her mouth on the back of her hand right after.

"I'm not so sure these two are end game," Grayson whispers next to me.

"If they are, they'll make it there by sheer spite."

He laughs. Monica's head whips around from the front row to glare at us. I purposefully don't meet her eyes, instead watching Brooke and Topher walk down the aisle toward the tent set up behind all of us. Monica and my dad stand together and begin to clap. I reluctantly join the crowd of people. Photographers race around, snapping photos of every angle possible. I hope they don't get any of me, I'm not a good enough actress to feign happiness for the bride and groom.

"If everyone could join us under the canopy, we will be celebrating Brooke and Christopher's impending nuptials with a four course meal as well as dancing and an open bar," Monica announces with a flourish of her hand.

Awesome. We get to spend our evening in a tent with people who have access to unlimited alcohol.

"If we make a break for it now, do you think anyone will notice?" I ask Grayson as we follow the crowd of people to the enclosed tent.

"I'm afraid you're too captivating to escape attention, Rose. We'd be caught in an instant."

"I'm not sure that everyone else sees me the way that you do, Gray."

"The amount of men I've had to glare at already this evening proves otherwise." His grip tightens on my hand. I look up at him to find his jaw clenched.

"You probably misunderstood their intentions. I'm sure they weren't looking at me in that way." It's sweet that he thinks so highly of me, but I'm not some supermodel who turns heads. I'm an averagely beautiful woman.

"I didn't misunderstand anything, trust me."

My skin is warm when we enter the canopy tent. He seems serious, but if I think about other guys looking at me in that way for too long I might combust. I'd rather no one look at me, *ever*. Grayson has become an exception to that rule, standing in line right beside Myla, Simone, and my mom.

There are thankfully no assigned seats, so Grayson and I choose a table in a back corner of the tent, furthest away from where Brooke and Topher are seated. Their table is on the opposite side of the dance floor, and the rest of the tables are situated in a way that makes it seem like we're the peasants while Brooke and Topher are the queen and king watching over us all from their royal dais.

No one sits with us, and judging by a few not-so-subtle glares, everyone here is a part of the Covington Cult. And since Monica heads it up, she's no doubt poisoned everyone against me. But instead of feeling slighted, I'm relieved. If no one sits with us, I don't have to make small talk with a snobby stranger. I can tune out the world and focus on Grayson.

"I'm not a fan of these looks you're getting," Grayson says, his frustration evident.

"Why do you assume they're glaring at me?" I joke to try and lighten the mood. "Maybe you've made some enemies amongst the southern elite."

He laughs. "Maybe so. Either way, if they don't ease up they're going to regret it."

My stomach flutters hearing the protective edge to his voice.

"They're harmless," I say, because even though I'd love to see Grayson take down any number of these rude people, it wouldn't be good for the already fragile relationship I have with my family.

Over the course of this trip–and well before it, if I'm honest–I've considered cutting ties with this side of my family entirely. But something in me just can't do it. Every time I hold the scissors to the fraying thread of our connection, I end up backing out. There's a part of me that's still holding out hope, I guess. Hope that one day my dad will wake up and see that he's hurt his daughter with the weight of his expectations. And more than that, he's allowed his new wife and daughter to disrespect me over and over again.

Until he sees the pain he's caused, I suppose I'll grin and bear it through these events and interactions. Even though each one seems to add a fresh cut to my already scarred heart.

"You're kinder than they deserve, Rose."

I give him a weak smile in response, since I don't know what to say. A waiter comes by and sets down the salad course. Grayson and I eat and talk about each of the books we're reading. Dinner goes by mercifully fast. During our last course, we watch an awkward 'last dance as an engaged couple' between Brooke and Topher. The applause at the end is quiet, as if even the people who love them felt uncomfortable watching. They kept each other at arm's length, and Brooke's smile looked as artificial as Splenda.

"I feel sorry for them," I say as they part ways at the end of their dance. Brooke heads over to a table of friends, while Topher heads straight to the bar.

"I don't, they deserve each other," Grayson says. I shoot him an admonishing look.

He's about to say more—no doubt something facetious—when he pulls his phone out of his pocket. He frowns down at it.

"It's my brother, Maverick. He's not one to call like this. Will you be okay if I step outside to answer him?"

"Of course," I say and he stands. "I hope everything is okay."

"Me too." He gives me a quick kiss before weaving his way through the tables and disappearing through the canopy opening.

I let my eyes bounce around the tent. Everyone seems to be having a great time. If I wasn't swimming in a sea of glares, I might actually be able to enjoy myself. There are twinkle lights strung above, giving everything a warm, romantic feel. Emphasis on the warm, though. I glance at my empty water glass. It's gotten pretty humid in here, and I'm sure Grayson would enjoy a nice cold drink when he comes back.

I decide to head to the bar and see if they have any nonalcoholic frozen drinks that could help us cool off. I'm not keen on the idea of not having my wits about me with all these people around, so I think staying away from alcohol is my best bet.

The closer I get to the bar, the more I regret my decision. Topher is leaning against the counter, tipping back a glass of dark amber liquid.

"Could I get two virgin piña coladas?" I ask. I can feel Topher's gaze slithering over me. I straighten my spine, wishing I would have waited for Grayson to be back before leaving the table.

"You sure can," the bartender answers. In my peripheral vision I see Topher still staring at me.

The man gets to work on the drinks right away. It's quiet, and I almost wish Topher would just say something so I didn't have to sit in this whirlpool of nerves.

"What are you doing here?" Topher grants my wish by speaking, his words slow. *Great.* He's drunk. That's going to make this interaction fun. The bartender sets one drink down and I thank him.

"Getting something to drink," I answer.

"No, I mean here, in Hawaii."

"Your *fiancée* invited me." The same fiancée that likely wouldn't appreciate how drunk he is right now. But I guess she's too busy being fawned over by her socialite friends to notice.

"Are you jealous? You sound jealous."

I roll my eyes. The bartender hands me my other drink and I shoot him a grateful smile before turning and walking away.

"Hey, don't walk away from me when I'm talking to you." I make it a few steps before a hand clamps down on my wrist and jerks me back. One of the drinks sloshes over my wrist and his fingers.

"Let me go, Christopher," I grit out and jerk on his hand. Fear floods my system. All rational thought abandons me until I'm stuck not knowing what to do. Topher's eyes run over my body and I feel sick.

"You never dressed like this when we were together. Is it because you want me back?" He jerks me closer and the force of it makes me drop both of the plastic cups I was holding. They clatter to the ground, splattering the cold drinks all over the floor and the bottom of my dress.

"Stop it!" I yell at him. *Why is no one doing anything?* Tears flood my eyes and my chest tightens.

"Quit pretending you don't want my attention," he slurs, his breath reeking of alcohol.

Through the blur of my tears I register a figure storming up to us. Before I can process what's happening, an arm wraps around Topher's neck from behind, choking off his next words.

"*Let her go,*" Grayson growls in a voice I've never heard from him before. It's dangerously low and sends chill bumps across my skin.

Topher drops my wrist and I stumble backward. I wipe my eyes just in time to watch Grayson let go of Topher, spin him around, rear back, and *punch him* square across the jaw. I gasp at the sight. Topher sways on his feet, kept standing only by Grayson grabbing the collar of his polo. Those nearest to us are wearing shocked expressions. I avoid looking at my family, unable to stomach their reactions.

"Don't *ever* touch her again. Don't look at her. Don't even come near her. If you so much as breathe in her general vicinity, I will make it your last." Grayson shoves him and he falls into the puddle of piña colada, groaning.

My tears haven't let up, but now I'm not sure if they're from shock or gratitude or both. Grayson dusts his hands off on his dress pants then looks over at me. The hardness of his expression melts away. His steps are quick and sure as he crosses the path to me. His arms wrap around me in a firm embrace and I collapse against him. I try to get out some kind of thank you, but I can't manage around my tears.

"Shhh, it's okay," he whispers as he runs a hand over my hair. "I'm here, Rose. I've got you."

I hold on to him as tight as I can, feeling like a ship caught in a hurricane. He's my anchor in the storm, the only thing keeping me from going under.

"Let's get you out of here," he says against my ear.

I let him lead me. I don't look up. If people are talking about me, I can't hear them over the ringing in my ears. My knees buckle when we leave the tent. Grayson catches me, not letting me fall into the sand. *He always catches me.* My world tilts when he scoops me up into his arms and carries me the rest of the way to our room. The entire time, I cling to him, hoping beyond hope that I'll wake up soon and this will have all been a terrible dream.

CHAPTER THIRTY-ONE

Sloane Covington

"You punched Topher," I say when Grayson sets me down on our bed.

"I did." He slides my sandals off my feet. "Are you okay? Do you need anything?"

"You *punched* him, for me."

"Yes, Rose, I did." He gives me a tender look while pulling the covers over my legs. "And I'd do it again in a heartbeat. He probably deserved worse than that. But right now I'm worried about you. Are you hurt?"

I look down at my wrist where he grabbed me. Grayson's hands come into view as he gently turns my hand over, then back the way it was.

"I think I'm okay. It was more scary than anything." I glance up just in time to see a dark look flicker over Grayson's face.

"I should have hit him harder."

"Then the repercussions of this would be worse than they're already going to be."

He frowns. "What are you talking about?"

"Any minute now, my dad is going to call me to have a *talk* about my behavior and yours."

"About *your* behavior? What about Topher's?" He laces Topher's ridiculous name with venom.

"I'm sure he'll find a way to pin it on me." I sigh.

"Sloane, listen to me." I meet Grayson's eyes, his use of my first name quickly drawing my attention. "None of this was your fault. Don't let your dad convince you of that. Don't even let him get away with saying it."

I look down at my hands, twisting my engagement ring.

"You're right." I rub my eyes and groan. "I *know* you're right. It's just the only times I've stood up to him have been when we weren't in the same room. When I decided to become an author, when I broke up with Topher, both of those pivotal life moments were choices he found out about through other people. I didn't even *call* him."

"Maybe if you told him face to face that what he's done and is doing is wrong, he'd know better for the future. He doesn't seem like Monica and Brooke. When we spent time together on the golf course, he seems mostly misguided, if a touch too proud."

"A touch?" I question his generosity with a raised brow. He gives me a wry grin in return.

"He's your dad, I'm trying to be sensitive." I laugh, and it feels *so* good. After everything that just happened, I needed a good laugh to expel all the tension in my limbs.

Grayson tucks a piece of hair behind my ear. "You should speak up. It might not change your dad, but I know it will be good for you."

"Okay," I say. "I won't back down when we talk. I'll tell them the truth and even if they don't accept it, I know I'll have said what I needed to."

"That's my girl."

I push up on my knees and throw my arms around him in a hug. He falls backward onto the bed, even though I know I'm not strong enough to push him over. His blue eyes meet mine, their tropical depths sparkling with affection.

I love him. My muscles stiffen at the realization. *Is it too soon?* His fingers lace into my hair before he guides me into a gentle kiss. As soon as his lips brush mine, I know it must be true, even if it is sooner than what some would consider normal. Every part of him calls out to me in a way that is undeniably based in love. It's as if my very soul has been waiting for him. Every awkward date, every bad relationship, all of it has been because there was a part of me holding out for *this*. For *him*. And now that he's here, I'm hopeless to do anything but fall.

He pulls back from the kiss. I lay my forehead on his with closed eyes, taking in the sound of his breathing, the feeling of his arms wrapped around me.

"Thank you," I whisper to him. "For saving me, for carrying me back here, and for encouraging me to stand up to my family. I don't know what would have happened if you weren't there to help."

His arms tighten around me. "I'm glad I was there. I might never leave your side again."

"I wouldn't mind that," I say, lifting my head to smile at him. "Though I do think it would be best for me to talk to my dad and Monica alone."

His expression is pained, but he nods. "I understand. I'd like to be nearby though, in case Topher comes by or you need me for any reason."

"That sounds like a good plan." Right as I'm about to thank him again, my phone buzzes on the nightstand.

I push up off of Grayson, then reach to grab my phone. Sure enough, there's a text from my father asking me to meet him and Monica in their room to discuss what happened.

"Ready to go to war again?"

"Darling, storming the battlefield with you would be my greatest honor."

My heart leaps at his direct quote from Simone's trilogy.

"You finished book two," I say and he grins.

"I did. After that dungeon kiss scene, I don't mind being compared to Castien at all." His smirk sends flames across my skin.

"I forgot about that scene."

"No, you didn't." *No, I didn't.* My face is too hot, much like that kiss scene. I believe that after reading it for the first time I had to use my paperback as a fan.

"I'll tease you about your fictional boyfriend later though. Right now we need to get the stuff with your dad out of the way."

I sigh. Even though Grayson's teasing always turns me into a puddle of embarrassment, I'd rather that over the nerves that accompany what I'm about to do.

"Okay, let's go."

We walk hand in hand down the hall to the elevator. My feet are sticking to my sandals because of the residual piña colada on them, but I don't care. I didn't bother to fix my makeup or hair, or even change my ruined dress. They should see the damage Topher caused.

The elevator ride and subsequent walk to my dad and Monica's room is quiet. Grayson doesn't say anything until we get to the door. He takes my face in his hands and kisses my forehead, then my lips.

"You are strong, Rose. And you deserve to have your voice be heard." I smile at his gentle tone, trying not to cry again. "I'll be right outside this door if you need me. Close the hinge on the lock before the door shuts so that it stays propped open, okay? I promise I won't come in unless I think something is very wrong."

"Okay, I will. Thank you again, Gray."

He kisses me once more before letting me go. "Anything for my fiancée," he says and my heart skips. It's not like he hasn't called me his fiancée before, but now after realizing my feelings, it feels different. It feels real, like a title I could see myself proudly wearing each day until the day I got a new one: *wife*.

I turn, draw my shoulders back, then knock on the door. It opens right away, as if my dad has been waiting by it.

"Come in," my father commands. I have to catch the door as he lets it go, since he's already heading further into their suite. Before the door shuts, I flip out the hinge so it's propped open. Grayson stands like a sentry across from the door, his hands clasped in front of him. His presence brings me the comfort I need to carry this out.

I hold my head high as I enter the ostentatious suite my dad and Monica are staying in. I thought our room was nice, but this blows it out of the water. It's at least twice the size of mine and Grayson's room, complete with a large seating area that Monica and Dad are occupying currently. Monica greets me with a scowl, and my Dad looks borderline furious. They sit next to one another on the couch, but there's a noticeable gap between them. I decide to stay standing. I don't want to feel small in front of them.

"Would you care to explain why you're set on ruining my daughter's wedding?" Monica takes the first shot. "First you attempt to upstage her with your own engagement, then you cause a scene at her rehearsal dinner. Topher is going to have a swollen lip tomorrow!"

"I did not cause a scene, Topher did. I have no intention of ruining their wedding, though I would caution Brooke against marrying him if I thought she'd listen to me."

"You will do no such thing!" Monica seethes, her eyes flashing. "I have had enough of you soiling the Covington name your father worked so hard to build."

At the mention of him, I look at my dad. The man who was supposed to raise and protect me but instead forced ideals on me and neglected our relationship. There's darkness around his eyes and it seems as if some of the fight that was in them when I walked in has gone out.

"What about you?" I ask him. "Are you going to tell me how I've ruined your reputation?"

"Do not get an attitude with me, young lady." I let out a bitter laugh, rolling my eyes. He shoots up to standing. "I am your father, you will listen to what I have to say and respect me."

"*Respect you?*" I shake my head. "I could never respect the kind of man who would watch his daughter get assaulted and then *blame* her. I've sat back and listened to your reprimands for years. I tried to be a good daughter, but it was never enough. Now I've come to see that trying to live up to your twisted expectations isn't worth it."

I turn to glare at Monica before continuing.

"As for the *Covington name*, you can keep it. I don't want to be associated with it anymore. When I marry Grayson, I'll be happy to get rid of this dreadful name and all that's associated with it."

I'm not sure what has me bringing up Grayson. I guess my feelings are starting to overflow, but I don't regret my words. They're true.

"You'll regret saying that when Charles takes you out of the will," Monica sneers. My dad looks at her, his brow furrowed.

"Not everything in this world is about money. And even if it was, I can assure you I have plenty on my own thanks to the career both of you put down all the time."

"Charles, are you going to sit there and let her speak to me this way?"

My dad lets out a weary sigh. "Sloane, I'm sure you understand that you can't stay for the wedding after what transpired today, no matter whose fault it was."

"No matter–" Monica sputters. "It was clearly her fault! She provoked the upstanding Toph–"

Dad cuts her off with a lift of his large hand. "*Enough*. I'm speaking to my daughter." I blink at him in surprise. Monica's jaw snaps shut with an audible click. "I will pay for you to take the next flight back to Georgia. As soon as the ticket details are sorted out, I will email them to you."

Wanting me to leave isn't entirely unreasonable. In a perfect world, the wedding would be canceled on account of the groom being a vulgar drunk, but since this is a decidedly *im*perfect world, this isn't a bad solution. It helps that he's not being rude, too.

"Okay, we'll prepare to leave tomorrow," I say and he nods. "Is there anything else?" I ask him. Emotion wars behind his eyes, stirring up all kinds of conflicting feelings within me. But in the end, he looks at Monica, then back at me and shakes his head.

"Okay, then I'll be going." I meet my dad's eyes. "Thank you for the trip. It was mostly fun." After another bob of his head, I turn around and head to the door.

As soon as it falls shut behind me, Grayson wraps me up in his arms.

"I am *so* proud of you, Rose."

"You heard everything?" I say into his rumpled dress shirt.

"Yes, and you were amazing." He looks down at me. "How are you feeling?"

So he's not bringing up the whole *I'm going to take his last name* comment. Maybe he thought I was just upping the ante to sound stronger. I'm not sure if I'm disappointed he didn't at least tease me about it, or grateful he's holding back while I collect my bearings.

"Okay." I shrug. "I'm sad that we're being forced to leave early, but this whole thing could have gone a lot worse. I wish my dad would have said more, too. But I don't expect him to realize all of his issues over the course of one conversation."

"Maybe this was the first step toward something better."

"Maybe." I smile up at him. "Either way, I'm glad I said what I said."

"I think all of this is reason to celebrate. How do you feel about changing into comfy clothes and getting ice cream?"

I feel like if I wasn't already in love with you, I would be now.

"That sounds absolutely perfect."

"You're absolutely perfect," he says with a cheesy grin before kissing me breathless.

Yeah, I'm in love with him. No doubt about it.

CHAPTER THIRTY-TWO

Grayson Carter

"I forgot to ask in the chaos of everything, what did your brother call about?" Sloane asks before taking another bite of her cookie dough ice cream. Her feet kick in the water beside mine, her tan skin illuminated by the pale pool lights.

After getting our dessert right before the shop closed, we came to camp out by the pool. It's fairly quiet, with only a handful of stragglers to keep us company as the area is about to close. I don't think either of us want to leave. From the pool we can hear the ocean's waves hitting the shore, and breathe in the salty air. When we go back to our room it will feel like our trip is really over. And even with all the bad parts, it's still the best vacation I've ever had.

"He's worried about a family friend of ours, Evie." I sigh and rake a hand through my hair. "I'm more worried about *him*. Evie is like family to all of us, but she used to follow Maverick and her brother Drew around like a little puppy. Mav is ultra-protective of everyone he cares about, and if he thinks Evie's in trouble, he might take matters into his own hands."

"I don't want to pry, but I don't understand what you mean."

"He thinks Evie's husband is purposely isolating her from her family and friends." Sloane's eyes widen. "I think there's a chance that Evie just wants to live her own life and has made a few reckless choices in the process. But at the same time, I don't know, Maverick and Drew are both set on something being wrong."

"What does he want to do about it?"

"Well he called me to ask if my company could be hired to protect someone against their will." I shake my head, letting out a half-laugh. "I told him *absolutely not*, which of course he already knew. I think he's panicking, but he also knows he can't go to New York to see Evie without her permission. It won't go well."

"He feels helpless," she says and I nod. "That must be hard to deal with."

"It is. Especially for Mav. He's a fix-it guy. After our mom died, he got into boxing. I think it was his way of feeling in control when he wasn't. Thankfully he eventually backed off of fighting *people*, and now he takes his frustrations out on a bag in his garage. Which I'm sure has seen ample use since Evie got married a few months ago."

I set my empty ice cream cup beside me and pat my legs.

"But we've had enough family drama for one night, don't you think?" I ask. Sloane nods enthusiastically, making me laugh. "How about a swim?"

"A swim?" Her brows draw together. "The pool is closing. I was going to say we should head back. I'm not even wearing a swimsuit." I open my mouth to respond, but she cuts me off. "And if you make a joke about skinny dipping I will not hesitate to drown you."

A burst of laughter escapes me. "I was going to say you can wear what you have on, but if you'd prefer to be a little more *free* I won't stop you."

She sets down her ice cream cup, then shoves me hard. It's not hard enough though, because I don't fall in.

"You're going to regret that, Rose," I say with a maniacal grin before grabbing her and throwing her right into the deep end.

As soon as her head is back above water, she's splashing me. I strip off my shirt and throw it to the side then jump in after her. I chase her down to the five-foot area, where she's on her tiptoes but I'm well above the water line. She's still splashing me as I get closer. It's not easy because of the constant stream of water going into my eyes, but I manage to catch both of her wrists.

"What are you going to do now, Rose?"

She bites her lip, looking up at me through wet lashes. I place her hands on my shoulders, she slides them to the back of my neck, pressing our bodies together. My hands find her waist next. Her shirt has come up in the water, causing my fingertips to brush against her bare skin. When I run my thumb over the bottom of her ribcage, her lips part.

I lean down toward her and it feels as if every star in the sky is leaning with me. Every galaxy burning bright above is watching, waiting. Our lips touch and a supernova explodes within my chest. Every cell in my body burns for her. I grip her waist. Close isn't close enough. I want to be branded by her. For everyone to see me in the days to come and know I'm hers and she's mine.

Her lips part and she's sweeter than honey, better than any dessert I've ever had. I can't get enough of her. Her touch is just as frenzied as my own. My heart aches with the desire to tell her how I feel.

Unable to keep myself from it any longer, I break our kiss. She looks up at me, panting in my arms from the intensity of our kiss.

I reach up and cup her face with one hand. She shivers as water cascades from my palm down her neck. I gaze into her eyes and ... a flash of light burns my retinas. I squint through the sudden bright beam, finding a man in a resort uniform glaring down at us.

"Pool's closed." His tone leaves no room for argument.

"Sorry about that, we'll leave," I say with a forced chuckle. Sloane is giving me a look that says *I told you so*. But I don't regret a thing. That kiss was worth the trouble. I'd get arrested before I gave up a kiss like that.

"Next time please adhere to the sign on the gate with the pool times," the worker says as we climb over the edge of the pool.

"Will do-" I strain my eyes to see his name tag. "Gary. We'll just be grabbing some towels from the shelf over there, then heading on our way."

He nods his approval. I snag my shirt off the ground on the way to the towel display. I hand a shivering Sloane a towel, then wrap one around myself.

"Now leave so I can lock up," Gary grumbles.

"Right away. Thanks for keeping the resort safe, Gary. You're a gentleman and a scholar." Gary looks unamused.

I shoot him one last grin then tuck Sloane under my arm and rush out of the pool area toward the resort.

"I can't believe you got us in trouble! Actually, I can. You *are* trouble," Sloane says under her breath.

"We aren't in trouble. Nothing happened."

I lead her onto an empty elevator, pressing our floor number.

"We were reprimanded and kicked out, that is the very definition of *in trouble.* All because you wanted to swim after hours."

"Tell me you didn't have fun," I say, looking down at her.

She bumps her shoulder into my side. "You know I had fun." Her cheeks tint an adorable pink.

"So then it was worth it."

"Yeah." She smiles up at me. "It was."

"Rose," I whisper in the dark. "Rose, wake up."

She makes a soft whining sound while snuggling closer. Her head is tucked under my chin and our legs are tangled together. She's soft and warm. If this wasn't so important, I'd close my eyes and sleep until it's time for us to get on the plane.

"Rose," I say again, running a hand up and down her back. "It's time to get up."

She lifts her head off my chest. "It's still dark out," she mumbles. The only light in our room is coming from the bathroom door that's cracked open.

"I know, I thought you might want to see the sunrise before we leave."

She blinks her eyes open and smiles. "Another bucket list item."

"We won't be able to fit in snorkeling before we have to go, but I figured we could at least go down to the beach one more time. You don't even have to change out of your pajamas."

"Yeah, that sounds fun," she says, her voice still laced with sleep.

We get out of bed and hunt around in the dark for our sandals. I slide mine on, then look across the room to find Sloane shivering near the door. I snag my Thrashers sweatshirt I brought to wear on the plane ride home and walk over to her.

"Here, put this on," I say as I hand it to her.

She gives me a grateful smile. "Thanks, Gray."

I'm sure it'll be chilly down by the water so early in the morning, but I'm fine with being cold if it means she's warm. We walk down the hall hand in hand. Once we're on the elevator, Sloane leans against me with her eyes closed. Her hair is wavy and wild around her face and her cheeks are pink from our time in the sun this week. She lifts one of her arms to swipe at a stray hair, her hand barely poking out of my sweatshirt. A sense of deep satisfaction fills me at the sight of her in my clothes. She looks like she was meant to wear them.

We get to the ground floor and step off the elevator into a quiet lobby. A few workers are milling about–thankfully none of them are Gary, who I'm sure wouldn't be happy to see us–but aside from that it's empty.

Cool, salty air greets us upon stepping outside. The sky is just beginning to light up and it's misting, but not quite raining. Everything around us is shrouded in the haze of blue hour. I reach over the fence and snag a towel from the pool area before taking Sloane's hand once more and walking down the sandy path to the water.

There's a peace enveloping the beach that makes me all the more happy I planned this last night. After a rollercoaster of a week, this is the perfect way to cap it off. It's also a great backdrop for heartfelt confessions. One where we–hopefully–won't be interrupted.

We walk as close to the water as we can without risk of getting wet. I fan out our towel and sit down. Sloane sits in between my legs and leans back against my chest. I wrap my arms around her. The sun is starting to peek over the horizon, its soft glow a stark contrast against the foaming waves of the ocean below. We watch in silence for a while before Sloane speaks up.

"I love it here," Sloane says, pressing a kiss to my arm. "I miss Myla and Simone and Roman, but I wish we could have had longer to explore."

"I'll bring you back whenever you want. And next time it'll be just us."

"I would love that." She shifts out of my arms and turns so she's on her knees in between my legs. "I can't thank you enough for everything you did on this trip, Gray."

"You don't need to thank me. I got to spend time in Hawaii with the most beautiful woman in the world. I couldn't have asked for a better week."

"Even though you had to deal with my toxic family and dumb ex-boyfriend?"

"I got to punch a guy. I haven't had the opportunity to do that in a while, it felt good. I should be thanking you."

She laughs, pushing one of my shoulders. "*Gray.*"

"*Rose,*" I reply in a teasing tone. I put my hands on her waist. "I'm serious. This week has been the time of my life. I'd do it all over again the exact same way." I tilt my head to the side.

She smiles and shakes her head at me. "It's hard to believe this was the time of your life. You've probably been on hundreds of adventures."

"But none of them have been with you." I lightly squeeze her waist. "I'd rather sit on a couch with you than be anywhere else in the world with anyone else."

She looks down, toying with her engagement ring. The one I hope she'll consider to be real in the future. I place a finger under her chin and lift her head. The sky is a watercolor painting of pale pinks and dusty blues behind her. Her hair is lifted away from her face by the wind and the mist has dampened her soft skin. She's so perfect it hurts.

"Rose, I'm in love with you." She sucks in a breath. "I've been falling for you for some time now, and I can't keep my feelings to myself any longer. I am hopelessly, recklessly, out-of-my-mind in love with you. It's okay if you don't feel the same yet–"

Soft fingertips on my mouth cut off my sentence.

"I love you too," she whispers. "Every part of you." Pure elation floods my veins, making a smile break out across my face. *She loves me.* She's seen the darkest parts of me and she still wants me.

I pull her to me and fall backward onto the towel. She lands on my chest with a giggle. I take her face in my hands and kiss her. I pour my emotions into the kiss, feeling her do the same. A drop of water hits my arm, then another, then it starts to flood. Sloane breaks our kiss, pulling back to look at me with a shy smile.

"It's raining." I point out the obvious, waiting for her to acknowledge what she's thinking.

"I've always wanted to be kissed in the rain," she echoes her words from that night on the golf course.

I waste no time by hesitating. I pull her back down to my lips. Her soaked hair creates a curtain around us. The warmth of her mouth on mine chases away the cold of the pouring rain. She deepens the kiss and I feel heat pool in my abdomen. There's a kind of wildness to this moment. As if we're a part of the storm too. Her lips the ocean crashing against my shore. My touch lightning, hers the cleansing rain.

When we break apart, we're both gasping for air. Sloane's eyes meet mine, dark and untamed. The desire churning in her gaze is an ocean I'd happily drown in. I'm about to kiss her again when a crack of thunder makes us both jump.

"We should go inside," she yells over the rain and waves. I nod in agreement. As much as I'd love to stay out here with her, I don't want anything bad to happen.

We jump up and I grab our towel, then her hand. We run toward the resort, our sandals slapping against the wet sand. When we make it inside, we stop to take a breath. A front desk worker bustles over with two fresh towels. I thank the worker, then turn to wrap the first one around Sloane. She tucks it under her chin and smiles up at me. I smile back down at her.

This is the love of my life. Drenched to the bone, but smiling like she just won an award. I press a kiss to her forehead. *I'm the luckiest man alive.*

CHAPTER THIRTY-THREE

Grayson Carter

TWO WEEKS LATER

Sloane hasn't taken off her engagement ring. Even now, as we prepare dinner for my family, it sparkles on her hand. She stirs marinara sauce on the stove while smiling at Maddie who is talking to her about ballet. My kitchen used to feel so empty, even with guests over, but not any longer. Sloane was the missing piece. She's only been over twice since we got back from Hawaii, but she already looks right at home.

We've spent the last two weeks spending as much time together as possible. It hasn't been easy, what with her manuscript deadline and my work hitting a busy streak. There have been plenty of nights where we fall asleep video chatting, and quick lunch breaks where we spend most of our time kissing rather than eating.

To celebrate her submitting her manuscript to her editor, I invited all my family over to make homemade pizza. It will also give me the opportunity to tell them how I've been feeling, which I'm not exactly looking forward to. Beginning this relationship with Sloane has helped, but I don't know how long it'll be before something else comes up. If I've learned anything over the years, it's that even in the best of times, anxiety can rear its ugly head. So Sloane encouraged me to invite them over for dinner to talk to them.

Everyone was happy to come under the guise of celebrating Sloane. My whole family loves her, even my dad. He talked to her on the phone the other night and when I spoke to him after, he said she was a *good one* and I *better not screw this up*. Which is his way of expressing his approval. He's not here tonight, because while I love him, he doesn't handle the concept of *mental health* all that well. But everyone else is here, even Dahlia's sister Jasmine. It makes my confession all the more scary, but I think it would be good for both Jasmine and Maddie to see me be vulnerable.

"You're staring at her like she's going to disappear," Levi jokes next to me. Dahlia giggles from the other side of Levi. We're sitting at my kitchen island. Adrian is out back throwing a football with Sebastian and Maverick. MJ, Juliette, and Jasmine are watching in lawn chairs while sipping the strawberry lemonade Sloane made earlier today.

"If you expect me to be embarrassed about staring at the most beautiful woman in the world, then you'll be disappointed," I reply, not taking my eyes off Sloane. Her gaze flicks over to me. She's wearing a faint smile that lets me know she heard me.

"You're such a sap." Levi laughs.

"Says the man who annotated Sloane's books for his fiancée," I point out.

"I still think that's one of the most romantic things ever," Sloane chimes in with a dreamy sigh. Maddie nods in agreement, her blonde curls bouncing with the movement.

Levi shrugs off the compliment, but the look he gives Dahlia is one that shows he'd do it again and again to see her smile. That sort of look would be the kind of thing that used to make loneliness flare in my chest. But not anymore.

"Everything is ready," Sloane says to me with a meaningful look. I take a deep breath, trying to ignore the stab of anxiety in my gut.

"Mad Dog, can you go tell everyone to come inside and hang out in the living room? I have something I want to talk about before dinner." Curiosity shines in Maddie's eyes, and the look is mirrored on the faces of Levi and Dahlia. Once Maddie is out the door, Levi turns to me.

"Y'all didn't elope in Hawaii did you?" Levi asks with a laugh.

"No, though that's not a half-bad idea." I wink at Sloane, who just shakes her head.

My back door opens, and in filters the rest of my family. I walk into the living room and wait for everyone to sit down. I've never minded the spotlight, but today it's more on the suffocating side. Everyone is watching me with their hyper observant gazes, no doubt making guesses on what they think is going on. Sloane passes by me, reaching out to squeeze my hand before perching on the arm of the couch. She's within arm's reach, which I know she's done for my sake.

"What's going on, Grayson?" Adrian is the first to speak up, which is a rarity.

I take in another deep breath, then speak. "I need to talk about something serious with all of you," I begin. "I've been struggling with anxiety lately. A few years back, I had a panic attack in front of Adrian. He had me get the help I needed, and not long after that I felt a lot better. But in the last few months, with all of the change happening in our family, I started to struggle again."

I'd thought the words would tumble out of me, but it feels like they keep getting stuck in my throat. Each one is a battle to get out in front of all of my family. I look to Sloane. She holds out her hand, mimicking every time I've done the same for her. I smile and take it. A weight lifts off my chest.

"I haven't wanted to tell you because I didn't want any of you to feel like you couldn't share the changes happening in your life with me." I look down. "And I'll admit, I didn't want to look weak." Sloane squeezes my hand. "But I think it would be better if y'all knew, in case anything happened."

It's quiet for a moment. The silence is tangible and heavy. But it's broken before the weight can become unbearable.

"I'm choosing not to be mad at you for keeping this from us," MJ says in her signature brash way.

"That sounds like you're mad," Levi says. I look up to see MJ glare at him.

"He'd be mad at us for keeping it from him," she argues.

"No, he'd be sorry for not noticing sooner," Maverick says. "Which is how I feel."

MJ shifts in her seat, looking conflicted for a moment before nodding. "You're right. I'm sorry."

"It's okay," I tell them, because I don't know what else to say.

"Are *you* okay?" Maddie asks, worry in her voice.

I smile at her. "I'm okay, Mad Dog. I just need everyone to know what's going on in case I need help. I don't want anyone to be caught off guard." She nods in understanding. I hope that I'm being a good example for her, but I feel too off balance to be sure that I am.

"Do you need anything from us?" Dahlia asks.

I shrug. "I don't really know. I just felt like I should tell you."

She nods. "Well if you do, we're here for you." All my family nods in agreement.

"Something happened in Hawaii," Adrian says. "That's why you're telling us, isn't it?"

Juliette shoots him an admonishing look. "You don't have to answer that, Grayson."

"No, it's okay." I sigh. "I had another attack, but Sloane helped me through it." I look to the woman in question, meeting her tender gaze. "She's actually the reason I'm talking to all of you."

"I already liked you before, but I definitely approve now," Dahlia says to her, making me chuckle.

"Will you keep us in the loop as much as you're comfortable?" Maverick asks. "That way we can try to help."

"I can do that. I don't want to be alone in this anymore."

"Good," Levi says as he stands. "Because we're not going to let you be alone." He comes over to give me a hug with a few too many aggressive back pats.

Dahlia joins in, and soon enough everyone is coming to hug me. My heart and head already feel lighter. I hug each of my family members with a smile on my face. Even Adrian and MJ hug me, and they're not huge fans of physical affection. I pick MJ up off the ground when it's her turn just to mess with her. Over her head I see Sebastian's eyes widen. I set my sister down and point an accusing finger at him.

"Why do you look like that?" I ask. His eyes widen.

"Like what?"

"Like you're worried I'll break my little sister. You've never looked that way before, and I've thrown her into the pool in front of you." I look down at MJ, then back at him. "Is something wrong?"

"It feels wrong to announce it after you just poured your heart out." MJ looks at Sebastian, who just shrugs with a small smile on his face. "But the longer we wait, the higher the chance of one of you figuring it out on your own ... I'm pregnant," she announces with the biggest smile I've ever seen her wear.

"Are you serious?" I ask and she nods with a laugh.

I look over to Maddie, who's wearing a giant smile of her own. Pure joy rushes through me.

"Congratulations!" Dahlia squeals before I can even formulate a response.

"This is the best news ever!" I go to pick MJ up again, but pause. "Probably shouldn't do that, actually."

"As much as I hate it when you do, it's really not a big deal. Sebastian is just over protective of me. He's making me send him pictures of windows being open in my classroom so I don't inhale paint fumes." She rolls her eyes.

I nod my head at Sebastian in appreciation. "Good man." I'm glad my sister has someone to take care of her. She'd never admit it, but I know she loves how he dotes on her.

Everyone gives their congratulations and starts asking MJ, Sebastian, and Maddie a million questions about the due date and when they found out and if they know the gender yet. A hand slips into mine in the midst of the chaos and I look down at Sloane.

"How are you feeling?" she asks, just loud enough for me to hear.

"I'm good," I tell her with a smile. "I know they'll be here for me if I need them."

"And about the news?"

I pull her into my arms. My chest warms knowing she's checking to make sure this good news isn't being spoiled in my brain by thoughts of my family moving on without me. "I'm happy for them. I'm excited to get to see Maddie be a big sister. And the fact that everyone made time to come today shows that them not having time for me is just in my head."

"That's good." She tilts her head back to look up at me. "I'm proud of you, Gray."

"Don't make me cry in front of my brothers." I try to joke away the lump in my throat. I've heard those words before, but something about them coming from her is special.

She places a hand on my cheek, swiping away a stray tear. "I love you."

"I love you, Rose."

CHAPTER THIRTY-FOUR

Sloane Covington

"One day you'll realize that you have no hope of beating me at pool," Levi says as he swipes up the money Grayson set down on the edge of the billiards table.

Levi and Grayson have been throwing playful barbs back and forth this entire game. All of the Carters are competitive, so to watch them go back and forth makes for great entertainment.

"I would have beat you this time if I wouldn't have let Sloane play a few rounds," Grayson says and I hit his shoulder.

"Hey! I got one in, thank you very much."

"Yes, you put a stripe in and we're solids," Grayson says in a dry tone. Levi throws his head back laughing.

"You lined up my shot," I huff.

"Sloane, it's okay, Grayson has had a losing streak long before you came along," Levi says with a smirk.

"Pride cometh before the fall, brother."

"Grayson, give up already," Dahlia yells from the couch where she's playing Mario Kart against Jasmine and Maddie. "He's too good."

"You tell 'em, Doll." Levi's grin only grows.

"Dahlia, don't build his ego up anymore," Grayson says. "If his head gets any bigger he won't be able to fit through the door."

I smile and shake my head at their antics.

"Says the guy who's constantly talking about how perfect his face is."

"Hey, I compliment Adrian too," Grayson says.

"Because you have the same face!"

I put a hand over my mouth to hide my laughter. Grayson grabs a sealed bag of chips off his snack bar and throws it at Levi.

"Don't get mad at me because you got the worst parts of the gene pool." As soon as Grayson's words leave his mouth, Levi is rushing around the table and attempting to get him into a headlock. They immediately begin to wrestle, grumbling nonsense to each other, and laughing occasionally.

I back away toward Dahlia. "Is this normal?"

"Yes," all the girls on the couch answer.

Not long ago, everyone else went home for the evening. When the rest of the family made the decision to leave, Levi and Grayson had just started their game. Maddie is staying the night with Dahlia and Jasmine, so they came downstairs to play Mario Kart while they waited.

Grayson and Levi stumble toward the couch. The girls squeal as Levi pushes Grayson over the back of the couch and halfway onto them. All of the girls start pushing and shoving Grayson. He falls onto the floor with a loud oof. It's not long before Levi is on him.

Perfect timing. With everyone here distracted, I start to make my way to the stairs. There's a surprise I want to hide for Grayson to find later. I didn't want to answer any questions from his family, and surprising Grayson is incredibly difficult, so this might be my only chance. Levi keeps him down long enough for me to be unnoticed.

I sneak up the stairs and slide the early copy of Simone's latest series out of my bag. She gave it to me and I read it within a day, then asked if she'd mind me gifting it to Grayson. Since he managed to get on her good side by gushing about her characters–and being good to me–she said she didn't mind at all.

I haven't gotten to snoop around Grayson's house much. He specifically told me that his library was off limits until he was ready to show me but ... I think it would be the best surprise if he came in and found the book already on his shelf with a note from me inside. So hopefully he'll forgive my intrusion.

After accidentally opening the door to a linen closet, I find the library. My mouth drops open. There are floor to ceiling bookshelves, a beautiful dark wood writing desk with a leather chair, and a daybed right under a large window. Why did he not feel ready to show me? I mean, sure, the shelves aren't completely full but that just means plenty of trips to the bookstore in the future.

I run my hand along the spines, searching for Simone's series among the shelves of others. I find mine before hers, though. He has every single book I've ever written, including the special edition hardbacks I had made earlier this year. I pull out my debut novel, noticing how worn the spine is. A gasp falls from my lips when I see a cascade of tabs along the side. *He annotated my books?*

I open it up to a random page and a laugh bursts out of me when I see *NO* in all caps beside a scene where the characters almost kiss, but are broken apart at the last second. I flip a few more pages. Tears burn in my eyes as I read note after note reacting to the book, complimenting my prose, declaring his love for certain characters and his hatred for others. There are more lines highlighted than not.

"I should have known you wouldn't listen." Grayson's voice comes from behind me.

I turn around, not bothering to hide my book or Simone's. Grayson leans against the doorframe, a smile on his lips. His hair is mussed and his clothes are wrinkled but he looks happy, if a bit nervous.

"When you said you read some of my books, you made it sound casual." I look down at the ink-soaked pages. "This isn't casual. When did you do this?"

"Before we met." His words hang in the air between us, suspended in disbelief. "I didn't want you to know how much of a fan I was. I thought it might put pressure on you, or that you would see me differently."

"You're a *fan*?" I let out a disbelieving laugh.

"I read your newsletter every week, I've read all the bonus content you put out, bought every special edition you've released, and annotated all of my copies. I'd say that makes me a fan."

I stare at him as his words sink in. As a writer, it's hard to know how those closest to you really feel about your work. You never know if someone is saying what they're saying because they're your friend or family member, or because they mean it. Even Myla and Simone are susceptible to bias because of our friendship, though Simone insists she'd tell me if I ever wrote something terrible. So to hear that he loved my work before we ever spoke shifts something inside me.

The threads of hesitation that once held me back are cut away. It's like I'm falling in love with him all over again. I look down at the ring I haven't been able to take off since we got back. Each time I've thought about giving it back to Grayson, I haven't been able to. I told myself it's because I think it's pretty, but the real reason is clear in the fresh light of this moment.

"I don't want to be your fake fiancée," I blurt out.

His forehead crinkles in confusion. "I know, we talked about this in Hawaii. Is everything okay? I know the whole book thing might be overwhelming. I was trying to figure out the best way to tell you."

He walks over to me, concern in his baby blue eyes.

I shake my head. "I mean I want to be engaged for real." Surprise washes over his expression. He doesn't move, just stands there frozen. I immediately regret my words.

"I-I shouldn't have said that. You probably think I'm crazy. I'm going to go and hope that you get a sudden bout of amnesia and–"

Grayson's lips on mine cut off my rambling. He takes the books from my hands and then I'm being pushed against the shelves. He cages me in, breaking the kiss to press his forehead against mine.

"You're not crazy," he breathes out. "Or if you are, so am I. My heart has been yours for some time now, Rose. It only makes sense for you to have my last name too."

"Really?" I whisper.

He steps back and gets down on one knee in a flash. I suck in a shaky breath, unable to keep my tears at bay. He takes my left hand in his, but doesn't remove my ring.

"Sloane Elizabeth Covington," he begins with a watery smile. "*My* Rose, will you marry me, for real this time?"

I let out a little laugh, then nod. "Yes, I would love to."

I'm in his arms in a heartbeat. His lips crash into mine with a riptide of passion, dragging me under in the most exhilarating way. He picks me up and sets me on his desk. I wrap my legs around him and drag him closer. His hands sink into my hair, tugging at the strands to tilt my head and deepen the kiss. We're sharing oxygen, lost in each other completely the way someone gets lost in a great novel. When we finally break apart all I can think is I never want this story to end.

"I love you," he whispers against my lips. "Thank you for saying yes."

"How could I ever say no?"

He smiles and I wonder at how this could be real. How a man so perfect could be mine.

"Since this is real this time, I want to make sure: do you love your ring?" he asks while running his fingers through my hair. "It's okay if you say no."

"I don't want a different one," I say quickly. "I love this one too much. I don't care if it's a fake diamond."

"I'm glad to hear it," he says with a smile. "I love it too, but since we're sharing secrets today you should know ... it's a real diamond."

I gape at him. "I've been wearing *real* diamonds this whole time and you didn't tell me? What if I would have lost it in the ocean?"

He shrugs, wearing a grin that is so *him* it's hard to hold back a smile of my own.

"Then I guess we would have had to get you a new ring."

"Why did you buy a real diamond ring? We barely knew each other!"

"I had a good feeling." He presses a kiss to my lips. "And my instincts were right."

"Do you have any other secrets I should know about?" I ask him.

"Well..." he trails off. I narrow my eyes. "I like the marshmallows in lucky charms best. I don't know why anyone would like just the cereal, it tastes like cardboard."

I laugh, dropping my forehead against his chest. I knew there was no way the marshmallows weren't his favorite.

"Of all things, why did you lie about that?"

"To make you think we were perfect for each other, of course," he jokes. "Are you going to rescind your yes now that you know the truth? We're doomed to fight over the marshmallows in every cereal box."

"I think we'll be okay. They make boxes of just the marshmallows now." I look up at him again, smiling.

"Thank goodness, I was worried I was going to lose you."

"Never," I whisper.

His smile softens. He bends down and kisses me and it feels both new and known all at once. There's a new layer to us now, one that holds the weight of commitment. It's a big step, but I'm not worried. Just like every other adventure with Grayson, I know as long as my hand is in his, it's safe to jump.

Epilogue

GRAYSON CARTER

September that same year

Sloane bites her lip, glancing across the room at her phone for the tenth time in the last ten minutes. Today is the release day for her latest novel, and she's been steadily climbing the ranks since this morning. She's limited herself to checking once every hour, but in between those times she's antsy as ever.

"You can check it, you know," I say as I move one of my chess pieces.

Usually, we're pretty evenly matched, but today I've already beaten her twice because of how distracted she is. So far today we've baked cookies, gone on a walk, packaged up paperback copies for her launch team, and played two—about to be three—games of chess. None of it has kept her from wanting to check every five minutes. I wouldn't care if she did, but she insists that the ranks don't change but once per hour so it's pointless to look.

"Has it been an hour?" She makes her move, then frowns when she sees a better one right after.

"Almost," I reply before making the last move needed to beat her. "I should have placed a bet on these games, I could have won some great stuff."

She scrunches her nose up. "I'm *distracted*. If I wasn't, I would have beat you every single time."

"I'm still adding these to the record. A win is a win." She chucks a pawn at me and I dodge out of the way with a laugh. "You could have taken out my eye!"

"And you would have deserved it!"

"Go check your rank. You're cranky when you're nervous." She sticks her tongue out at me, making me laugh harder.

"I'm not checking it until it's been an hour."

I sigh and get up, going to grab her phone off the bookshelf nearby. She pushes up off the floor where we were playing chess and grabs my arm, attempting to tug me backward.

"You can't check it yet," she says while pulling on my arm. I easily make it to the shelf even while dragging her behind me and grab her phone.

"We need to work on your arm strength during our training sessions," I tease and she hits me.

"I'm not weak, you're just a giant." I chuckle and hold her phone up out of her reach as she tries to get it. I type in the passcode and she huffs. "I regret giving my password to you."

She jumps and wraps her legs around my waist as I'm hitting refresh. I laugh as I readjust my grip, holding onto her and the phone.

She swipes it from me before I can see the new number. Instead of locking it or setting it down though, she looks at the screen. Blinks. Blinks again.

"Well, what does it say?" I ask her.

"It says ... I'm *number one*!" My eyes get big. I squeeze her tight.

"Yeah you are! I knew you'd get it. My girl is a number one bestseller!" I spin her around in my arms and she laughs, the sound is pure sunshine.

"I can't believe it," she breathes out, placing her fingertips to her mouth. "I was so scared of trying a new subgenre, but this is the best my work has ever done."

"You deserve it, Rose." I give her a soft kiss. "I'm so proud of you."

Her eyes well up with tears and she wraps her arms around my neck. I close my eyes and breathe in her sweet cinnamon scent. She swapped her perfume for the change in seasons, along with her wardrobe. A few months ago I wondered if I'd get to see her once the leaves changed, and here I am, holding her close as autumn approaches. For this season, and every one after, I'm hers, and she's mine.

Sloane Covington

Grayson lifts the box of books out of his back seat, then kicks the door shut.

"I can't believe the store asked for this many signed copies," I say as we walk toward The Secret Door bookstore.

We're dropping off a box of books for them to sell before heading to a celebratory dinner. They asked for triple the copies I normally bring. I was grateful that they wanted so many, but it was an odd request considering they had no idea how my book would sell.

"I can," he says and I smile at him.

"That's because you see me through *rose* colored glasses."

He laughs. "That was a *terrible* pun. You call yourself an author?"

"A bestselling one, thank you," I say with a flip of my hair.

"The fame has gone to your head quick."

I open the door for him to walk through since he's holding the books.

"I should tone it down. Our relationship will be unbalanced if more than one of us has an insufferably large ego," I say as I walk in behind him. The scent of books and coffee floats in the air. I breathe in deep with a smile.

"*Ouch*. That almost makes me regret planning this surprise." He sets the books on the counter with a *thump*.

"What–"

"SURPRISE!"

I jump as a crowd of people pops out from behind various book-shelves in the store. My mouth drops open as I see the entire Carter family, my mom and stepdad, as well as Myla and Simone standing amongst the shelves.

I look to Grayson, who just grins.

"Told you I knew you could do it. I invited everyone a month ago." I throw my arms around him. He presses a kiss to the top of my head.

"Thank you," I say with a sniffle.

"You're welcome, now go let everyone fawn all over you. I know they're dying to congratulate you."

I give him a quick kiss before walking over to my mom first. Person after person comes up to hug and congratulate me. I keep wiping my face with the sleeves of my cardigan because I can't stop crying.

Once the line has dwindled, I hear Myla yell out, "Speech!"

I shake my head, but everyone starts chanting it. Grayson grabs my hips and lifts me up to sit on top of one of the shelves.

"I don't think the owners will appreciate me being up here," I say to him.

"They love me, they won't mind." He winks before stepping back and raising his voice. "Quiet down people, my wife is about to make a speech!"

"You're not married yet," Levi says from a few feet away.

"Semantics," Grayson replies, and everyone laughs.

The room quiets eventually, and all eyes are on me. I'm not nervous though. As I stare out at the small crowd smiling at me, I know everyone here cares about me. The thought almost chokes off my words, but I manage to work around it.

"I obviously wasn't prepared to give a speech," I say, eliciting a laugh from everyone. "I guess all I have to say is thank you, all of you. Your support means the world to me. I've–" I tilt my head back, trying to keep in the tears. "I've never had a big support system before. But now I do, and I promise not to take it for granted."

I wipe away my tears for the millionth time today, and look to Grayson.

"And a special thank you to my fiancé Grayson, who helped me stay calm–" He raises a brow at my words. "Relatively calm," I say with a giggle. "As well as helping me with the logistics of some of the suspense elements."

"And the kiss scenes," he adds rather loudly. "Don't forget about my help there."

I cover my burning face while everyone else laughs. I feel him lift me off the shelf and set me down on my feet. He tugs my hands away.

"You are the worst," I say with a smile.

"You love me." He pulls me to him. I wrap my arms around him. "I do."

"Mmm, I like the sound of those words," he says in a low voice against my ear.

"Soon," I whisper to him.

"Not soon enough."

"You're the one who wanted a spring wedding," I tease.

"I know." He sighs. "In the meantime..." He presses his lips to mine. A few whoops and cheers break out around us, and I can't help but smile into the kiss.

"I love you, Rose," he whispers and I'm so happy it feels like sun is shining on my very soul.

"I love you, Gray."

—

Keep reading for a glimpse into Maverick's story!
Maverick Carter

I take a sip of the punch that no doubt is turning my tongue blue the more I drink it. Grayson made sure that every detail of this celebration matched either the theme of Sloane's book, or the cover—which is blue. He spared no expense renting out the entire bookstore and having the event catered by MJ and Sebastian's friend

Sophie. I guess that's what you do when you're in love. I can't say I remember the feeling well enough to know.

It's strange knowing that soon I'll be the only one of my siblings left who's not married. Levi got married last month, Adrian gets married next month, and Grayson will get married next spring. MJ, the youngest of all of us, somehow got married first. I'm not bitter about it though. After my ex-fiancé cheated on me, I worked through all my anger and bitterness. Some of that work resulted in a broken hand from hitting the punching bag in my garage a little too hard, but in the end, I got all that pain out.

Now I'm happy with my life. I live in a quiet farmhouse on a couple acres of land, and I run a successful bakery. My family is amazing and we all live close enough that I can see them whenever our schedules allow. I've got the kind of life people dream about. Maybe on cold nights it gets a little lonely, but that's not too bad. There are worse things than being lonely.

I watch Grayson wrap Sloane up in his arms. A dull ache begins to pulse behind my ribcage. *There are worse things than being lonely.* The ache doesn't fade even when I remind myself.

My phone begins to buzz in my pocket, so I slide it out. My best friend Drew's name and a photo of us fishing on the lake together come up on the screen. I immediately answer.

"Hey, everything okay?" I ask, unable to keep the worry from my voice. After the past few months of Drew giving me terrible updates about his sister Evie, it's hard not to expect the worst. I turn away from my siblings and walk further into the store.

"No," he replies and my blood runs cold. "We were right about everything. Evie's in trouble."

Preorder *But He's My Roommate* to find out how Maverick and Evie fall in love! And sign up for my newsletter to get a BONUS scene set in Grayson and Sloane's future!

Author's Note

Dear lovely reader,

My hope is that whether you've been a Grayson girl since *One Last Play*, or if he's not your Carter brother, you still enjoyed this book. Gray and Rose stole my heart fairly quickly. I related all too well to Sloane's shy nature. It was a beautiful journey for me to write her slowly making her own choices and coming out of her shell. I didn't want her to become this social butterfly by the end. I just wanted her to be confident in her own choices and able to stand up for herself, while maybe having a little fun making out under waterfalls ;)

I think Grayson was the perfect foil for her. He's wild and crazy and unafraid of being the center of attention, while also being kind and thoughtful. In my opinion, he pushed her just enough, but let her know it was her decision in the end.

Overall, this is one of my favorite books I've written. While I'm an autumn and winter lover, this summer romance reminded me of the beauty of the warmer months. It made me excited to get to the beach this summer and drink smoothies while tilting my face up to the sun.

I hope it did that for you too! And if you already are a summer girl, I hope this is your perfect beach read.

Be sure to reach out on socials or over email to let me know what you thought of the book!

IG: @authorannahconwell

Email: annahconwell@annahconwell.com

FB Group: Annah's Book Babes

All my love,

AC

Acknowledgements

Everything I achieve, every word I write, every breath I breathe, consider it yours, Lord. All glory and honor to You forever. Amen.

To my husband, Ryan, I know you said you relate to Grayson the least of all my MMCs, but he helped Sloane believe in herself, and you've been helping me with that since the day we met. Thank you for never letting me say I can't do something. I'm publishing my *ninth* book because you looked me in the eyes and told me if I wanted to I could. And then time and time again you backed that statement up with immeasurable support. *Thank you* doesn't cover it, but it's all I have. I love you forever and always.

To Sarah and Rachel aka Gray's Girls aka Mrs. Carter x2, thank you for loving Grayson as much as you do. When I was stressed or worried that I wasn't going to be able to do him justice, you both reassured me. So thank you for all of the inspiration your edits, song choices, and general monologues about him. Oh and the knife emojis. Can't forget those.

To Baylie St. James, I know you're a Bennett girl, but your love of summertime and the beach inspired me so much for this book. I'll be curious to see if Grayson will beat out Bennett after this. More than any inspiration though, I'm grateful for your friendship. You've helped me through a ton and encouraged me more than you know. Thank you.

Thank you to my editor, Caitlin, for being as kind and amazing as you are. You're the best out there! And I'm not biased at all.

A big thanks to my proofreader, Charity, for catching everything I miss!

Thanks to my cover designer, Stephanie, for all your hard work creating such gorgeous covers.

Special thanks to my Insider Book Babes for all that you do on social media. Your reels, aesthetics, graphics, and reviews are stunning!

Thanks to my ARC team for reading and reviewing this early. Y'all are what makes my books successful!

Lastly, thank you, lovely reader, for spending time with my characters. Your support lets me live out my dreams.

Also By Annah

Sweet Peach Series

The Love Audit

One More Song

Out of Office (FREE)

The First Taste

One Last Play

But He's a Carter Brother Series

But He's My Grumpy Neighbor

But He's My One Regret

But He's My Fake Fiancé

But He's My Roommate (08/08/24)

More Than a Game Series

The Golden Goal

The Perfect Putt (06/06/24)

About the Author

Annah Conwell is an Amazon bestselling sweet romcom author who loves witty banter, sassy heroines, and swoony heroes. She has a passion for writing books that make you LOL one minute and melt into a puddle of 'aw' the next. You can find her living out her days in a small town in Sweet Home Alabama (roll tide roll!) with the love of her life (aka her husband), Ryan, and her two goofball pups, Prince and Ella.

She loves coffee, the color pink, and playing music way too loud in the car. Most of the time she's snuggled up under her favorite blanket on the couch, reading way too many books to call it anything other than an addiction, or writing her little hopeless romantic heart out.

Check out her website: annahconwell.com

Made in United States
Troutdale, OR
11/24/2024

25259515R00171